Mary Mapes Dodge

MARY MAPES DODGE (1831–1905) grew up in New York City, where her family's home was a meeting center for literary groups. When she was widowed in 1858, she began writing children's stories for a number of magazines to support herself and her two young sons.

Mrs. Dodge's deep interest in the history and culture of Holland led to the publication in 1858 of one of the best-loved children's books of all time, *Hans Brinker, or The Silver Skates*. It was one of the first novels written to entertain rather than instruct young readers—a welcome change from the many "improving" moral tales written for children in the nineteenth century.

Filled with vivid glimpses of daily life on the canals, *Hans Brinker* was praised by the people of Holland as the best picture of Dutch life ever written. It includes the famous tale of the boy who stuck his finger in a dike to hold back the sea, thereby saving his country, and the Dutch even erected a statue of the tale's hero.

In 1873 Mary Mapes Dodge was asked by a New York publisher to be the editor of a new children's magazine called *St. Nicholas*. In it Mrs. Dodge published stories by such writers as Mark Twain, Louisa May Alcott, Robert Louis Stevenson, and Rudyard Kipling. The magazine owed much of its success to Mrs. Dodge's creative and inspired understanding of what children most like to read.

YEARLING CLASSICS

Works of lasting literary merit by English
and American classic and contemporary writers

HANS BRINKER, OR THE SILVER SKATES, *Mary Mapes Dodge*
EIGHT COUSINS, OR THE AUNT HILL, *Louisa May Alcott*
FIVE LITTLE PEPPERS AND HOW THEY GREW, *Margaret Sidney*
THE MIDNIGHT FOLK, *John Masefield*
FIVE CHILDREN AND IT, *E. Nesbit*
THE PRINCE AND THE PAUPER, *Mark Twain*
THE PRINCESS AND THE GOBLIN, *George MacDonald*
ROSE IN BLOOM, *Louisa May Alcott*
TOM'S MIDNIGHT GARDEN, *Philippa Pearce*
LITTLE LORD FAUNTLEROY, *Frances Hodgson Burnett*
THE BOOK OF DRAGONS, *E. Nesbit*
REBECCA OF SUNNYBROOK FARM, *Kate Douglas Wiggin*

YEARLING BOOKS are designed especially to entertain and
enlighten young people. Charles F. Reasoner, Professor
Emeritus of Children's Literature and Reading, New York
University, is consultant to this series.

For a complete listing of all Yearling titles, write to
Dell Publishing Co., Inc., Promotion Department,
P.O. Box 3000, Pine Brook, N.J. 07058.

Hans Brinker,
or
The Silver Skates

Mary Mapes Dodge

With an Afterword by E. L. Konigsburg

Published by
Dell Publishing Co., Inc.
1 Dag Hammarskjold Plaza
New York, New York 10017

Yearling ® TM 913705, Dell Publishing Co., Inc.

ISBN: 0-440-43446-7

RL: 6.9

Printed in the United States of America
First Yearling Classic printing
November 1985

10 9 8 7 6 5 4 3 2 1

W

To my father,
JAMES J. MAPES
This book
is dedicated in gratitude
and love

Hans Brinker,
or
The Silver Skates

Preface

*T*his little work aims to combine the instructive features of a book of travels with the interest of a domestic tale. Throughout its pages the descriptions of Dutch localities, customs, and general characteristics have been given with scrupulous care. Many of its incidents are drawn from life, and the story of Raff Brinker is founded strictly upon fact.

While acknowledging my obligations to many well-known writers on Dutch history, literature, and art, I turn with especial gratitude to those kind Holland friends, who, with generous zeal, have taken many a backward glance at their country for my sake, seeing it as it looked twenty years ago, when the Brinker home stood unnoticed in sunlight and shadow.

Should this simple narrative serve to give my young readers a just idea of Holland and its resources, or present true pictures of its inhabitants and their everyday life, or free them from certain current prejudices concerning that noble and enterprising people, the leading desire in writing it will have been satisfied.

Should it cause even one heart to feel a deeper trust in God's goodness and love, or aid any in weaving a life, wherein, through knots and entanglements, the golden thread shall never be tarnished or broken, the prayer with which it was begun and ended will have been answered.

M. M. D.

A Letter from Holland

Dear Boys and Girls at Home:

If you all could be here with me today, what fine times we might have walking through this beautiful Dutch city! How we should stare at the crooked houses, standing with their gable ends to the street; at the little slanting mirrors fastened outside of the windows; at the wooden shoes and dogcarts nearby; the windmills in the distance; at the great warehouses; at the canals, doing the double duty of streets and rivers, and at the singular mingling of trees and masts to be seen in every direction. Ah, it would be pleasant, indeed! But here I sit in a great hotel looking out upon all these things, knowing quite well that not even the spirit of the Dutch, which seems able to accomplish anything, can bring you at this moment across the ocean. There is one comfort, however, in going through these wonderful Holland towns without you—it would be dreadful to have any of the party tumble into the canals; and then these lumbering Dutch wagons, with their heavy wheels, so very far apart: what should I do if a few dozen of you were to fall under *them?* And, perhaps, one of the wildest of my boys might harm a stork, and then all Holland would be against us! No. It is better as it is. You will be coming, one by one, as years go on, to see the whole thing for yourselves.

Holland is as wonderful today as it was when, more than twenty years ago, Hans and Gretel skated on the frozen Y. In fact, more wonderful, for every day increases the marvel of its not being washed away by the sea. Its cities have grown, and some of its peculiarities have been brushed away by contact with other nations; but it is Holland still, and always will be—full of oddity, courage and industry—the pluckiest little country on earth. I shall not tell you in this letter of its customs, its cities, its palaces, churches, picture galleries and museums—for these are described in the story—except to say that they are here still, just the same, in this good year 1873, for I have seen them nearly all within a week.

Today an American boy and I, seeing some children enter an old house in the business part of Amsterdam, followed them in—and what do you think we found? An old woman, here in the middle of summer, selling hot water and fire! She makes her living by it. All day long she sits tending her great fires of peat and keeping the shining copper tanks above them filled with water. The children who come and go carry away in a curious stone pail their kettle of boiling water and their blocks of burning peat. For these they give her a Dutch cent, which is worth less than half of one of ours. In this way persons who cannot afford to keep a fire burning in hot weather may yet have their cup of tea or coffee and bit of boiled fish and potato.

After leaving the old fire woman, who nodded a pleasant good-bye to us, and willingly put our stivers in her great outside pocket, we drove through the streets enjoying the singular sights of a public washing day. Yes, in certain quarters of the city, away from the canals, the streets were lively with washerwomen hard at work. Hundreds of them in clumsy wooden shoes, with their tucked-up skirts, bare arms, and close-fitting caps, were bending over tall wooden tubs that reached as high as their waists—gossiping and rubbing, rubbing and gossiping—with perfect unconcern, in the public thoroughfare, and all washing with cold water instead of using hot, as we do. What a grand thing it would be for our old fire woman if boiling water were suddenly to become the fashion on these public washing days!

And now good-bye. Oh! I must tell you one more thing. We found today in an Amsterdam bookstore this story of Hans Brinker told in Dutch. It is a queer-looking volume, beautifully printed, and with colored pictures, but filled with such astonishing words that it really made me feel sorry for the little Hollanders who are to read them.

Good-bye again, in the touching words of our Dutch translator with whom I'm sure you'll heartily agree: *Toch ben ik er mijn landgenooten dank baar voor, die mijn arbeid steeds zoo welwillend outvangen en wier genegenheid ik voortdurend hoop te verdienen.*

Yours affectionately,

The Author

Contents

Chapter 1

Hans and Gretel

*O*n a bright December morning long ago, two thinly clad children were kneeling upon the bank of a frozen canal in Holland.

The sun had not yet appeared, but the gray sky was parted near the horizon, and its edges shone crimson with the coming day. Most of the good Hollanders were enjoying a placid morning nap. Even Mynheer van Stoppelnoze, that worthy old Dutchman, was still slumbering "in beautiful repose."

Now and then some peasant woman, poising a well-filled basket upon her head, came skimming over the glassy surface of the canal; or a lusty boy, skating to his day's work in the town, cast a good-natured grimace toward the shivering pair as he flew along.

Meanwhile, with many a vigorous puff and pull, the brother and sister, for such they were, seemed to be fastening something upon their feet—not skates, certainly, but clumsy pieces of wood narrowed and smoothed at their lower edge, and pierced with holes, through which were threaded strings of rawhide.

These queer-looking affairs had been made by the boy Hans. His mother was a poor peasant woman, too poor even to think of such a thing as buying skates for her little ones. Rough as these were, they had afforded the children many a happy hour upon the ice. And now, as with cold, red fingers our young Hollanders tugged at the strings—their solemn faces bending closely over their knees—no vision of impossible iron runners came to dull the satisfaction glowing within.

In a moment the boy arose and, with a pompous swing of the arms and a careless "Come on, Gretel," glided easily across the canal.

"Ah, Hans," called his sister plaintively, "this foot is not well yet. The strings hurt me on last market day, and now I cannot bear them tied in the same place."

"Tie them higher up, then," answered Hans, as without looking at her he performed a wonderful cat's-cradle step on the ice.

"How can I? The string is too short."

Giving vent to a good-natured Dutch whistle, the English of which was that girls were troublesome creatures, he steered toward her.

"You are foolish to wear such shoes, Gretel, when you have a stout leather pair. Your *klompen** would be better than these."

"Why, Hans! Do you forget? The father threw my beautiful new shoes in the fire. Before I knew what he had done, they were all curled up in the midst of the burning peat. I can skate with these but not with my wooden ones. Be careful now—"

Hans had taken a string from his pocket. Humming a tune as he knelt beside her, he proceeded to fasten Gretel's skate with all the force of his strong young arm.

"Oh! Oh!" she cried, in real pain.

With an impatient jerk Hans unwound the string. He would

---

*Wooden shoes.

have cast it upon the ground in true big-brother style had he
not just then spied a tear trickling down his sister's cheek.

"I'll fix it—never fear," he said with sudden tenderness, "but
we must be quick. The mother will need us soon."

Then he glanced inquiringly about him, first at the ground,
next at some bare willow branches above his head, and finally
at the sky, now gorgeous with streaks of blue, crimson, and
gold.

Finding nothing in any of these localities to meet his need,
his eye suddenly brightened as, with the air of a fellow who
knew what he was about, he took off his cap and, removing the
tattered lining, adjusted it in a smooth pad over the top of
Gretel's worn-out shoe.

"Now," he cried triumphantly, at the same time arranging
the strings as briskly as his benumbed fingers would allow, "can
you bear some pulling?"

Gretel drew up her lips as if to say "Hurt away," but made no
further response.

In another moment they were laughing together, as hand in
hand they flew along the canal, never thinking whether the ice
would bear them or not, for in Holland, ice is generally an all-
winter affair. It settles itself upon the water in a determined kind
of way, and so far from growing thin and uncertain every time the
sun is a little severe upon it, it gathers its forces day by day and
flashes defiance to every beam.

Presently, squeak! squeak! sounded something beneath Hans's
feet. Next his strokes grew shorter, ending ofttimes with a jerk,
and finally, he lay sprawling upon the ice, kicking against the
air with many a fantastic flourish.

"Ha! ha!" laughed Gretel. "That was a fine tumble!" But a
tender heart was beating under her coarse blue jacket, and even
as she laughed, she came, with a graceful sweep, close to her
prostrate brother.

"Are you hurt, Hans? Oh, you are laughing! Catch me now!"
And she darted away, shivering no longer, but with cheeks all
aglow and eyes sparkling with fun.

Hans sprang to his feet and started in brisk pursuit, but it was
no easy thing to catch Gretel. Before she had traveled very far,
her skates, too, began to squeak.

Believing that discretion was the better part of valor, she
turned suddenly and skated into her pursuer's arms.

"Ha! ha! I've caught you!" cried Hans.

"Ha! ha! I caught *you*," she retorted, struggling to free
herself.

Just then a clear, quick voice was heard calling "Hans!
Gretel!"

"It's the mother," said Hans, looking solemn in an instant.

By this time the canal was gilded with sunlight. The pure
morning air was very delightful, and skaters were gradually
increasing in numbers. It was hard to obey the summons. But
Gretel and Hans were good children; without a thought of
yielding to the temptation to linger, they pulled off their skates,
leaving half the knots still tied. Hans, with his great square
shoulders and bushy yellow hair, towered high above his blue-
eyed little sister as they trudged homeward. He was fifteen years
old and Gretel was only twelve. He was a solid, hearty-looking
boy, with honest eyes and a brow that seemed to bear a sign
GOODNESS WITHIN just as the little Dutch *zomerhuis** wears a
motto over its portal. Gretel was lithe and quick; her eyes had a
dancing light in them, and while you looked at her cheek, the
color paled and deepened just as it does upon a bed of pink and
white blossoms when the wind is blowing.

As soon as the children turned from the canal, they could see
their parents' cottage. Their mother's tall form, arrayed in

---

*Summer house.

jacket and petticoat and close-fitting cap, stood, like a picture, in the crooked frame of the doorway. Had the cottage been a mile away, it would still have seemed near. In that flat country every object stands out plainly in the distance; the chickens show as distinctly as the windmills. Indeed, were it not for the dikes and the high banks of the canals, one could stand almost anywhere in middle Holland without seeing a mound or a ridge between the eye and the "jumping-off place."

None had better cause to know the nature of these same dikes than Dame Brinker and the panting youngsters now running at her call. But before stating *why*, let me ask you to take a rocking-chair trip with me to that far country where you may see, perhaps for the first time, some curious things that Hans and Gretel saw every day.

Chapter 2

Holland

*H*olland is one of the queerest countries under the sun. It should be called Odd-land or Contrary-land, for in nearly everything it is different from other parts of the world. In the first place, a large portion of the country is lower than the level of the sea. Great dikes, or bulwarks, have been erected at a heavy cost of money and labor to keep the ocean where it belongs. On certain parts of the coast it sometimes leans with all its weight against the land, and it is as much as the poor country can do to stand the pressure. Sometimes the dikes give way or spring a leak, and the most disastrous results ensue. They are high and wide, and the tops of some of them are covered with buildings and trees. They have even fine public roads upon them, from which horses may look down upon wayside cottages. Often the keels of floating ships are higher than the roofs of the dwellings. The stork clattering to her young on the house peak may feel that her nest is lifted far out of danger, but the croaking frog in neighboring bulrushes is nearer the stars than she. Water bugs dart backward and forward above the heads of the chimney swallows, and willow trees seem drooping with shame, because they cannot reach as high as the reeds nearby.

Ditches, canals, ponds, rivers, and lakes are everywhere to be seen. High, but not dry, they shine in the sunlight, catching nearly all the bustle and the business, quite scorning the tame fields stretching damply beside them. One is tempted to ask, "Which is Holland—the shores or the water?" The very verdure that should be confined to the land has made a mistake and settled upon the fish ponds. In fact, the entire country is a kind of saturated sponge or, as the English poet Butler called it,

> A land that rides at anchor, and is moor'd,
> In which they do not live, but go aboard.

Persons are born, live, and die, and even have their gardens on canal boats. Farmhouses, with roofs like great slouched hats pulled over their eyes, stand on wooden legs with a tucked-up sort of air, as if to say, "We intend to keep dry if we can." Even the horses wear a wide stool on each hoof to lift them out of the mire. In short, the landscape everywhere suggests a paradise for ducks. It is a glorious country in summer for barefoot girls and boys. Such wading! Such mimic ship-sailing! Such rowing, fishing, and swimming! Only think of a chain of puddles where one can launch chip boats all day long and never make a return trip! But enough. A full recital would set all young America rushing in a body toward the Zuider Zee.

Dutch cities seem at first sight to be a bewildering jungle of houses, bridges, churches, and ships, sprouting into masts, steeples, and trees. In some cities vessels are hitched like horses to their owners' doorposts and receive their freight from the upper windows. Mothers scream to Lodewyk and Kassy not to swing on the garden gate for fear they may be drowned! Water roads are more frequent there than common roads and railways; water fences in the form of lazy green ditches enclose playground, farms, and garden.

Sometimes fine green hedges are seen; but wooden fences such as we have in America are rarely met with in Holland. As for stone fences, a Dutchman would lift his hands with astonishment at the very idea. There is no stone there, except for those great masses of rock that have been brought from other lands to strengthen and protect the coast. All the small stones or pebbles, if there ever were any, seem to be imprisoned in pavements or quite melted away. Boys with strong, quick arms may grow from pinafores to full beards without ever finding one to start the water rings or set the rabbits flying. The water roads are nothing less than canals intersecting the country in every direction. These are of all sizes, from the great North Holland Ship Canal, which is the wonder of the world, to those which a boy can leap. Water omnibuses, called *trekschuiten*,* constantly ply up and down these roads for the conveyance of passengers; and water drays, called *pakschuyten*,* are used for carrying fuel and merchandise. Instead of green country lanes, green canals stretch from field to barn and from barn to garden; and the farms, or *polders*, as they are termed, are merely great lakes pumped dry. Some of the busiest streets are water, while many of the country roads are paved with brick. The city boats with their rounded sterns, gilded prows, and gaily painted sides are unlike any others under the sun; and a Dutch wagon, with its funny little crooked pole, is a perfect mystery of mysteries.

"One thing is clear," cries Master Brightside, "the inhabi-

---

*Canal boats. Some of the first named are over thirty feet long. They look like green houses lodged on barges and are drawn by horses walking along the bank of the canal. The *trekschuiten* are divided into two compartments, first and second class, and when not too crowded, the passengers make themselves quite at home in them; the men smoke, the women knit or sew, while children play upon the small outer deck. Many of the canal boats have white, yellow, or chocolate-colored sails. This last color is caused by a tanning preparation which is put on to preserve them.

tants need never be thirsty." But no, Odd-land is true to itself still. Notwithstanding the sea pushing to get in, and the lakes struggling to get out, and the overflowing canals, rivers, and ditches, in many districts there is no water fit to swallow; our poor Hollanders must go dry or drink wine and beer or send far into the inland to Utrecht and other favored localities for that precious fluid older than Adam yet young as the morning dew. Sometimes, indeed, the inhabitants can swallow a shower when they are provided with any means of catching it; but generally they are like the albatross-haunted sailors in Coleridge's famous poem "The Rime of the Ancient Mariner." They see

> Water, Water, everywhere,
> Nor any drop to drink!

Great flapping windmills all over the country make it look as if flocks of huge sea birds were just settling upon it. Everywhere one sees the funniest trees, bobbed into fantastical shapes, with their trunks painted a dazzling white, yellow, or red. Horses are often yoked three abreast. Men, women, and children go clattering about in wooden shoes with loose heels; peasant girls who cannot get beaux for love, hire them for money to escort them to the *kermis;*[*] and husbands and wives lovingly harness themselves side by side on the bank of the canal and drag their *pakschuyts* to market.

Another peculiar feature of Holland is the dune, or sand hill. These are numerous along certain portions of the coast. Before they were sown with coarse reed grass and other plants, to hold them down, they used to send great storms of sand over the inland. So, to add to the oddities, farmers sometimes dig down under the surface to find their soil, and on windy days *dry*

---

[*]Fair.

showers (of sand) often fall upon fields that have grown wet under a week of sunshine.

In short, almost the only familiar thing we Yankees can meet with in Holland is a harvest song which is quite popular there, though no linguist could translate it. Even then we must shut our eyes and listen only to the tune, which I leave you to guess.

> *Yanker didee dudel down*
> *Didee dudel lawnter;*
> *Yankee viver, voover, vown,*
> *Botermelk und Tawnter!*

On the other hand, many of the oddities of Holland serve only to prove the thrift and perseverance of the people. There is not a richer or more carefully tilled garden spot in the whole world than this leaky, springy little country. There is not a braver, more heroic race than its quiet, passive-looking inhabitants. Few nations have equaled it in important discoveries and inventions; none has excelled it in commerce, navigation, learning, and science—or set as noble examples in the promotion of education and public charities; and none in proportion to its extent has expended more money and labor upon public works.

Holland has its shining annals of noble and illustrious men and women; its grand, historic records of patience, resistance, and victory; its religious freedom; its enlightened enterprise; its art, music, and literature. It has truly been called "the battle-field of Europe"; as truly may we consider it the asylum of the world, for the oppressed of every nation have there found shelter and encouragement. If we Americans, who after all are homeopathic preparations of Holland stock, can laugh at the Dutch and call them human beavers and hint that their country may float off any day at high tide, we can also feel proud and say they have proved themselves heroes and that their country will *not* float off while there is a Dutchman left to grapple it.

There are said to be at least ninety-nine hundred large windmills in Holland, with sails ranging from eighty to one hundred and twenty feet long. They are employed in sawing timber, beating hemp, grinding, and many other kinds of work; but their principal use is for pumping water from the lowlands into the canals and for guarding against the inland freshets that so often deluge the country. Their yearly cost is said to be nearly ten million dollars. The large ones are of great power. The huge circular tower, rising sometimes from the midst of factory buildings, is surmounted with a smaller one tapering into a caplike roof. This upper tower is encircled at its base with a balcony, high above which juts the axis turned by its four prodigious ladder-back sails.

Many of the windmills are primitive affairs, seeming sadly in need of Yankee "improvements," but some of the new ones are admirable. They are constructed so that by some ingenious contrivance they present their fans, or wings, to the wind in precisely the right direction to work with the requisite power. In other words, the miller may take a nap and feel quite sure that his mill will study the wind and make the most of it, until he wakens. Should there be but a slight current of air, every sail will spread itself to catch the faintest breath, but if a heavy "blow" should come, they will shrink at its touch, like great mimosa leaves, and only give it half a chance to move them.

One of the old prisons of Amsterdam, called the Rasphouse, because the thieves and vagrants who were confined there were employed in rasping logwood, had a cell for the punishment of lazy prisoners. In one corner of this cell was a pump, and in another, an opening through which a steady stream of water was admitted. The prisoner could take his choice, either to stand still and be drowned or to work for dear life at the pump and keep the flood down until his jailer chose to relieve him. Now it seems to me that, throughout Holland, nature has introduced this little diversion on a grand scale. The Dutch have always been forced to pump for their very existence and probably must continue to do so to the end of time.

Every year millions of dollars are spent in repairing dikes and regulating water levels. If these important duties were neglected, the country would be uninhabitable. Already dreadful consequences, as I have said, have followed the bursting of these dikes. Hundreds of villages and towns have from time to time been buried beneath the rush of waters, and nearly a million persons have been destroyed. One of the most fearful inundations ever known occurred in the autumn of the year 1570. Twenty-eight terrible floods had before that time overwhelmed portions of Holland, but this was the most terrible of all. The unhappy country had long been suffering under Spanish tyranny; now, it seemed, the crowning point was given to its troubles. When we read Motley's history of the rise of the Dutch republic, we learn to revere the brave people who have endured, suffered, and dared so much.

Mr. Motley, in his thrilling account of the great inundation, tells us how a long-continued and violent gale had been sweeping the Atlantic waters into the North Sea, piling them against the coasts of the Dutch provinces; how the dikes, tasked beyond their strength, burst in all directions; how even the Hand-bos, a bulwark formed of oaken piles, braced with iron, moored with heavy anchors, and secured by gravel and granite, was snapped to pieces like thread; how fishing boats and bulky vessels floating up into the country became entangled among the trees or beat in the roofs and walls of dwellings, and how, at last, all Friesland was converted into an angry sea. "Multitudes of men, women, children, of horses, oxen, sheep, and every domestic animal, were struggling in the waves in every direction. Every boat and every article which could serve as a boat was eagerly seized upon. Every house was inundated; even the graveyards gave up their dead. The living infant in his cradle and the long-buried corpse in his coffin floated side by side. The ancient flood seemed about to be renewed. Everywhere, upon the tops of trees, upon the steeples of churches, human beings were clustered, praying to God for mercy and to their fellowmen for assistance. As the storm at last was subsiding, boats began to ply in every direction, saving those who were struggling in the water, picking fugitives from roofs and treetops, and collecting the bodies of those already drowned." No less than one hundred thousand human beings had perished in a few hours. Thousands upon thousands of dumb creatures lay dead upon the waters, and the damage to property was beyond calculation.

Robles, the Spanish governor, was foremost in noble efforts to save life and lessen the horrors of the catastrophe. He had formerly been hated by the Dutch because of his Spanish or Portuguese blood, but by his goodness and activity in their hour of disaster, he won all hearts to gratitude. He soon introduced an improved method of constructing the dikes and passed a law that they should in future be kept up by the owners of the soil. There were fewer heavy floods from this time, though within less than three hundred years, six fearful inundations swept over the land.

In the spring there is always great danger of inland freshets, especially in times of thaw, because the rivers, choked with blocks of ice, overflow before they can discharge their rapidly rising waters into the ocean. Adding to this that the sea chafes and presses against the dikes, it is no wonder that Holland is often in a state of alarm. The greatest care is taken to prevent accidents. Engineers and workmen are stationed all along in threatened places, and a close watch is kept up night and day. When a general signal of danger is given, the inhabitants all rush to the rescue, eager to combine against their common foe.

As, everywhere else, straw is supposed to be of all things the most helpless in the water, of course, in Holland, it must be rendered the mainstay against a rushing tide. Huge straw mats are pressed against the embankments, fortified with clay and heavy stone, and once adjusted, the ocean dashes against them in vain.

Raff Brinker, the father of Gretel and Hans, had for years been employed upon the dikes. It was at the time of a threatened inundation, when in the midst of a terrible storm, in darkness and sleet, the men were laboring at a weak spot near the Veermyk sluice, that he fell from the scaffolding and was taken home insensible. From that hour he never worked again; though he lived on, mind and memory were gone.

Gretel could not remember him otherwise than as the strange, silent man whose eyes followed her vacantly whichever way she turned, but Hans had recollections of a hearty, cheerful-voiced father who was never tired of bearing him upon his shoulder and whose careless song still seemed echoing near when he lay awake at night and listened.

Chapter 3

The Silver Skates

*D*ame Brinker earned a scanty support for her family by raising vegetables, spinning, and knitting. Once she had worked on board the barges plying up and down the canal and had occasionally been harnessed with other women to the towing rope of a *pakschuyt* plying between Broek and Amsterdam. But when Hans had grown strong and large, he had insisted upon doing all such drudgery in her place. Besides, her husband had become so very helpless of late that he required her constant care. Although not having as much intelligence as a little child, he was yet strong of arm and very hearty, and Dame Brinker had sometimes great trouble in controlling him.

"Ah! children, he was so good and steady," she would sometimes say, "and as wise as a lawyer. Even the burgomaster would stop to ask him a question, and now, alack! he don't know his wife and little ones. You remember the father, Hans, when he was himself—a great brave man—don't you?"

"Yes, indeed, Mother, he knew everything and could do anything under the sun—and how he would sing! Why, you used to laugh and say it was enough to set the windmills dancing."

"So I did. Bless me! how the boy remembers! Gretel, child, take that knitting needle from your father, quick; he'll get it in his eyes maybe; and put the shoe on him. His poor feet are like ice half the time, but I can't keep 'em covered, all I can do—" And then, half wailing, half humming, Dame Brinker would sit down and fill the low cottage with the whir of her spinning wheel.

Nearly all the outdoor work, as well as the household labor, was performed by Hans and Gretel. At certain seasons of the year the children went out day after day to gather peat, which they would stow away in square, bricklike pieces, for fuel. At other times, when homework permitted, Hans rode the towing horses on the canals, earning a few *stivers** a day, and Gretel tended geese for the neighboring farmers.

Hans was clever at carving in wood, and both he and Gretel were good gardeners. Gretel could sing and sew and run on great, high homemade stilts better than any girl for miles around. She could learn a ballad in five minutes and find, in its season, any weed or flower you could name; but she dreaded books, and often the very sight of the figuring board in the old schoolhouse would set her eyes swimming. Hans, on the contrary, was slow and steady. The harder the task, whether in study or daily labor, the better he liked it. Boys who sneered at him out of school, on account of his patched clothes and scant leather breeches, were forced to yield him the post of honor in nearly every class. It was not long before he was the only youngster in the school who had not stood at least *once* in the corner of horrors, where hung a dreaded whip, and over it this motto: *"Leer, leer! jou luigaart, of dit endje touw zal je leeren!"***

It was only in winter that Gretel and Hans could be spared to

---

*A *stiver* is worth about two cents of our money.

**Learn! learn! you idler, or this rope's end shall teach you.

attend school, and for the past month they had been kept at home because their mother needed their services. Raff Brinker required constant attention, and there was black bread to be made, and the house to be kept clean, and stockings and other things to be knitted and sold in the marketplace.

While they were busily assisting their mother on this cold December morning, a merry troop of girls and boys came skimming down the canal. There were fine skaters among them, and as the bright medley of costumes flitted by, it looked from a distance as though the ice had suddenly thawed and some gay tulip bed were floating along on the current.

There was the rich burgomaster's daughter Hilda van Gleck, with her costly furs and loose-fitting velvet sack; and, nearby, a pretty peasant girl, Annie Bouman, jauntily attired in a coarse scarlet jacket and a blue skirt just short enough to display the gray homespun hose to advantage. Then there was the proud Rychie Korbes, whose father, Mynheer van Korbes, was one of the leading men of Amsterdam; and, flocking closely around her, Carl Schummel, Peter and Ludwig* van Holp, Jacob Poot, and a very small boy rejoicing in the tremendous name of Voostenwalbert Schimmelpenninck. There were nearly twenty other boys and girls in the party, and one and all seemed full of excitement and frolic.

Up and down the canal within the space of a half mile they skated, exerting their racing powers to the utmost. Often the swiftest among them was seen to dodge from under the very nose of some pompous lawgiver or doctor who, with folded arms, was skating leisurely toward the town; or a chain of girls would suddenly break at the approach of a fat old burgomaster who, with gold-headed cane poised in air, was puffing his way

---

*Ludwig, Gretel, and Carl were named after German friends. The Dutch form would be Lodewyk, Grietje, and Karel.

to Amsterdam. Equipped in skates wonderful to behold, with
their superb strappings and dazzling runners curving over the
instep and topped with gilt balls, he would open his fat eyes a
little if one of the maidens chanced to drop him a curtsy but
would not dare to bow in return for fear of losing his balance.

Not only pleasure seekers and stately men of note were upon
the canal. There were workpeople, with weary eyes, hastening
to their shops and factories; market women with loads upon
their heads; peddlers bending with their packs; bargemen with
shaggy hair and bleared faces, jostling roughly on their way;
kind-eyed clergymen speeding perhaps to the bedsides of the
dying; and, after a while, groups of children with satchels slung
over their shoulders, whizzing past, toward the distant school.
One and all wore skates except, indeed, a muffled-up farmer
whose queer cart bumped along on the margin of the canal.

Before long our merry boys and girls were almost lost in the
confusion of bright colors, the ceaseless motion, and the gleaming of skates flashing back the sunlight. We might have known
no more of them had not the whole party suddenly come to a
standstill and, grouping themselves out of the way of the passersby, all talked at once to a pretty little maiden, whom they
had drawn from the tide of people flowing toward the town.

"Oh, Katrinka!" they cried in one breath, "Have you heard of
it? The race—we want you to join!"

"What race?" asked Katrinka, laughing. "Don't all talk at
once, please. I can't understand."

Everyone panted and looked at Rychie Korbes, who was their
acknowledged spokeswoman.

"Why," said Rychie, "we are to have a grand skating match
on the twentieth, on *Mevrouw** van Gleck's birthday. It's all

---

*Mrs. or Madame (pronounced Meffrow).

Hilda's work. They are going to give a splendid prize to the best skater."

"Yes," chimed in half a dozen voices, "a beautiful pair of silver skates—perfectly magnificent—with, oh! such straps and silver bells and buckles!"

"*Who* said they had bells?" put in a small voice of the boy with the big name.

"*I* say so, Master Voost," replied Rychie.

"So they have"; "No, I'm sure they haven't"; "*Oh*, how can you say so?"; "It's an arrow"; "And Mynheer van Korbes told *my* mother they had bells"—came from the excited group, but Mynheer Voostenwalbert Schimmelpenninck essayed to settle the matter with a decisive "Well, you don't any of you know a single thing about it; they haven't a sign of a bell on them, they—"

"Oh! oh!" and the chorus of conflicting opinions broke forth again.

"The girls' pair are to have bells," interposed Hilda quietly, "but there is to be another pair for the boys with an arrow engraved upon the sides."

"*There*! I told you so!" cried nearly all the youngsters in one breath.

Katrinka looked at them with bewildered eyes.

"Who is to try?" she asked.

"All of us," answered Rychie. "It will be such fun! And you must, too, Katrinka. But it's schooltime now, we will talk it all over at noon. Oh! you will join, of course."

Katrinka, without replying, made a graceful pirouette and laughing out a coquettish "Don't you hear the last bell? Catch me!" darted off toward the schoolhouse, standing half a mile away on the canal.

All started, pell-mell, at this challenge, but they tried in vain to catch the bright-eyed, laughing creature who, with

golden hair streaming in the sunlight, cast back many a sparkling glance of triumph as she floated onward.

Beautiful Katrinka! Flushed with youth and health, all life
and mirth and motion, what wonder thine image, ever floating
in advance, sped through one boy's dreams that night! What
wonder that it seemed his darkest hour when, years afterward,
thy presence floated away from him forever.

Chapter 4

Hans and Gretel
Find a Friend

At noon our young friends poured forth from the schoolhouse, intent upon having an hour's practice upon the canal.

They had skated but a few moments when Carl Schummel said mockingly to Hilda, "There's a pretty pair just coming upon the ice! The little ragpickers! Their skates must have been a present from the king direct."

"They are patient creatures," said Hilda gently. "It must have been hard to learn to skate upon such queer affairs. They are very poor peasants, you see. The boy has probably made the skates himself."

Carl was somewhat abashed.

"Patient they may be, but as for skating, they start off pretty well only to finish with a jerk. They could move well to your new *staccato* piece, I think."

Hilda laughed pleasantly and left him. After joining a small detachment of the racers and sailing past every one of them, she halted beside Gretel, who, with eager eyes, had been watching the sport.

"What is your name, little girl?"

"Gretel, my lady," answered the child, somewhat awed by Hilda's rank, though they were nearly of the same age, "and my brother is called Hans."

"Hans is a stout fellow," said Hilda cheerily, "and seems to have a warm stove somewhere within him, but *you* look cold. You should wear more clothing, little one."

Gretel, who had nothing else to wear, tried to laugh as she answered, "I am not so very little. I am past twelve years old."

"Oh, I beg your pardon. You see, I am nearly fourteen, and so large for my age that other girls seem small to me, but that is nothing. Perhaps you will shoot up far above me yet, but not unless you dress more warmly, though. Shivering girls never grow."

Hans flushed as he saw tears rising in Gretel's eyes.

"My sister has not complained of the cold, but this is bitter weather, they all say." And he looked sadly upon Gretel.

"It is nothing," said Gretel. "I am often warm—too warm when I am skating. You are good, *jufvrouw,** to think of it."

"No, no," answered Hilda, quite angry at herself. "I am careless, cruel, but I meant no harm. I wanted to ask you—I mean, if—" And here Hilda, coming to the point of her errand, faltered before the poorly clad but noble-looking children she wished to serve.

"What is it, young lady?" exclaimed Hans eagerly. "If there is any service I can do, any—"

"Oh, no, no," laughed Hilda, shaking off her embarrassment. "I only wished to speak to you about the grand race. Why do you not join it? You both can skate well, and the ranks are free. Anyone may enter for the prize."

---

*Miss; young lady (pronounced yuffrow). In studied or polite address it would be *jongvrowe* (pronounced youngfrow).

Gretel looked wistfully at Hans, who, tugging at his cap, answered respectfully, "Ah, *jufvrouw*, even if we could enter, we could skate only a few strokes with the rest. Our skates are hard wood, you see"—(holding up the sole of his foot)—"but they soon become damp, and then they stick and trip us."

Gretel's eyes twinkled with fun as she thought of Hans's mishap in the morning, but she blushed as she faltered out timidly, "Oh, no, we can't join, but may we be there, my lady, on the great day to look on?"

"Certainly," answered Hilda, looking kindly into the two earnest faces and wishing from her heart that she had not spent so much of her monthly allowance for lace and finery. She had but eight *kwartjes** left, and they would buy but one pair of skates, at the furthest.

Looking down with a sigh at the two pairs of feet so very different in size, she asked, "Which of you is the better skater?"

"Gretel," replied Hans promptly.

"Hans," answered Gretel in the same breath.

Hilda smiled.

"I cannot buy you each a pair of skates, or even one good pair, but here are eight *kwartjes*. Decide between you which stands the best chance of winning the race and buy the skates accordingly. I wish I had enough to buy better ones. Good-bye!" And, with a nod and a smile, Hilda, after handing the money to the electrified Hans, glided swiftly away to rejoin her companions.

"*Jufvrouw! Jufvrouw* van Gleck!" called Hans in a loud tone, stumbling after her as well as he could, for one of his skate strings was untied.

Hilda turned and, with one hand raised to shield her eyes

---

*A *kwartje* is a small silver coin worth one-quarter of a guilder, or ten cents in American currency.

from the sun, seemed to him to be floating through the air, nearer and nearer.

"We cannot take this money," panted Hans, "though we know your goodness in giving it."

"Why not indeed?" asked Hilda, flushing.

"Because," replied Hans, bowing like a clown but looking with the eye of a prince at the queenly girl, "we have not earned it."

Hilda was quick-witted. She had noticed a pretty wooden chain upon Gretel's neck.

"Carve me a chain, Hans, like the one your sister wears."

"That I will, lady, with all my heart. We have whitewood in the house, fine as ivory. You shall have one tomorrow," and Hans hastily tried to return the money.

"No, no," said Hilda decidedly. "That sum will be but a poor price for the chain." And off she darted, outstripping the fleetest among the skaters.

Hans sent a long, bewildered gaze after her; it was useless, he felt, to make any further resistance.

"It is right," he muttered, half to himself, half to his faithful shadow, Gretel. "I must work hard every minute and sit up half the night if the mother will let me burn a candle, but the chain shall be finished. We may keep the money, Gretel."

"What a good little lady!" cried Gretel, clapping her hands with delight. "Oh! Hans, was it for nothing the stork settled on our roof last summer? Do you remember how the mother said it would bring us luck and how she cried when Janzoon Kolp shot him? And she said it would bring him trouble. But the luck has come to us at last! Now, Hans, if the mother sends us to town tomorrow, you can buy the skates in the marketplace."

Hans shook his head. "The young lady would have given us the money to buy skates, but if I *earn* it, Gretel, it shall be spent for wool. You must have a warm jacket."

"Oh!" cried Gretel in real dismay, "not buy the skates? Why, I am not often cold! Mother says the blood runs up and down in poor children's veins, humming, 'I must keep 'em warm! I must keep 'em warm.'

"Oh, Hans," she continued with something like a sob, "don't say you won't buy the skates. It makes me feel just like crying. Besides, I want to be cold. I mean, I'm real, awful warm—so now!"

Hans looked up hurriedly. He had a true Dutch horror of tears, or emotion of any kind, and, most of all, he dreaded to see his sister's blue eyes overflowing.

"Now, mind," cried Gretel, seeing her advantage, "I'll feel awful if you give up the skates. *I* don't want them. I'm not so stingy as that; but I want *you* to have them, and then when I get bigger, they'll do for me—oh—count the pieces, Hans. Did ever you see so many!"

Hans turned the money thoughtfully in his palm. Never in all his life had he longed so intensely for a pair of skates, for he had known of the race and had fairly ached for a chance to test his powers with the other children. He felt confident that with a good pair of steel runners he could readily outdistance most of the boys on the canal. Then, too, Gretel's argument was so plausible. On the other hand, he knew that she, with her strong but lithe little frame, needed but a week's practice on good runners to make her a better skater than Rychie Korbes or even Katrinka Flack. As soon as this last thought flashed upon him, his resolve was made. If Gretel would not have the jacket, she should have the skates.

"No, Gretel," he answered at last, "I can wait. Someday I may have money enough saved to buy a fine pair. You shall have these."

Gretel's eyes sparkled, but in another instant she insisted, rather faintly, "The young lady gave the money to *you*, Hans. I'd be real bad to take it."

Hans shook his head resolutely as he trudged on, causing his sister to half skip and half walk in her effort to keep beside him. By this time they had taken off their wooden "rockers" and were hastening home to tell their mother the good news.

"Oh! *I* know!" cried Gretel in a sprightly tone. "You can do this. You can get a pair a little too small for you, and too big for me, and we can take turns and use them. Won't that be fine?" Gretel clapped her hands again.

Poor Hans! This was a strong temptation, but he pushed it away from him, brave-hearted fellow that he was.

"Nonsense, Gretel. You could never get on with a big pair. You stumbled about with these, like a blind chicken, before I curved off the ends. No, you must have a pair to fit exactly, and you must practice every chance you can get, until the twentieth comes. My little Gretel shall win the silver skates."

Gretel could not help laughing with delight at the very idea.

"Hans! Gretel!" called out a familiar voice.

"Coming, Mother!"

They hastened toward the cottage, Hans still shaking the pieces of silver in his hand.

On the following day there was not a prouder nor a happier boy in all Holland than Hans Brinker as he watched his sister, with many a dexterous sweep, flying in and out among the skaters who at sundown thronged the canal. A warm jacket had been given her by the kindhearted Hilda, and the burst-out shoes had been cobbled into decency by Dame Brinker. As the little creature darted backward and forward, flushed with enjoyment and quite unconscious of the many wondering glances bent upon her, she felt that the shining runners beneath her feet had suddenly turned earth into fairyland while "Hans, dear, good Hans!" echoed itself over and over again in her grateful heart.

"By *den donder*!" exclaimed Peter van Holp to Carl Schummel, "but that little one in the red jacket and patched petticoat skates well. *Gunst*! She has toes on her heels and eyes in the back of her head. See her! It will be a joke if she gets in the race and beats Katrinka Flack, after all."

"Hush! not so loud!" returned Carl, rather sneeringly. "That little lady in rags is the special pet of Hilda van Gleck. Those shining skates are her gift, if I make no mistake."

"So! so!" exclaimed Peter with a radiant smile, for Hilda was his best friend. "She has been at her good work there too!" And Mynheer van Holp, after cutting a double figure eight on the ice, to say nothing of a huge *P*, then a jump and an *H*, glided onward until he found himself beside Hilda.

Hand in hand, they skated together, laughingly at first, then staidly talking in a low tone.

Strange to say, Peter van Holp soon arrived at a sudden conviction that his little sister needed a wooden chain just like Hilda's.

Two days afterward, on Saint Nicholas's Eve, Hans, having burned three candle ends and cut his thumb into the bargain, stood in the marketplace at Amsterdam, buying another pair of skates.

Chapter 5

Shadows in the Home

*G*ood Dame Brinker! As soon as the scanty dinner had been cleared away that noon, she had arrayed herself in her holiday attire in honor of Saint Nicholas. It will brighten the children, she thought to herself, and she was not mistaken. This festival dress had been worn very seldom during the past ten years; before that time it had done good service and had flourished at many a dance and *kermis*, when she was known, far and wide, as the pretty Meitje Klenck. The children had sometimes been granted rare glimpses of it as it lay in state in the old oaken chest. Faded and threadbare as it was, it was gorgeous in their eyes, with its white linen tucker, now gathered to her plump throat and vanishing beneath the trim bodice of blue homespun, and its reddish-brown skirt bordered with black. The knitted woolen mitts and the dainty cap showing her hair, which generally was hidden, made her seem almost like a princess to Gretel, while Master Hans grew staid and well behaved as he gazed.

Soon the little maid, while braiding her own golden tresses, fairly danced around her mother in an ecstasy of admiration.

"Oh, Mother, Mother, Mother, how pretty you are! Look, Hans! Isn't it just like a picture?"

"Just like a picture," assented Hans cheerfully. "*Just* like a picture—only I don't like those stocking things on the hands."

"Not like the mitts, brother Hans! Why, they're very important. See, they cover up all the red. Oh, Mother, how white your arm is where the mitt leaves off, whiter than mine, oh, ever so much whiter. I declare, Mother, the bodice is tight for you. You're growing! You're surely growing!"

Dame Brinker laughed.

"This was made long ago, lovey, when I wasn't much thicker about the waist than a churn dasher. And how do you like the cap?" she asked, turning her head from side to side.

"Oh, *ever* so much, Mother. It's b-e-a-u-tiful! See, the father is looking!"

Was the father looking? Alas, only with a dull stare. His *vrouw* turned toward him with a start, something like a blush rising to her cheeks, a questioning sparkle in her eye. The bright look died away in an instant.

"No, no." She sighed. "He sees nothing. Come, Hans"—and the smile crept faintly back again—"don't stand gaping at me all day, and the new skates waiting for you at Amsterdam."

"Ah, Mother," he answered, "you need many things. Why should I buy skates?"

"Nonsense, child. The money was given to you on purpose, or the work was—it's all the same thing. Go while the sun is high."

"Yes, and hurry back, Hans!" laughed Gretel. "We'll race on the canal tonight if the mother lets us."

At the very threshold he turned to say, "Your spinning wheel wants a new treadle, Mother."

"You can make it, Hans."

"So I can. That will take no money. But you need feathers and wool and meal and—"

"There, there! That will do. Your silver cannot buy everything. Ah! Hans, if our stolen money would but come back on this bright Saint Nicholas's Eve, how glad we would be! Only last night I prayed to the good saint—"

"Mother!" interrupted Hans in dismay.

"Why not, Hans? Shame on you to reproach me for that! I'm as true a Protestant, in sooth, as any fine lady that walks into church, but it's no wrong to turn sometimes to the good Saint Nicholas. Tut! It's a likely story if one can't do that, without one's children flaring up at it—and the boys' and girls' own saint. Hoot! Mayhap the colt is a steadier horse than the mare?"

Hans knew his mother too well to offer a word in opposition when her voice quickened and sharpened as it did now (it was often sharp and quick when she spoke of the missing money), so he said gently, "And what did you ask of good Saint Nicholas, Mother?"

"Why, to never give the thieves a wink of sleep till they brought it back, to be sure, if he has power to do such things, or else to brighten our wits that we might find it ourselves. Not a sight have I had of it since the day before the dear father was hurt—as you well know, Hans."

"That I do, Mother," he answered sadly, "though you have almost pulled down the cottage in searching."

"Aye, but it was of no use," moaned the dame. " 'Hiders make best finders.' "

Hans started. "Do you think the father could tell aught?"

"Aye, indeed," said Dame Brinker, nodding her head. "I think so, but that is no sign. I never hold the same belief in the matter two days. Mayhap the father paid it off for the great silver watch we have been guarding since that day. But, no— I'll never believe it."

"The watch was not worth a quarter of the money, Mother."

"No, indeed, and your father was a shrewd man up to the last moment. He was too steady and thrifty for silly doings."

"Where *did* the watch come from, I wonder," muttered Hans, half to himself.

Dame Brinker shook her head and looked sadly toward her husband, who sat staring blankly at the floor. Gretel stood near him, knitting.

"That we shall never know, Hans. I have shown it to the father many a time, but he does not know it from a potato. When he came in that dreadful night to supper, he handed the watch to me and told me to take good care of it until he asked for it again. Just as he opened his lips to say more, Broom Klatterboost came flying in with word that the dike was in danger. Ah! The waters were terrible that holy Pinxter-week! My man, alack, caught up his tools and ran out. That was the last I ever saw of him in his right mind. He was brought in again by midnight, nearly dead, with his poor head all bruised and cut. The fever passed off in time but never the dullness—*that* grew worse every day. We shall never know."

Hans had heard all this before. More than once he had seen his mother, in hours of sore need, take the watch from its hiding place, half resolved to sell it, but she had always conquered the temptation.

"No, Hans," she would say, "we must be nearer starving than this before we turn faithless to the father!"

A memory of some such scene crossed her son's mind now, for, after giving a heavy sigh and flipping a crumb of wax at Gretel across the table, he said, "Aye, Mother, you have done bravely to keep it—many a one would have tossed it off for gold long ago."

"And more shame for them!" exclaimed the dame indignantly. "*I* would not do it. Besides, the gentry are so hard on us poor folks that if they saw such a thing in our hands, even if we told all, they might suspect the father of—"

Hans flushed angrily.

"They would not *dare* to say such a thing, Mother! If they did, I'd . . ."

He clenched his fist and seemed to think that the rest of his sentence was too terrible to utter in her presence.

Dame Brinker smiled proudly through her tears at this interruption.

"Ah, Hans, thou'rt a true, brave lad. We will never part company with the watch. In his dying hour the dear father might wake and ask for it."

"Might *wake*, Mother!" echoed Hans. "Wake—and know us?"

"Aye, child," almost whispered his mother. "Such things have been."

By this time Hans had nearly forgotten his proposed errand to Amsterdam. His mother had seldom spoken so familiarly with him. He felt himself now to be not only her son, but her friend, her adviser.

"You are right, Mother. We must never give up the watch. For the father's sake we will guard it always. The money, though, may come to light when we least expect it."

"Never!" cried Dame Brinker, taking the last stitch from her needle with a jerk and laying the unfinished knitting heavily on her lap. "There is no chance! One thousand guilders—and all gone in a day! One thousand guilders. Oh, what ever *did* become of them? If they went in an evil way, the thief would have confessed it on his dying bed. He would not dare to die with such guilt on his soul!"

"He may not be dead yet," said Hans soothingly. "Any day we may hear of him."

"Ah, child," she said in a changed tone, "what thief would

ever have come *here?* It was always neat and clean, thank God, but not fine, for the father and I saved and saved that we might have something laid by. 'Little and often soon fills the pouch.' We found it so, in truth. Besides, the father had a goodly sum already, for service done to the Heernocht lands, at the time of the great inundation. Every week we had a guilder left over, sometimes more; for the father worked extra hours and could get high pay for his labor. Every Saturday night we put something by, except the time when you had the fever, Hans, and when Gretel came. At last the pouch grew so full that I mended an old stocking and commenced again. Now that I look back, it seems that the money was up to the heel in a few sunny weeks. There was great pay in those days if a man was quick at engineer work. The stocking went on filling with copper and silver—aye, and gold. You may well open your eyes, Gretel. I used to laugh and tell the father it was not for poverty that I wore my old gown. And the stocking went on filling, so full that sometimes when I woke at night, I'd get up, soft and quiet, and go feel it in the moonlight. Then, on my knees, I would thank our Lord that my little ones could in time get good learning and that the father might rest from labor in his old age. Sometimes, at supper, the father and I would talk about a new chimney and a good winter room for the cow, but my man had finer plans even than that. 'A big sail,' says he, 'catches the wind—we can do what we will soon,' and then we would sing together as I washed my dishes. Ah, 'a smooth sea makes an easy rudder.' Not a thing vexed me from morning till night. Every week the father would take out the stocking and drop in the money and laugh and kiss me as we tied it up together. Up with you, Hans! There you sit gaping, and the day a-wasting!" added Dame Brinker tartly, blushing to find that she had been speaking too freely to her boy. "It's high time you were on your way."

Hans had seated himself and was looking earnestly into her face. He arose and, in almost a whisper, asked, "Have you ever *tried*, Mother?"

She understood him.

"Yes, child, often. But the father only laughs, or he stares at me so strange I am glad to ask no more. When you and Gretel had the fever last winter, and our bread was nearly gone, and I could earn nothing, for fear you would die while my face was turned, oh! I tried then! I smoothed his hair and whispered to him soft as a kitten, about the money—where it was, who had it? Alack! He would pick at my sleeve and whisper gibberish till my blood ran cold. At last, while Gretel lay whiter than snow and you were raving on the bed, I screamed to him—it seemed as if he *must* hear me—'Raff, where is our money? Do you know aught of the money, Raff? The money in the pouch and the stocking, in the big chest?' But I might as well have talked to a stone. I might as—"

The mother's voice sounded so strange, and her eye was so bright, that Hans, with a new anxiety, laid his hand upon her shoulder.

"Come, Mother," he said, "let us try to forget this money. I am big and strong. Gretel, too, is very quick and willing. Soon all will be prosperous with us again. Why, Mother, Gretel and I would rather see thee bright and happy than to have all the silver in the world, wouldn't we, Gretel?"

"The mother knows it," said Gretel, sobbing.

Chapter 6

Sunbeams

*D*ame Brinker was startled at her children's emotion; glad, too, for it proved how loving and true they were.

Beautiful ladies in princely homes often smiled suddenly and sweetly, gladdening the very air around them, but I doubt if their smile be more welcome in God's sight than that which sprang forth to cheer the roughly clad boy and girl in the humble cottage. Dame Brinker felt that she had been selfish. Blushing and brightening, she hastily wiped her eyes and looked upon them as only a mother can.

"Hoity! Toity! Pretty talk we're having, and Saint Nicholas's Eve almost here! What wonder the yarn pricks my fingers! Come, Gretel, take this *cent,* * and while Hans is trading for the skates, you can buy a waffle in the marketplace."

"Let me stay home with you, Mother," said Gretel, looking up with eyes that sparkled through their tears. "Hans will buy me the cake."

"As you will, child, and Hans—wait a moment. Three turns of the needle will finish this toe, and then you may have as good a pair of hose as ever were knitted (owning the yarn is a grain

---

*The Dutch cent is worth less than half of an American cent.

too sharp) to sell to the hosier on the Herengracht.* That will give us three quarter-guilders if you make good trade; and as it's right hungry weather, you may buy four waffles. We'll keep the Feast of Saint Nicholas after all."

Gretel clapped her hands. "That will be fine! Annie Bouman told me what grand times they will have in the big houses tonight. But we will be merry too. Hans will have beautiful new skates—and then there'll be the waffles! Oh! Don't break them, brother Hans. Wrap them well, and button them under your jacket very carefully."

"Certainly," replied Hans, quite gruff with pleasure and importance.

"Oh! Mother!" cried Gretel in high glee, "soon you will be busied with the father, and now you are only knitting. Do tell us all about Saint Nicholas!"

Dame Brinker laughed to see Hans hang up his hat and prepare to listen. "Nonsense, children," she said. "I have told it to you often."

"Tell us again! Oh, *do* tell us again!" cried Gretel, throwing herself upon the wonderful wooden bench that her brother had made on the mother's last birthday. Hans, not wishing to appear childish, and yet quite willing to hear the story, stood carelessly swinging his skates against the fireplace.

"Well, children, you shall hear it, but we must never waste the daylight again in this way. Pick up your ball, Gretel, and let your sock grow as I talk. Opening your ears needn't shut your fingers. Saint Nicholas, you must know, is a wonderful saint. He keeps his eye open for the good of sailors, but he cares most of all for boys and girls. Well, once upon a time, when he was living on the earth, a merchant of Asia sent his three sons to a great city, called Athens, to get learning."

---

*A street in Amsterdam.

"Is Athens in Holland, Mother?" asked Gretel.

"I don't know, child. Probably it is."

"Oh, no, Mother," said Hans respectfully. "I had that in my geography lessons long ago. Athens is in Greece."

"Well," resumed the mother, "what matter? Greece may belong to the king, for aught we know. Anyhow, this rich merchant sent his sons to Athens. While they were on their way, they stopped one night at a shabby inn, meaning to take up their journey in the morning. Well, they had very fine clothes—velvet and silk, it may be, such as rich folks' children all over the world think nothing of wearing—and their belts, likewise, were full of money. What did the wicked landlord do but contrive a plan to kill the children and take their money and all their beautiful clothes himself. So that night, when all the world was asleep, he got up and killed the three young gentlemen."

Gretel clasped her hands and shuddered, but Hans tried to look as if killing and murder were everyday matters to him.

"That was not the worst of it," continued Dame Brinker, knitting slowly and trying to keep count of her stitches as she talked. "That was not near the worst of it. The dreadful landlord went and cut up the young gentlemen's bodies into little pieces and threw them into a great tub of brine, intending to sell them for pickled pork!"

"Oh!" cried Gretel, horror-stricken, though she had often heard the story before. Hans was still unmoved and seemed to think that pickling was the best that could be done under the circumstances.

"Yes, he pickled them, and one might think that would have been the last of the young gentlemen. But no. That night Saint Nicholas had a wonderful vision, and in it he saw the landlord cutting up the merchant's children. There was no need of his hurrying, you know, for he was a saint, but in the morning he went to the inn and charged the landlord with the murder. Then the wicked landlord confessed it from beginning to end and fell down on his knees, begging forgiveness. He felt so sorry for what he had done that he asked the saint to bring the young masters to life."

"And did the saint do it?" asked Gretel, delighted, well knowing what the answer would be.

"Of course he did. The pickled pieces flew together in an instant, and out jumped the young gentlemen from the brine tub. They cast themselves at the feet of Saint Nicholas, and he gave them his blessing, and—oh! mercy on us, Hans, it will be dark before you get back if you don't start this minute!"

By this time Dame Brinker was almost out of breath and quite out of commas. She could not remember when she had seen the children idle away an hour of daylight in this manner, and the thought of such luxury quite appalled her. By way of compensation she now flew about the room in extreme haste. Tossing a block of peat upon the fire, blowing invisible dust from the table, and handing the finished hose to Hans, all in an instant . . .

"Come, Hans," she said as her boy lingered by the door. "What keeps thee?"

Hans kissed his mother's plump cheek, rosy and fresh yet, in spite of all her troubles.

"My mother is the best in the world, and I would be right glad to have a pair of skates, but"—and as he buttoned his jacket he looked, in a troubled way, toward a strange figure crouching by the hearthstone—"if my money would bring a *meester** from Amsterdam to see the father, something might yet be done."

"A *meester* would not come, Hans, for twice that money, and

---

*Doctor (*dokter* in Dutch) called *meester* by the lower class.

it would do no good if he did. Ah, how many guilders I once spent for that, but the dear, good father would not waken. It is God's will. Go, Hans, and buy the skates."

Hans started with a heavy heart, but since the heart was young and in a boy's bosom, it set him whistling in less than five minutes. His mother had said "thee" to him, and that was quite enough to make even a dark day sunny. Hollanders do not address each other, in affectionate intercourse, as the French and Germans do. But Dame Brinker had embroidered for a Heidelberg family in her girlhood, and she had carried its *thee* and *thou* into her rude home, to be used in moments of extreme love and tenderness.

Therefore, "What keeps thee, Hans?" sang an echo song beneath the boy's whistling and made him feel that his errand was blessed.

Chapter 7

Hans Has His Way

*B*roek, with its quiet, spotless streets, its frozen rivulets, its yellow brick pavements and bright wooden houses, was nearby. It was a village where neatness and show were in full blossom, but the inhabitants seemed to be either asleep or dead.

Not a footprint marred the sanded paths where pebbles and seashells lay in fanciful designs. Every window shutter was closed as tightly, as though air and sunshine were poison, and the massive front doors were never opened except on the occasion of a wedding, a christening, or a funeral.

Serene clouds of tobacco smoke were floating through hidden apartments, and children, who otherwise might have awakened the place, were studying in out-of-the-way corners or skating upon the neighboring canal. A few peacocks and wolves stood in the gardens, but they had never enjoyed the luxury of flesh and blood. They were made out of boxwood hedges and seemed to be guarding the grounds with a sort of green ferocity. Certain lively automata, ducks, women, and sportsmen, were stowed away in summer houses, waiting for the springtime when they could be wound up and rival their owners in animation; and the shining tiled roofs, mosaic courtyards, and polished house trimmings flashed up a silent homage to the sky, where never a speck of dust could dwell.

Hans glanced toward the village as he shook his silver *kwartjes* and wondered whether it were really true, as he had often heard, that some of the people of Broek were so rich that they used kitchen utensils of solid gold.

He had seen Mevrouw van Stoop's sweet cheeses in market, and he knew that the lofty dame earned many a bright silver guilder in selling them. But did she set the cream to rise in golden pans? Did she use a golden skimmer? When her cows were in winter quarters, were their tails really tied up with ribbons?

These thoughts ran through his mind as he turned his face toward Amsterdam, not five miles away, on the other side of the frozen Y.* The ice upon the canal was perfect but his wooden runners, so soon to be cast aside, squeaked a dismal farewell as he scraped and skimmed along.

When crossing the Y, whom should he see skating toward him but the great Dr. Boekman, the most famous physician and surgeon in Holland. Hans had never met him before, but he had seen his engraved likeness in many of the shop windows of Amsterdam. It was a face that one could never forget. Thin and lank, though a born Dutchman, with stern blue eyes, and queer compressed lips that seemed to say "No smiling permitted," he certainly was not a very jolly or sociable-looking personage, nor one that a well-trained boy would care to accost unbidden.

But Hans *was* bidden, and that, too, by a voice he seldom disregarded—his own conscience.

"Here comes the greatest doctor in the world," whispered the voice. "God has sent him. You have no right to buy skates

---

*Pronounced eye, an arm of the Zuider Zee.

when you might, with the same money, purchase such aid for your father!"

The wooden runners gave an exultant squeak. Hundreds of beautiful skates were gleaming and vanishing in the air above him. He felt the money tingle in his fingers. The old doctor looked fearfully grim and forbidding. Hans's heart was in his throat, but he found voice enough to cry out, just as he was passing, "Mynheer Boekman!"

The great man halted and, sticking out his thin underlip, looked scowlingly about him.

Hans was in for it now.

"*Mynheer*," he panted, drawing close to the fierce-looking doctor, "I knew you could be none other than the famous Boekman. I have to ask a great favor—"

"Humph!" muttered the doctor, preparing to skate past the intruder. "Get out of the way. I've no money—never give to beggars."

"I am no beggar, *mynheer*," retorted Hans proudly, at the same time producing his mite of silver with a grand air. "I wish to consult with you about my father. He is a living man but sits like one dead. He cannot think. His words mean nothing, but he is not sick. He fell on the dikes."

"Hey? What?" cried the doctor, beginning to listen.

Hans told the whole story in an incoherent way, dashing off a tear once or twice as he talked, and finally ending with an earnest "Oh, do see him, *mynheer*. His body is well—it is only his mind. I know this money is not enough, but take it, *mynheer*, I will earn more, I know I will. Oh! I will toil for you all my life, if you will but cure my father!"

What was the matter with the old doctor? A brightness like sunlight beamed from his face. His eyes were kind and moist; the hand that had lately clutched his cane, as if preparing to strike, was laid gently upon Hans's shoulder.

"Put up your money, boy, I do not want it. We will see your father. It's hopeless, I fear. How long did you say?"

"Ten years, *mynheer*," sobbed Hans, radiant with sudden hope.

"Ah! a bad case, but I shall see him. Let me think. Today I start for Leyden, to return in a week, then you may expect me. Where is it?"

"A mile north of Broek, *mynheer*, near the canal. It is only a poor, broken-down hut. Any of the children thereabout can point it out to your honor," added Hans with a heavy sigh. "They are all half afraid of the place; they call it the idiot's cottage."

"That will do," said the doctor, hurrying on with a bright backward nod at Hans. "I shall be there. A hopeless case," he muttered to himself, "but the boy pleases me. His eye is like my poor Laurens. Confound it, shall I never forget that young scoundrel!" And, scowling more darkly than ever, the doctor pursued his silent way.

Again Hans was skating toward Amsterdam on the squeaking wooden runners; again his fingers tingled against the money in his pocket; again the boyish whistle rose unconsciously to his lips.

Shall I hurry home, he was thinking, to tell the good news, or shall I get the waffles and the new skates first? Whew! I think I'll go on!

And so Hans bought the skates.

Chapter 8

Introducing Jacob Poot
and His Cousin Ben

*H*ans and Gretel had a fine frolic early on that Saint Nicholas's Eve. There was a bright moon, and their mother, though she believed herself to be without any hope of her husband's improvement, had been made so happy at the prospect of the *meester*'s visit, that she had yielded to the children's entreaties for an hour's skating before bedtime.

Hans was delighted with his new skates and, in his eagerness to show Gretel how perfectly they "worked," did many things upon the ice that caused the little maid to clasp her hands in solemn admiration. They were not alone, though they seemed quite unheeded by the various groups assembled upon the canal.

The two Van Holps and Carl Schummel were there, testing their fleetness to the utmost. Out of four trials Peter van Holp had beaten three times. Consequently Carl, never very amiable, was in anything but a good humor. He had relieved himself by taunting young Schimmelpenninck, who, being smaller than the others, kept meekly near them without feeling exactly like one of the party, but now a new thought seized Carl, or rather he seized the new thought and made an onset upon his friends.

"I say, boys, let's put a stop to those young ragpickers from the idiot's cottage joining the race. Hilda must be crazy to think of it. Katrinka Flack and Rychie Korbes are furious at the very idea of racing with the girl; and, for my part, I don't blame them. As for the boy, if we've a spark of manhood in us, we will scorn the very idea of—"

"Certainly we will!" interposed Peter van Holp, purposely mistaking Carl's meaning. "Who doubts it? No fellow with a spark of manhood in him would refuse to let in two good skaters just because they were poor!"

Carl wheeled about savagely. "Not so fast, master! And I'd thank you not to put words in other people's mouths. You'd best not try it again."

"Ha! ha!" laughed little Voostenwalbert Schimmelpenninck, delighted at the prospect of a fight, and sure that, if it should come to blows, his favorite Peter could beat a dozen excitable fellows like Carl.

Something in Peter's eye made Carl glad to turn to a weaker offender. He wheeled furiously upon Voost.

"What are you shrieking about, you little weasel? You skinny herring you, you little monkey with a long name for a tail!"

Half a dozen bystanders and byskaters set up an applauding shout at this brave witticism; and Carl, feeling that he had fairly vanquished his foes, was restored to partial good humor. He, however, prudently resolved to defer plotting against Hans and Gretel until some time when Peter should not be present.

Just then, his friend, Jacob Poot, was seen approaching. They could not distinguish his features at first, but as he was the stoutest boy in the neighborhood, there could be no mistaking his form.

"Halloo! Here comes Fatty!" exclaimed Carl. "And there's someone with him, a slender fellow, a stranger."

"Ha! ha! That's like good bacon," cried Ludwig. "A streak of lean and a streak of fat."

"That's Jacob's English cousin," put in Master Voost, delighted at being able to give the information. "That's his English cousin, and oh, he's got such a funny little name—Ben Dobbs. He's going to stay with him until after the grand race."

All this time the boys had been spinning, turning, rolling, and doing other feats upon their skates, in a quiet way, as they talked, but now they stood still, bracing themselves against the frosty air as Jacob Poot and his friend drew near.

"This is my cousin, boys," said Jacob, rather out of breath. "Benjamin Dobbs. He's a John Bull, and he's going to be in the race."

All crowded, boy-fashion, about the newcomers. Benjamin soon made up his mind that the Hollanders, notwithstanding their queer gibberish, were a fine set of fellows.

If the truth must be told, Jacob had announced his cousin as Penchamin Dopps, and called him a Shon Pull, but as I translate every word of the conversation of our young friends, it is no more than fair to mend their little attempts at English. Master Dobbs felt at first decidedly awkward among his cousin's friends. Though most of them had studied English and French, they were shy about attempting to speak either, and he made very funny blunders when he tried to converse in Dutch. He had learned that *vrouw* meant wife; and *ja*, yes; and *spoorweg*, railway; *kanaals*, canals; *stoomboot*, steamboat; *ophaalbruggen*, drawbridges; *buiten plasten*, country seats; *mynheer*, mister; *tweegevegt*, duel or "two fights"; *koper*, copper; *zadel*, saddle; but he could not make a sentence out of these, nor use the long list of phrases he had learned in his "Dutch dialogues." The topics of the latter were fine but were never alluded to by the boys. Like the poor fellow who had learned in Ollendorf to ask in faultless German, "Have you seen my grandmother's red cow?" and, when he reached Germany, discovered that he had no occasion to inquire after that interesting animal, Ben found that his book-Dutch did not avail him as much as he had hoped. He acquired a hearty contempt for Jan van Gorp, a Hollander who wrote a book in Latin to prove that Adam and Eve spoke Dutch, and he smiled a knowing smile when his uncle Poot assured him that Dutch "had great likeness mit Zinglish but it vash much petter languish, much petter."

However, the fun of skating glides over all barriers of speech. Through this, Ben soon felt that he knew the boys well, and when Jacob (with a sprinkling of French and English for Ben's benefit) told of a grand project they had planned, his cousin could now and then put in a *ja*, or a nod, in quite a familiar way.

The project *was* a grand one, and there was to be a fine opportunity for carrying it out; for, besides the allotted holiday of the Festival of Saint Nicholas, four extra days were to be allowed for a general cleaning of the schoolhouse.

Jacob and Ben had obtained permission to go on a long skating journey—no less a one than from Broek to The Hague, the capital of Holland, a distance of nearly fifty miles!*

"And now, boys," added Jacob, when he had told the plan, "who will go with us?"

"I will! I will!" cried the boys eagerly.

"And so will I!" ventured little Voostenwalbert.

"Ha! ha!" laughed Jacob, holding his fat sides and shaking his puffy cheeks. "*You* go? Such a little fellow as you? Why, youngster, you haven't left off your pads yet!"

Now, in Holland very young children wear a thin, padded

---

*Throughout this narrative distances are given according to our standard, the English statute mile of 5,280 feet. The Dutch mile is more than four times as long as ours.

cushion around their heads, surmounted with a framework of whalebone and ribbon, to protect them in case of a fall; and it is the dividing line between babyhood and childhood when they leave it off. Voost had arrived at this dignity several years before; consequently Jacob's insult was rather too great for endurance.

"Look out what you say!" he squeaked. "Lucky for you when you can leave off *your* pads—you're padded all over!"

"Ha! ha!" roared all the boys except Master Dobbs, who could not understand. "Ha! ha!"—and the good-natured Jacob laughed more than any.

"It ish my fat—yaw—he say I bees pad mit fat!" he explained to Ben.

So a vote was passed unanimously in favor of allowing the now-popular Voost to join the party, if his parents would consent.

"Good night!" sang out the happy youngster, skating homeward with all his might.

"Good night!"

"We can stop at Haarlem, Jacob, and show your cousin the big organ," said Peter van Holp eagerly, "and at Leyden, too, where there's no end to the sights; and spend a day and night at The Hague, for my married sister, who lives there, will be delighted to see us; and the next morning we can start for home."

"All right!" responded Jacob, who was not much of a talker.

Ludwig had been regarding his brother with enthusiastic admiration.

"Hurrah for you, Pete! It takes you to make plans! Mother'll be as full of it as we are when we tell her we can take her love direct to sister Van Gend. My, but it's cold!" he added. "Cold enough to take a fellow's head off his shoulders. We'd better go home."

"What if it is cold, old Tender-skin?" cried Carl, who was busily practicing a step he called the "double edge." "Great skating we should have by this time, if it was as warm as it was last December. Don't you know if it wasn't an extra cold winter, and an early one into the bargain, we couldn't go?"

"I know it's an extra cold night anyhow," said Ludwig. "Whew! I'm going home!"

Peter van Holp took out a bulgy gold watch and, holding it toward the moonlight as well as his benumbed fingers would permit, called out, "Halloo! It's nearly eight o'clock! Saint Nicholas is about by this time, and I, for one, want to see the little ones stare. Good night!"

"Good night!" cried one and all, and off they started, shouting, singing, and laughing as they flew along.

Where were Gretel and Hans?

Ah, how suddenly joy sometimes comes to an end!

They had skated about an hour, keeping aloof from the others, quite contented with each other, and Gretel exclaimed, "Ah, Hans, how beautiful! How fine! To think that we both have skates! I tell you, the stork brought us good luck!" When they heard something!

It was a scream—a very faint scream! No one else upon the canal observed it, but Hans knew its meaning too well. Gretel saw him turn white in the moonlight as he hastily tore off his skates.

"The father!" he cried. "He has frightened our mother!" And Gretel ran after him toward the house as rapidly as she could.

Chapter 9

The Festival of Saint Nicholas

*W*e all know how, before the Christmas tree began to flourish in the home life of our country, a certain "right jolly old elf," with "eight tiny reindeer," used to drive his sleigh-load of toys up to our housetops, and then bounded down the chimney to fill the stockings so hopefully hung by the fireplace. His friends called him Santa Claus, and those who were most intimate ventured to say "Old Nick." It was said that he originally came from Holland. Doubtless he did, but, if so, he certainly, like many other foreigners, changed his ways very much after landing upon our shores. In Holland Saint Nicholas is a veritable saint and often appears in full costume, with his embroidered robes glittering with gems and gold, his miter, his crosier and his jeweled gloves. *Here* Santa Claus comes rollicking along, on the twenty-fifth of December, our holy Christmas morn. But in Holland, Saint Nicholas visits earth on the fifth, a time especially appropriated to him. Early on the morning of the sixth, he distributes his candies, toys, and treasures, then vanishes for a year.

Christmas Day is devoted by the Hollanders to church rites

and pleasant family visiting. It is on Saint Nicholas's Eve that their young people become half wild with joy and expectation. To some of them it is a sorry time, for the saint is very candid, and if any of them have been bad during the past year, he is quite sure to tell them so. Sometimes he carries a birch rod under his arm and advises the parents to give them scoldings in place of confections, and floggings instead of toys.

It was well that the boys hastened to their abodes on that bright winter evening, for in less than an hour afterward, the saint made his appearance in half the homes of Holland. He visited the king's palace and in the selfsame moment appeared in Annie Bouman's comfortable home. Probably one of our silver half-dollars would have purchased all that his saintship left at the peasant Bouman's; but a half-dollar's worth will sometimes do for the poor what hundreds of dollars may fail to do for the rich; it makes them happy and grateful, fills them with new peace and love.

Hilda van Gleck's little brothers and sisters were in a high state of excitement that night. They had been admitted into the grand parlor; they were dressed in their best and had been given two cakes apiece at supper. Hilda was as joyous as any. Why not? Saint Nicholas would never cross a girl of fourteen from his list, just because she was tall and looked almost like a woman. On the contrary, he would probably exert himself to do honor to such an august-looking damsel. Who could tell? So she sported and laughed and danced as gaily as the youngest and was the soul of all their merry games. Her father, mother, and grandmother looked on approvingly; so did her grandfather, before he spread his large red handkerchief over his face, leaving only the top of his skullcap visible. This kerchief was his ensign of sleep.

Earlier in the evening all had joined in the fun. In the general hilarity there had seemed to be a difference only in bulk between the grandfather and the baby. Indeed a shade of solemn expectation, now and then flitting across the faces of the younger members, had made them seem rather more thoughtful than their elders.

Now the spirit of fun reigned supreme. The very flames danced and capered in the polished grate. A pair of prim candles that had been staring at the astral lamp began to wink at other candles far away in the mirrors. There was a long bell rope suspended from the ceiling in the corner, made of glass beads netted over a cord nearly as thick as your wrist. It generally hung in the shadow and made no sign, but tonight it twinkled from end to end. Its handle of crimson glass sent reckless dashes of red at the papered wall, turning its dainty blue stripes into purple. Passersby halted to catch the merry laughter floating, through curtain and sash, into the street, then skipped on their way with a startled consciousness that the village was wide-awake. At last matters grew so uproarious that the grandsire's red kerchief came down from his face with a jerk. What decent old gentleman could sleep in such a racket! Mynheer van Gleck regarded his children with astonishment. The baby even showed symptoms of hysterics. It was high time to attend to business. Madame suggested that if they wished to see the good Saint Nicholas, they should sing the same loving invitation that had brought him the year before.

The baby stared and thrust his fist into his mouth as *mynheer* put him down upon the floor. Soon he sat erect and looked with a sweet scowl at the company. With his lace and embroideries and his crown of blue ribbon and whalebone (for he was not quite past the tumbling age), he looked like the king of the babies.

The other children, each holding a pretty willow basket, formed a ring at once, and moved slowly around the little fellow, lifting their eyes, for the saint to whom they were about to address themselves was yet in mysterious quarters.

Madame commenced playing softly upon the piano. Soon the voices rose—gentle, youthful voices—rendered all the sweeter for their tremor:

> "Welcome, friend! Saint Nicholas, welcome!
>   Bring no rod for us tonight!
> While our voices bid thee welcome,
>   Every heart with joy is light!
>
>   Tell us every fault and failing,
>   We will bear thy keenest railing,
>   So we sing—so we sing—
>   Thou shalt tell us everything!
>
> Welcome, friend! Saint Nicholas, welcome!
>   Welcome to this merry band!
> Happy children greet thee, welcome!
>   Thou art glad'ning all the land!
>
>   Fill each empty hand and basket,
>   'Tis thy little ones who ask it,
>   So we sing—so we sing—
>   Thou wilt bring us everything!"

During the chorus sundry glances, half in eagerness, half in dread, had been cast toward the polished folding doors. Now a loud knocking was heard. The circle was broken in an instant. Some of the little ones, with a stange mixture of fear and delight, pressed against their mother's knee. Grandfather bent forward with his chin resting upon his hand; Grandmother lifted her spectacles; Mynheer van Gleck, seated by the fireplace, slowly drew his meerschaum from his mouth while Hilda and the other children settled themselves beside him in an expectant group.

The knocking was heard again.

"Come in," said madame softly.

The door slowly opened, and Saint Nicholas, in full array, stood before them.

You could have heard a pin drop.

Soon he spoke. What a mysterious majesty in his voice! What kindliness in his tones!

"Karel van Gleck, I am pleased to greet thee, and thy honored *vrouw* Kathrine, and thy son and his good *vrouw* Annie!

"Children, I greet ye all! Hendrick, Hilda, Broom, Katy, Huygens, and Lucretia! And thy cousins, Wolfert, Diedrich, Mayken, Voost, and Katrina! Good children ye have been, in the main, since I last accosted ye. Diedrich was rude at the Haarlem fair last fall, but he has tried to atone for it since. Mayken has failed of late in her lessons, and too many sweets and trifles have gone to her lips, and too few stivers to her charity box. Diedrich, I trust, will be a polite, manly boy for the future, and Mayken will endeavor to shine as a student. Let her remember, too, that economy and thrift are needed in the foundation of a worthy and generous life. Little Katy has been cruel to the cat more than once. Saint Nicholas can hear the cat cry when its tail is pulled. I will forgive her if she will remember from this hour that the smallest dumb creatures have feeling and must not be abused."

As Katy burst into a frightened cry, the saint graciously remained silent until she was soothed.

"Master Broom," he resumed, "I warn thee that boys who are in the habit of putting snuff upon the foot stove of the school-mistress may one day be discovered and receive a flogging—"

Master Broom colored and stared in great astonishment.

"But thou art such an excellent scholar, I shall make thee no further reproof.

"Thou, Hendrick, didst distinguish thyself in the archery match last spring, and hit the *Doel*,* though the bird was swung before it to unsteady thine eye. I give thee credit for excelling in manly sport and exercise, though I must not unduly countenance thy boat racing, since it leaves thee too little time for thy proper studies.

"Lucretia and Hilda shall have a blessed sleep tonight. The consciousness of kindness to the poor, devotion in their souls, and cheerful, hearty obedience to household rule will render them happy.

"With one and all I avow myself well content. Goodness, industry, benevolence, and thrift have prevailed in your midst. Therefore, my blessing upon you—and may the new year find all treading the paths of obedience, wisdom, and love. Tomorrow you shall find more substantial proofs that I have been in your midst. Farewell!"

With these words came a great shower of sugarplums, upon a linen sheet spread out in front of the doors. A general scramble followed. The children fairly tumbled over each other in their eagerness to fill their baskets. Madame cautiously held the baby down in their midst, till the chubby little fists were filled. Then the bravest of the youngsters sprang up and burst open the closed doors. In vain they peered into the mysterious apartment. Saint Nicholas was nowhere to be seen.

Soon there was a general rush to another room, where stood a table, covered with the finest and whitest of linen damask. Each child, in a flutter of excitement, laid a shoe upon it. The door was then carefully locked, and its key hidden in the mother's bedroom. Next followed good-night kisses, a grand

---

*Bull's-eye.

family procession to the upper floor, merry farewells at bedroom doors, and silence, at last, reigned in the Van Gleck mansion.

Early the next morning the door was solemnly unlocked and opened in the presence of the assembled household, when lo! a sight appeared, proving Saint Nicholas to be a saint of his word!

Every shoe was filled to overflowing, and beside each stood many a colored pile. The table was heavy with its load of presents—candies, toys, trinkets, books, and other articles. Everyone had gifts, from the grandfather down to the baby.

Little Katy clapped her hands with glee and vowed inwardly that the cat should never know another moment's grief.

Hendrick capered about the room, flourishing a superb bow and arrows over his head. Hilda laughed with delight as she opened a crimson box and drew forth its glittering contents. The rest chuckled and said "Oh!" and "Ah!" over their treasures, very much as we did here in America on last Christmas Day.

With her glittering necklace in her hands and a pile of books in her arms, Hilda stole toward her parents and held up her beaming face for a kiss. There was such an earnest, tender look in her bright eyes that her mother breathed a blessing as she leaned over her.

"I am delighted with this book. Thank you, father," she said, touching the top one with her chin. "I shall read it all day long."

"Aye, sweetheart," said *mynheer*, "you cannot do better. There is no one like Father Cats. If my daughter learns his 'Moral Emblems' by heart, the mother and I may keep silent. The work you have there is the Emblems—his best work. You will find it enriched with rare engravings from Van de Venne."

Considering that the back of the book was turned away, *mynheer* certainly showed a surprising familiarity with an unopened volume, presented by Saint Nicholas. It was strange, too, that the saint should have found certain things made by the elder children and had actually placed them upon the table, labeled with parents' and grandparents' names. But all were too much absorbed in happiness to notice slight inconsistencies. Hilda saw, on her father's face, the rapt expression he always wore when he spoke of Jakob Cats, so she put her armful of books upon the table and resigned herself to listen.

"Old Father Cats, my child, was a great poet, not a writer of plays like the Englishman, Shakespeare, who lived in his time. I have read them in the German and very good they are—very, very good—but not like Father Cats. Cats sees no daggers in the air; he has no white women falling in love with dusky Moors; no young fools sighing to be a lady's glove; no crazy princes mistaking respectable old gentlemen for rats. No, no. He writes only sense. It is great wisdom in little bundles, a bundle for every day of your life. You can guide a state with Cats's poems, and you can put a little baby to sleep with his pretty songs. He was one of the greatest men of Holland. When I take you to The Hague, I will show you the Kloosterkerk where he lies buried. *There* was a man for you to study, my sons! He was good through and through. What did he say?

> "O Lord, let me obtain this from Thee
>   To live with patience, and to die with pleasure!*

"Did patience mean folding his hands? No, he was a lawyer, statesman, ambassador, farmer, philosopher, historian, and poet. He was keeper of the Great Seal of Holland! He was a—Bah! there is too much noise here, I cannot talk." And *mynheer*,

---

*O Heere! laat my dat van uwen hand verwerven,
Te leven met gedult, en met vermaak te sterven.*

looking with astonishment into the bowl of his meerschaum, for it had gone out, nodded to his *vrouw* and left the apartment in great haste.

The fact is, his discourse had been accompanied throughout with a subdued chorus of barking dogs, squeaking cats, and bleating lambs, to say nothing of a noisy ivory cricket that the baby was whirling with infinite delight. At the last, little Huygens, taking advantage of the increasing loudness of *mynheer*'s tones, had ventured a blast on his new trumpet, and Wolfert had hastily attempted an accompaniment on the drum. This had brought matters to a crisis, and it was good for the little creatures that it had. The saint had left no ticket for them to attend a lecture on Jakob Cats. It was not an appointed part of the ceremonies. Therefore when the youngsters saw that the mother looked neither frightened nor offended, they gathered new courage. The grand chorus rose triumphant, and frolic and joy reigned supreme.

Good Saint Nicholas! For the sake of the young Hollanders, I, for one, am willing to acknowledge him and defend his reality against all unbelievers.

Carl Schummel was quite busy during that day, assuring little children, confidentially, that not Saint Nicholas, but their own fathers and mothers, had produced the oracle and loaded the tables. But *we* know better than that.

And yet if this were a saint, why did he not visit the Brinker cottage that night? Why was that one home, so dark and sorrowful, passed by?

Chapter 10

What the Boys Saw and Did in Amsterdam

"**A**re we all here?" cried Peter, in high glee, as the party assembled upon the canal early the next morning, equipped for their skating journey. "Let me see. As Jacob has made me captain, I must call the roll. Carl Schummel, you here?"

"Ya!"

"Jacob Poot!"

"Ya!"

"Benjamin Dobbs!"

"Ya-a!"

"Lambert van Mounen!"

"Ya!"

"That's lucky! Couldn't get on without *you*, as you're the only one who can speak English. Ludwig van Holp!"

"Ya!"

"Voostenwalbert Schimmelpenninck!"

No answer.

"Ah, the little rogue has been kept at home! Now, boys, it's just eight o'clock—glorious weather, and the Y is as firm as a rock. We'll be at Amsterdam in thirty minutes. One, two, three, START!"

True enough, in less than half an hour they had crossed a dike of solid masonry and were in the very heart of the great metropolis of the Netherlands—a walled city of ninety-five islands and nearly two hundred bridges. Although Ben had been there twice since his arrival in Holland, he saw much to excite wonder, but his Dutch comrades, having lived nearby all their lives, considered it the most matter-of-course place in the world. Everything interested Ben: the tall houses with their forked chimneys and gable ends facing the street; the merchants' ware rooms, perched high up under the roofs of their dwellings, with long, armlike cranes hoisting and lowering goods past the household windows; the grand public buildings erected upon wooden piles driven deep into the marshy ground; the narrow streets; the canals crossing the city everywhere; the bridges; the locks; the various costumes; and, strangest of all, shops and dwellings crouching close to the fronts of the churches, sending their long, disproportionate chimneys far upward along the sacred walls.

If he looked up, he saw tall, leaning houses, seeming to pierce the sky with their shining roofs. If he looked down, there was the queer street, without crossing or curb—nothing to separate the cobblestone pavement from the footpath of brick— and if he rested his eyes halfway, he saw complicated little mirrors (*spionnen*) fastened upon the outside of nearly every window, so arranged that the inmates of the houses could observe all that was going on in the street or inspect whoever might be knocking at the door, without being seen themselves.

Sometimes a dogcart, heaped with wooden ware, passed him; then a donkey bearing a pair of panniers filled with crockery or glass; then a sled driven over the bare cobblestones (the runners kept greased with a dripping oil rag so that it might run easily);

and then, perhaps, a showy but clumsy family carriage, drawn by the brownest of Flanders horses, swinging the whitest of snowy tails.

The city was in full festival array. Every shop was gorgeous in honor of Saint Nicholas. Captain Peter was forced, more than once, to order his men away from the tempting show windows, where everything that is, has been, or can be thought of in the way of toys was displayed. Holland is famous for this branch of manufacture. Every possible thing is copied in miniature for the benefit of the little ones; the intricate mechanical toys that a Dutch youngster tumbles about in stolid unconcern would create a stir in our patent office. Ben laughed outright at some of the mimic fishing boats. They were so heavy and stumpy, so like the queer craft that he had seen about Rotterdam. The tiny *trekschuiten*, however, only a foot or two long, and fitted out, complete, made his heart ache. He so longed to buy one at once for his little brother in England. He had no money to spare, for, with true Dutch prudence, the party had agreed to take with them merely the sum required for each boy's expenses and to consign the purse to Peter for safekeeping. Consequently Master Ben concluded to devote all his energies to sight-seeing and to think as seldom as possible of little Robby.

He made a hasty call at the Marine school and envied the sailor students their full-rigged brig and their sleeping berths swung over their trunks or lockers; he peeped into the Jews' Quarter of the city, where the rich diamond cutters and squalid old-clothesmen dwell, and wisely resolved to keep away from it; he also enjoyed hasty glimpses of the four principal avenues of Amsterdam—the Prinsengracht, Keizersgracht, Herengracht, and Singel. These are semicircular in form, and the first three average more than two miles in length. A canal runs through the center of each, with a well-paved road on either side, lined with stately buildings. Rows of naked elms, bordering the ca-

nal, cast a network of shadows over its frozen surface, and
everything was so clean and bright that Ben told Lambert it
seemed to him like petrified neatness.

Fortunately the weather was cold enough to put a stop to the
usual street flooding, and window washing, or our young excur-
sionists might have been drenched more than once. Sweeping,
mopping, and scrubbing form a passion with Dutch housewives,
and to soil their spotless mansions is considered scarcely less
than a crime. Everywhere a hearty contempt is felt for those
who neglect to rub the soles of their shoes to a polish before
crossing the doorsill; and, in certain places, visitors are expected to remove their heavy shoes before entering.

Sir William Temple, in his memoirs of "What Passed in
Christendom from 1672 to 1679" tells a story of a pompous
magistrate going to visit a lady of Amsterdam. A stout Holland
lass opened the door and told him in a breath that the lady was
at home and that his shoes were not very clean. Without
another word she took the astonished man up by both arms,
threw him across her back, carried him through two rooms, set
him down at the bottom of the stairs, seized a pair of slippers
that stood there, and put them upon his feet. Then, and not
until then, she spoke, telling him that her mistress was on the
floor above and that he might go up.

While Ben was skating with his friends upon the crowded
canals of the city, he found it difficult to believe that the sleepy
Dutchmen he saw around him, smoking their pipes so leisurely
and looking as though their hats might be knocked off their
heads without their making any resistance, were capable of
those outbreaks that had taken place in Holland—that they
were really fellow countrymen of the brave, devoted heroes of
whom he had read in Dutch history.

As his party skimmed lightly along he told Van Mounen of a
burial riot which in 1696 had occurred in that very city, where

the women and children turned out, as well as the men, and formed mock funeral processions through the town, to show the burgomasters that certain new regulations, with regard to burying the dead, would not be acceded to—how at last they grew so unmanageable and threatened so much damage to the city that the burgomasters were glad to recall the offensive law.

"There's the corner," said Jacob, pointing to some large buildings, "where, about fifteen years ago, the great corn houses sank down in the mud. They were strong affairs and set up on good piles, but they had over seven million pounds of corn in them, and that was too much."

It was a long story for Jacob to tell, and he stopped to rest.

"How do you know there were seven million pounds in them?" asked Carl sharply. "You were in your swaddling clothes then."

"My father knows all about it" was Jacob's suggestive reply. Rousing himself with an effort, he continued, "Ben likes pictures. Show him some."

"All right," said the captain.

"If we had time, Benjamin," said Lambert van Mounen in English, "I should like to take you to the City Hall, or *Stadhuis*. There are building piles for you! It is built on nearly fourteen thousand of them, driven seventy feet into the ground. But what I wish you to see there is the big picture of Van Speyk blowing up his ship—great picture."

"Van *who*?" asked Ben.

"Van Speyk. Don't you remember? He was in the height of an engagement with the Belgians, and when he found that they had the better of him and would capture his ship, he blew it up, and himself, too, rather than yield to the enemy."

"Wasn't that Van Tromp?"

"Oh, no. Van Tromp was another brave fellow. They've a

monument to him down at Delftshaven—the place where the
Pilgrims took ship for America."

"Well, what about Van Tromp? He was a great Dutch admiral, wasn't he?"

"Yes, he was in more than thirty sea fights. He beat the
Spanish fleet and an English one, and then fastened a broom to
his masthead to show that he had swept the English from the
sea. Takes the Dutch to beat, my boy!"

"Hold up!" cried Ben. "Broom or no broom, the English
conquered him at last. I remember all about it now. He was
killed somewhere on the Dutch coast in an engagement in
which the British fleet was victorious. Too bad," he added
maliciously, "wasn't it?"

"Ahem! Where are we?" exclaimed Lambert, changing the
subject. "Halloo! The others are way ahead of us—all but
Jacob. Whew! How fat he is! He'll break down before we're
halfway."

Ben, of course, enjoyed skating beside Lambert, who, though
a staunch Hollander, had been educated near London and could
speak English as fluently as Dutch, but he was not sorry when
Captain van Holp called out, "Skates off! There's the museum!"

It was open, and there was no charge on that day for admission. In they went, shuffling, as boys will when they have a
chance, just to hear the sound of their shoes on the polished
floor.

This museum is in fact a picture gallery where some of the
finest works of the Dutch masters are to be seen, besides nearly
two hundred portfolios of rare engravings.

Ben noticed, at once, that some of the pictures were hung on
panels fastened to the wall with hinges. These could be swung
forward like a window shutter, thus enabling the subject to be
seen in the best light. The plan served them well in viewing a
small group by Gerard Douw, called the "Evening School,"

enabling them to observe its exquisite finish and the wonderful way in which the picture seemed to be lit through its own windows. Peter pointed out the beauties of another picture by Douw, called "The Hermit," and he also told them some interesting anecdotes of the artist, who was born at Leyden in 1613.

"Three days painting a broom handle!" echoed Carl in astonishment, while the captain was giving some instances of Douw's extreme slowness of execution.

"Yes, sir, three days. And it is said that he spent five in finishing one hand in a lady's portrait. You see how very bright and minute everything is in this picture. His unfinished works were kept carefully covered and his painting materials were put away in airtight boxes as soon as he had finished using them for the day. According to all accounts, the studio itself must have been as close as a bandbox. The artist always entered it on tiptoe, besides sitting still, before he commenced work, until the slight dust caused by his entrance had settled. I have read somewhere that his paintings are improved by being viewed through a magnifying glass. He strained his eyes so badly with this extra finishing that he was forced to wear spectacles before he was thirty. At forty he could scarcely see to paint, and he couldn't find a pair of glasses anywhere that would help his sight. At last, a poor old German woman asked him to try hers. They suited him exactly and enabled him to go on painting as well as ever."

"Humph!" exclaimed Ludwig indignantly. "That was high! What did *she* do without them, I wonder?"

"Oh," said Peter, laughing, "likely she had another pair. At any rate she insisted upon his taking them. He was so grateful that he painted a picture of the spectacles for her, case and all, and she sold it to a burgomaster for a yearly allowance that made her comfortable for the rest of her days."

"Boys!" called Lambert in a loud whisper, "come look at this 'Bear Hunt.' "

It was a fine painting by Paul Potter, a Dutch artist of the seventeenth century, who produced excellent works before he was sixteen years old. The boys admired it because the subject pleased them. They passed carelessly by the masterpieces of Rembrandt and Van der Helst and went into raptures over an ugly picture by Van der Venne, representing a sea fight between the Dutch and English. They also stood spellbound before a painting of two little urchins, one of whom was taking soup and the other eating an egg. The principal merit in this work was that the young egg-eater had kindly slobbered his face with the yolk for their entertainment.

An excellent representation of the "Feast of Saint Nicholas" next had the honor of attracting them.

"Look, Van Mounen," said Ben to Lambert. "Could anything be better than this youngster's face? He looks as if he *knows* he deserves a whipping but hopes Saint Nicholas may not have found him out. That's the kind of painting *I* like; something that tells a story."

"Come, boys!" cried the captain. "Ten o'clock, time we were off!"

They hastened to the canal.

"Skates on! Are you ready? One, two—halloo! Where's Poot?"

Sure enough, where *was* Poot?

A square opening had just been cut in the ice not ten yards off. Peter observed it and, without a word, skated rapidly toward it.

All the others followed, of course.

Peter looked in. They all looked in; then stared anxiously at each other.

"Poot!" screamed Peter, peering into the hole again. All was still. The black water gave no sign; it was already glazing on top.

Van Mounen turned mysteriously to Ben.

"*Didn't he have a fit once?*"

"My goodness! yes!" answered Ben in a great fright.

"Then, depend upon it, he's been taken with one in the museum!"

The boys caught his meaning. Every skate was off in a twinkling. Peter had the presence of mind to scoop up a capful of water from the hole, and off they scampered to the rescue.

Alas! They did indeed find poor Jacob in a fit, but it was a fit of sleepiness. There he lay in a recess of the gallery, snoring like a trooper! The chorus of laughter that followed this discovery brought an angry official to the spot.

"What now! None of this racket! Here, you beer barrel, wake up!" And Master Jacob received a very unceremonious shaking.

As soon as Peter saw that Jacob's condition was not serious, he hastened to the street to empty his unfortunate cap. While he was stuffing in his handkerchief to prevent the already frozen crown from touching his head, the rest of the boys came down, dragging the bewildered and indignant Jacob in their midst.

The order to start was again given. Master Poot was wide-awake at last. The ice was a little rough and broken just there, but every boy was in high spirits.

"Shall we go on by the canal or the river?" asked Peter.

"Oh, the river, by all means," said Carl. "It will be such fun; they say it is perfect skating all the way, but it's much farther."

Jacob Poot instantly became interested.

"*I* vote for the canal!" he cried.

"Well, the canal it shall be," responded the captain, "if all are agreed."

"Agreed!" they echoed, in rather a disappointed tone, and Captain Peter led the way.

"All right, come on. We can reach Haarlem in an hour!"

Chapter 11

Big Manias and Little Oddities

*W*hile skating along at full speed, they heard the cars from Amsterdam coming close behind them.

"Halloo!" cried Ludwig, glancing toward the rail track, "who can't beat a locomotive? Let's give it a race!"

The whistle screamed at the very idea—so did the boys—and at it they went.

For an instant the boys were ahead, hurrahing with all their might—only for an instant, but even *that* was something.

This excitement over, they began to travel more leisurely and indulge in conversation and frolic. Sometimes they stopped to exchange a word with the guards who were stationed at certain distances along the canal. These men, in winter, attend to keeping the surface free from obstruction and garbage. After a snowstorm they are expected to sweep the feathery covering away before it hardens into a marble pretty to look at but very unwelcome to skaters. Now and then the boys so far forgot their dignity as to clamber among the icebound canal boats crowded together in a widened harbor off the canal, but the watchful guards would soon spy them out and order them down with a growl.

Nothing could be straighter than the canal upon which our party were skating, and nothing straighter than the long rows of willow trees that stood, bare and wispy, along the bank. On the opposite side, lifted high above the surrounding country, lay the carriage road on top of the great dike built to keep the Haarlem Lake within bounds; stretching out far in the distance, until it became lost in a point, was the glassy canal with its many skaters, its brown-winged iceboats, its push-chairs, and its queer little sleds, light as cork, flying over the ice by means of iron-pronged sticks in the hands of the riders. Ben was in ecstasy with the scene.

Ludwig van Holp had been thinking how strange it was that the English boy should know so much of Holland. According to Lambert's account, he knew more about it than the Dutch did. This did not quite please our young Hollander. Suddenly he thought of something that he believed would make the "Shon Pull" open his eyes; he drew near Lambert with a triumphant "Tell him about the tulips!"

Ben caught the word *tulpen.*

"Oh, yes!" he said eagerly, in English, "the Tulip Mania— are you speaking of that? I have often heard it mentioned but know very little about it. It reached its height in Amsterdam, didn't it?"

Ludwig moaned; the words were hard to understand, but there was no mistaking the enlightened expression on Ben's face. Lambert, happily, was quite unconscious of his young countryman's distress as he replied, "Yes, here and in Haarlem, principally; but the excitement ran high all over Holland, and in England, too, for that matter."

"Hardly in England,* I think," said Ben, "but I am not sure, as I was not there at the time."

"Ha! ha! that's true, unless you are over two hundred years old. Well, I tell you, sir, there was never anything like it before or since. Why, persons were so crazy after tulip bulbs in those days that they paid their weight in gold for them."

"What, the weight of a man?" cried Ben, showing such astonishment in his eyes that Ludwig fairly capered.

"No, no, the weight of a *bulb*. The first tulip was sent here from Constantinople about the year 1560. It was so much admired that the rich people of Amsterdam sent to Turkey for more. From that time they grew to be the rage, and it lasted for years. Single roots brought from one to four thousand florins; and one bulb, the Semper Augustus, brought fifty-five hundred."

---

*Although the Tulip Mania did not prevail in England as in Holland, the flower soon became an object of speculation and brought very large prices. In 1636, tulips were publicly sold on the Exchange of London. Even as late as 1800, a common price was fifteen guineas for one bulb. Ben did not know that in his own day a single tulip plant, called the "Fanny Kemble," had been sold in London for more than seventy guineas.

Mr. Mackay in his *Memoirs of Popular Delusions* tells a funny story of an English botanist who happened to see a tulip bulb lying in the conservatory of a wealthy Dutchman. Ignorant of its value, he took out his penknife and, cutting the bulb in two, became very much interested in his investigations. Suddenly the owner appeared and, pouncing furiously upon him, asked him if he knew what he was doing. "Peeling a most extraordinary onion," replied the philosopher. "*Hundert tousant tuyvel!*" shouted the Dutchman, "it's an Admiral Van der Eyk!" "Thank you," replied the traveler, immediately writing the name in his notebook. "Pray are these very common in your country?" "Death and the *tuyvel!*" screamed the Dutchman. "Come before the Syndic and you shall see!" In spite of his struggles the poor investigator, followed by an indignant mob, was taken through the streets to a magistrate. Soon he learned to his dismay that he had destroyed a bulb worth 4,000 florins ($1,600). He was lodged in prison until securities could be procured for the payment of the sum.

"That's more than four hundred guineas of our money," interposed Ben.

"Yes, and I know I'm right, for I read it in a translation from Beckman, only day before yesterday. Well, sir, it was great. Everyone speculated in tulips, even the bargemen and rag women and chimney sweeps. The richest merchants were not ashamed to share the excitement. People bought bulbs and sold them again at a tremendous profit without ever seeing them. It grew into a kind of gambling. Some became rich by it in a few days, and some lost everything they had. Land, houses, cattle, and even clothing went for tulips when people had no ready money. Ladies sold their jewels and finery to enable them to join in the fun. Nothing else was thought of. At last the States-General interfered. People began to see what geese they were making of themselves, and down went the price of tulips. Old tulip debts couldn't be collected. Creditors went to law, and the law turned its back upon them; debts made in gambling were not binding, it said. Then there was a time! Thousands of rich speculators reduced to beggary in an hour. As old Beckman says, 'The bubble was burst at last.' "

"Yes, and a big bubble it was," said Ben, who had listened with great interest. "By the way, did you know that the word *tulip* came from the Turkish, signifying *turban?*"

"I had forgotten that," answered Lambert, "but it's a capital idea. Just fancy a party of Turks in full headgear, squatted upon a lawn—perfect tulip bed! Ha! ha! Capital idea!"

"There," groaned Ludwig to himself, "he's been telling Lambert something wonderful about tulips—I knew it!"

"The fact is," continued Lambert, "you can conjure up quite a human picture out of a tulip bed in bloom, especially when it is nodding and bobbing in the wind. Did you ever notice it?"

"Not I. It strikes me, Van Mounen, that you Hollanders are prodigiously fond of the flower to this day."

"Certainly. You can't have a garden without them; prettiest flower that grows, I think. My uncle has a magnificent bed of the finest varieties at his summer house on the other side of Amsterdam."

"I thought your uncle lived in the city?"

"So he does; but his summer house, or pavilion, is a few miles off. He has another one built out over the river. We passed near it when we entered the city. Everybody in Amsterdam has a pavilion somewhere, if he can."

"Do they ever live there?" asked Ben.

"Bless you, no! They are small affairs, suitable only to spend a few hours in on summer afternoons. There are some beautiful ones on the southern end of the Haarlem Lake—now that they've commenced to drain it into *polders,* it will spoil *that* fun. By the way, we've passed some red-roofed ones since we left home. You noticed them, I suppose, with their little bridges and ponds and gardens, and their mottoes over the doorway."

Ben nodded.

"They make but little show now," continued Lambert, "but in warm weather they are delightful. After the willows sprout, uncle goes to his summer house every afternoon. He dozes and smokes; aunt knits, with her feet perched upon a foot stove, never mind how hot the day; my cousin Rika and the other girls fish in the lake from the windows or chat with their friends rowing by; and the youngsters tumble about, or hang upon the little bridges over the ditch. Then they have coffee and cakes, beside a great bunch of water lilies on the table. It's very fine, I can tell you; only (between ourselves), though I was born here, I shall never fancy the odor of stagnant water that hangs about most of the summer houses. Nearly every one you see is built over a ditch. Probably I feel it more, from having lived so long in England."

"Perhaps I shall notice it too," said Ben, "if a thaw comes. This early winter has covered up the fragrant waters for my benefit—much obliged to it. Holland without this glorious skating wouldn't be the same thing to me at all."

"How very different you are from the Poots!" exclaimed Lambert, who had been listening in a sort of brown study, "and yet you are cousins—I cannot understand it."

"We *are* cousins, or rather we have always considered ourselves such, but the relationship is not very close. Our grandmothers were half-sisters. My side of the family is entirely English, while his is entirely Dutch. Old Great-grandfather Poot married twice, you see, and I am a descendant of his English wife. I like Jacob, though, better than half of my English cousins put together. He is the truest-hearted, best-natured boy I ever knew. Strange as you may think it, my father became accidentally acquainted with Jacob's father while on a business visit to Rotterdam. They soon talked over their relationship—in French, by the way—and they have corresponded in that language ever since. Queer things come about in this world. My sister Jenny would open her eyes at some of Aunt Poot's ways. Aunt is a thorough lady, but so different from mother—and the house, too, and the furniture, and way of living, everything is different."

"Of course," assented Lambert complacently, as if to say, You could scarcely expect such general perfection anywhere else than in Holland. "But you will have all the more to tell Jenny when you go back."

"Yes, indeed. I can say one thing—if cleanliness is, as they claim, next to godliness, Broek is safe. It is the cleanest place I ever saw in my life. Why, my Aunt Poot, rich as she is, scrubs half the time, and her house looks as if it were varnished all over. I wrote to mother yesterday that I could see my double always with me, feet to feet, in the polished floor of the dining room."

"Your *double*! That word puzzles me; what do you mean?"

"Oh, my reflection, my apparition. Ben Dobbs number two."

"Ah, I see," exclaimed Van Mounen. "Have you ever been in your Aunt Poot's grand parlor?"

Ben laughed. "Only once, and that was on the day of my arrival. Jacob says I shall have no chance of entering it again until the time of his sister Kenau's wedding, the week after Christmas. Father has consented that I shall remain to witness the great event. Every Saturday Aunt Poot and her fat Kate go into that parlor and sweep and polish and scrub; then it is darkened and closed until Saturday comes again; not a soul enters it in the meantime; but the *schoonmaken*, as she calls it, must be done, just the same."

"That is nothing. Every parlor in Broek meets with the same treatment," said Lambert. "What do you think of those moving figures in her neighbor's garden?"

"Oh, they're well enough; the swans must seem really alive gliding about the pond in summer; but that nodding mandarin in the corner, under the chestnut trees, is ridiculous, only fit for children to laugh at. And then the stiff garden patches, and the trees all trimmed and painted. Excuse me, Van Mounen, but I shall never learn to admire Dutch taste."

"It will take time," answered Lambert condescendingly, "but you are sure to agree with it at last. I saw much to admire in England, and I hope I shall be sent back with you to study at Oxford, but take everything together, I like Holland best."

"Of course you do," said Ben in a tone of hearty approval. "You wouldn't be a good Hollander if you didn't. Nothing like loving one's country. It is strange, though, to have such a warm feeling for such a cold place. If we were not exercising all the time, we should freeze outright."

Lambert laughed.

"That's your English blood, Benjamin. *I'm* not cold. And

look at the skaters here on the canal—they're red as roses and happy as lords. Halloo! good Captain van Holp," called out Lambert in Dutch, "what say you to stopping at yonder farmhouse and warming our toes?"

"Who is cold?" asked Peter, turning around.

"Benjamin Dobbs."

"Benjamin Dobbs shall be warmed," and the party was brought to a halt.

Chapter 12

On the Way to Haarlem

*O*n approaching the door of the farmhouse the boys suddenly found themselves in the midst of a lively domestic scene. A burly Dutchman came rushing out, closely followed by his dear *vrouw*, and she was beating him smartly with a long-handled warming pan. Her expression gave our boys so little promise of a kind reception that they prudently resolved to carry their toes elsewhere to be warmed.

The next cottage proved to be more inviting. Its low roof of bright red tiles extended over the cow stable that, clean as could be, nestled close to the main building. A neat, peaceful-looking old woman sat at one window, knitting. At the other could be discerned part of the profile of a fat figure that, pipe in mouth, sat behind the shining little panes and snowy curtain. In answer to Peter's subdued knock, a fair-haired, rosy-cheeked lass in holiday attire opened the upper half of the green door (which was divided across the middle) and inquired their errand.

"May we enter and warm ourselves, *jufvrouw?*" asked the captain respectfully.

"Yes, and welcome" was the reply as the lower half of the door swung softly toward its mate. Every boy, before entering, rubbed long and faithfully upon the rough mat, and each made his best bow to the old lady and gentleman at the windows. Ben was half inclined to think that these personages were automata like the moving figures in the garden at Broek; for they both nodded their heads slowly, in precisely the same way, and both went on with their employment as steadily and stiffly as though they worked by machinery. The old man puffed-puffed, and his *vrouw* clicked her knitting needles, as if regulated by internal cogs. Even the real smoke issuing from the motionless pipe gave no convincing proof that they were human.

But the rosy-cheeked maiden. Ah, how she bustled about. How she gave the boys polished high-backed chairs to sit upon, how she made the fire blaze up as if it were inspired, how she made Jacob Poot almost weep for joy by bringing forth a great square of gingerbread and a stone jug of sour wine! How she laughed and nodded as the boys ate like wild animals on good behavior, and how blank she looked when Ben politely but firmly refused to take any black bread and sauerkraut! How she pulled off Jacob's mitten, which was torn at the thumb, and mended it before his eyes, biting off the thread with her white teeth and saying "Now it will be warmer" as she bit; and finally, how she shook hands with every boy in turn and, throwing a deprecating glance at the female automaton, insisted upon filling their pockets with gingerbread!

All this time the knitting needles clicked on, and the pipe never missed a puff.

When the boys were fairly on their way again, they came in sight of Zwanenburg Castle with its massive stone front and its gateway towers, each surmounted with a sculptured swan.

"*Halfweg,* * boys," said Peter, "off with your skates."

"You see," explained Lambert to his companion, "the Y and the Haarlem Lake meeting here make it rather troublesome.

---

*Halfway.

The river is five feet higher than the land, so we must have everything strong in the way of dikes and sluice gates or there would be wet work at once. The sluice arrangements here are supposed to be something extra. We will walk over them and you shall see enough to make you open your eyes. The spring water of the lake, they say, has the most wonderful bleaching powers of any in the world; all the great Haarlem bleacheries use it. I can't say much upon that subject, but I can tell you *one* thing from personal experience."

"What is that?"

"Why, the lake is full of the biggest eels you ever saw. I've caught them here, often—perfectly prodigious! I tell you they're sometimes a match for a fellow; they'd almost wriggle your arm from the socket if you were not on your guard. But you're not interested in eels, I perceive. The castle's a big affair, isn't it?"

"Yes. What do those swans mean? Anything?" asked Ben, looking up at the stone gate towers.

"The swan is held almost in reverence by us Hollanders. These give the building its name—Zwanenburg, swan castle. That is all I know. This is a very important spot; for it is here that the wise ones hold council with regard to dike matters. The castle was once the residence of the celebrated Christiaan Brünings."

"What about *him?*" asked Ben.

"Peter could answer you better than I," said Lambert, "if you could only understand each other or were not such cowards about leaving your mother tongues. But I have often heard my grandfather speak of Brünings. He is never tired of telling us of the great engineer—how good he was and how learned, and how, when he died, the whole country seemed to mourn as for a friend. He belonged to a great many learned societies and was at the head of the State Department, entrusted with the care of the dikes and other defenses against the sea. There's no counting the improvements he made in dikes and sluices and water mills and all that kind of thing. We Hollanders, you know, consider our great engineers as the highest of public benefactors. Brünings died years ago; they've a monument to his memory in the cathedral of Haarlem. I have seen his portrait, and I tell you, Ben, he was right noble-looking. No wonder the castle looks so stiff and proud. It is something to have given shelter to such a man!"

"Yes, indeed," said Ben. "I wonder, Van Mounen, whether you or I will ever give any old building a right to feel proud. Heigh-ho! There's a great deal to be done yet in this world, and some of us, who are boys now, will have to do it. Look to your shoe latchet, Van. It's unfastened."

Chapter 13

A Catastrophe

*I*t was nearly one o'clock when Captain van Holp and his command entered the grand old city of Haarlem. They had skated nearly seventeen miles since morning and were still as fresh as young eagles. From the youngest (Ludwig van Holp, who was just fourteen) to the eldest, no less a personage than the captain himself, a veteran of seventeen, there was but one opinion—that this was the greatest frolic of their lives. To be sure, Jacob Poot had become rather short of breath during the last mile or two, and perhaps he felt ready for another nap, but there was enough jollity in him yet for a dozen. Even Carl Schummel, who had become very intimate with Ludwig during the excursion, forgot to be ill-natured. As for Peter, he was the happiest of the happy and had sung and whistled so joyously while skating that the staidest passersby had smiled as they listened.

"Come, boys! It's nearly *tiffin** hour," he said as they neared a coffeehouse on the main street. "We must have something more solid than the pretty maiden's gingerbread"—and the captain plunged his hands into his pockets as if to say, "There's money enough here to feed an army!"

---

*Lunch.

"Halloo!" cried Lambert. "What ails the man?"

Peter, pale and staring, was clapping his hands upon his breast and sides. He looked like one suddenly becoming deranged.

"He's sick!" cried Ben.

"No, he's lost something," said Carl.

Peter could only gasp, "The pocketbook with all our money in it—it's gone!"

For an instant all were too startled to speak.

Carl at last came out with a gruff, "No sense in letting one fellow have all the money. I said so from the first. Look in your other pocket."

"I did. It isn't there."

"Open your underjacket."

Peter obeyed mechanically. He even took off his hat and looked into it, then thrust his hand desperately into every pocket.

"It's gone, boys," he said at last in a hopeless tone. "No *tiffin* for us, nor dinner, either. What is to be done? We can't get on without money. If we were in Amsterdam, I could get as much as we want, but there is not a man in Haarlem from whom I can borrow a stiver. Don't one of you know anyone here who would lend us a few guilders?"

Each boy looked into five blank faces. Then something like a smile passed around the circle, but it got sadly knotted up when it reached Carl.

"That wouldn't do," he said crossly. "I know some people here, rich ones, too, but father would flog me soundly if I borrowed a cent from anyone. He has 'An honest man need not borrow' written over the gateway of his summer house."

"Humph!" responded Peter, not particularly admiring the sentiment just at that moment.

The boys grew desperately hungry at once.

"It wash my fault," said Jacob, in a penitent tone, to Ben. "I say first, petter all de boys put zair pursh into Van Holp's monish."

"Nonsense, Jacob. You did it all for the best."

Ben said this in such a sprightly tone that the two Van Holps and Carl felt sure he had proposed a plan that would relieve the party at once.

"What? what? Tell us, Van Mounen," they cried.

"He says it is not Jacob's fault that the money is lost—that he did it for the best when he proposed that Van Holp should put all of our money into his purse."

"Is that all?" said Ludwig dismally. "He need not have made such a fuss in just saying *that*. How much money have we lost?"

"Don't you remember?" said Peter. "We each put in exactly ten guilders. The purse had sixty guilders in it. I am the stupidest fellow in the world; little Schimmelpenninck would have made you a better captain. I could pommel myself for bringing such a disappointment upon you."

"Do it, then," growled Carl. "Pooh," he added, "we all know it was an accident, but that doesn't help matters. We must have money, Van Holp—even if you have to sell your wonderful watch."

"Sell my mother's birthday present! Never! I will sell my coat, my hat, anything but my watch."

"Come, come," said Jacob pleasantly, "we are making too much of this affair. We can go home and start again in a day or two."

"*You* may be able to get another ten-guilder piece," said Carl, "but the rest of us will not find it so easy. If we go home, we stay home, you can depend on it."

Our captain, whose good nature had not yet forsaken him for a moment, grew indignant.

"Do you think I will let you suffer for my carelessness?" he exclaimed. "I have three times sixty guilders in my strongbox at home!"

"Oh, I beg your pardon," said Carl hastily, adding in a surlier tone, "Well, I see no better way than to go back hungry."

"I see a better plan than that," said the captain.

"What is it?" cried all the boys.

"Why, to make the best of a bad business and go back pleasantly and like men," said Peter, looking so gallant and handsome as he turned his frank face and clear blue eyes upon them that they caught his spirit.

"Ho for the captain!" they shouted.

"Now, boys, we may as well make up our minds, there's no place like Broek, after all—and that we mean to be there in two hours. Is that agreed to?"

"Agreed!" cried all as they ran to the canal.

"On with your skates! Are you ready? Here, Jacob, let me help you."

"Now. One, two, three, start!"

And the boyish faces that left Haarlem at that signal were nearly as bright as those that had entered it with Captain Peter half an hour before.

Chapter 14

Hans

"*D*onder and Blixin!" cried Carl angrily, before the party had skated twenty yards from the city gates, "if here isn't that wooden-skate ragamuffin in the patched leather breeches. That fellow is everywhere, confound him! We'll be lucky," he added, in as sneering a tone as he dared to assume, "if our captain doesn't order us to halt and shake hands with him."

"Your captain is a terrible fellow," said Peter pleasantly, "but this is a false alarm, Carl. I cannot spy your bugbear anywhere among the skaters. Ah, there he is! Why, what is the matter with the lad?"

Poor Hans! His face was pale, his lips compressed. He skated like one under the effects of a fearful dream. Just as he was passing, Peter hailed him. "Good day, Hans Brinker!"

Hans's countenance brightened at once. "Ah, *mynheer*, is that you? It is well we meet!"

"Just like his impertinence," hissed Carl Schummel, darting scornfully past his companions, who seemed inclined to linger with their captain.

"I am glad to see you, Hans," responded Peter cheerily, "but you look troubled. Can I serve you?"

"I have a trouble, *mynheer*," answered Hans, casting down his eyes. Then, lifting them again with almost a happy expression, he added, "But it is Hans who can help Mynheer van Holp *this* time."

"How?" asked Peter, making, in his blunt Dutch way, no attempt to conceal his surprise.

"By giving you *this, mynheer.*" And Hans held forth the missing purse.

"Hurrah!" shouted the boys, taking their cold hands from their pockets to wave them joyfully in the air. But Peter said "Thank you, Hans Brinker" in a tone that made Hans feel as if the king had knelt to him.

The shout of the delighted boys reached the muffled ears of the fine young gentleman who, under a full pressure of pent-up wrath, was skating toward Amsterdam. A Yankee boy would have wheeled about at once and hastened to satisfy his curiosity. But Carl only halted and, with his back toward his party, wondered what on earth had happened. There he stood, immovable, until, feeling sure that nothing but the prospect of something to eat could have made them hurrah so heartily, he turned and skated slowly toward his excited comrades.

In the meantime Peter had drawn Hans aside from the rest.

"How did you know it was my purse?" he asked.

"You paid me three guilders yesterday, *mynheer*, for making the whitewood chain, telling me that I must buy skates."

"Yes, I remember."

"I saw your purse then. It was of yellow leather."

"And where did you find it today?"

"I left my home this morning, *mynheer*, in great trouble, and as I skated, I took no heed until I stumbled against some lumber, and while I was rubbing my knee, I saw your purse nearly hidden under a log."

"That place! Ah, I remember now. Just as we were passing it

I pulled my tippet from my pocket and probably flipped out the purse at the same time. It would have been gone but for you, Hans. Here"—pouring out the contents—"you must give us the pleasure of dividing the money with you."

"No, *mynheer,*" answered Hans. He spoke quietly, without pretense or any grace of manner, but Peter, somehow, felt rebuked, and put the silver back without a word.

I like that boy, rich or poor, he thought to himself, then added aloud, "May I ask about this trouble of yours, Hans?"

"Ah, *mynheer,* it is a sad case, but I have waited here too long. I am going to Leyden to see the great Dr. Boekman."

"Dr. Boekman!" exclaimed Peter in astonishment.

"Yes, *mynheer,* and I have not a moment to lose. Good day!"

"Say, I am going that way. Come, my lads! Shall we return to Haarlem?"

"Yes," cried the boys eagerly—and off they started.

"Now," said Peter, drawing near Hans, both skimming the ice so easily and lightly as they skated on together that they seemed scarcely conscious of moving. "We are going to stop at Leyden, and if you are going there with only a message for Dr. Boekman, cannot I do the errand for you? The boys may be too tired to skate so far today, but I will promise to see him early tomorrow if he is to be found in the city."

"Ah, *mynheer,* that would be serving me indeed; it is not the distance I dread but leaving my mother so long."

"Is she ill?"

"No, *mynheer.* It is the father. You may have heard it; how he has been without wit for many a year—ever since the great Schlossen Mill was built; but his body has been well and strong. Last night the mother knelt upon the hearth to blow the peat (it is his only delight to sit and watch the live embers, and she will blow them into a blaze every hour of the day to please him). Before she could stir, he sprang upon her like a giant and held her close to the fire, all the time laughing and shaking his head. I was on the canal, but I heard the mother scream and ran to her. The father had never loosened his hold, and her gown was smoking. I tried to deaden the fire, but with one hand, he pushed me off. There was no water in the cottage or I could have done better, and all that time he laughed—such a terrible laugh, *mynheer*, hardly a sound, but all in his face. I tried to pull her away, but that only made it worse. Then—it was dreadful, but could I see the mother burn? I beat him—beat him with a stool. He tossed me away. The gown was on fire! I *would* put it out. I can't remember well after that. I found myself upon the floor, and the mother was praying. It seemed to me that she was in a blaze, and all the while I could hear that laugh. My sister Gretel screamed out that he was holding the mother close to the very coals. *I* could not tell! Gretel flew to the closet and filled the porringer with the food he liked and put it upon the floor. Then, *mynheer*, he left the mother and crawled to it like a little child. She was not burned, only a part of her clothing. Ah, how kind she was to him all night, watching and tending him. He slept in a high fever, with his hand pressed to his head. The mother says he has done that so much of late, as though he felt pain there. Ah, *mynheer*, I did not mean to tell you. If the father was himself, he would not harm even a kitten."

For a moment the two boys moved on in silence.

"It is terrible," said Peter at last. "How is he today?"

"Very sick, *mynheer*."

"Why go for Dr. Boekman, Hans? There are others in Amsterdam who could help him, perhaps. Boekman is a famous man, sought only by the wealthiest, and they often wait upon him in vain."

"He *promised, mynheer*. He promised me yesterday to come to the father in a week. But now that the change has come, we cannot wait. We think the poor father is dying. Oh, *mynheer*, you can plead with him to come quick. He will not wait a whole week and our father dying, the good *meester* is so kind."

"*So kind!*" echoed Peter in astonishment. "Why, he is known as the crossest man in Holland!"

"He looks so because he has no fat and his head is busy, but his heart is kind, I know. Tell the *meester* what I have told you, *mynheer*, and he will come."

"I hope so, Hans, with all my heart. You are in haste to turn homeward, I see. Promise me that should you need a friend you will go to my mother at Broek. Tell her I bade you see her. And, Hans Brinker, not as a reward, but as a gift, take a few of these guilders."

Hans shook his head resolutely.

"No, no, *mynheer*. I cannot take it. If I could find work in Broek or at the South Mill, I would be glad, but it is the same story everywhere—'Wait till spring.' "

"It is well you speak of it," said Peter eagerly, "for my father needs help at once. Your pretty chain pleased him much. He said, 'That boy has a clean cut; he would be good at carving.' There is to be a carved portal to our new summer house, and father will pay well for the job."

"God is good!" cried Hans in sudden delight. "Oh, *mynheer*, that would be too much joy! I have never tried big work, but I can do it. I know I can."

"Well, tell my father you are the Hans Brinker of whom I spoke. He will be glad to serve you."

Hans stared in honest surprise.

"Thank you, *mynheer*."

"Now, captain," shouted Carl, anxious to appear as good-humored as possible, by way of atonement, "here we are in the midst of Haarlem, and no word from you yet. We await your orders, and we're as hungry as wolves."

Peter made a cheerful answer and turned hurriedly to Hans.

"Come, get something to eat, and I will detain you no longer."

What a quick, wistful look Hans threw upon him! Peter wondered that he had not noticed before that the poor boy was hungry.

"Ah, *mynheer*, even now the mother may need me, the father may be worse—I must not wait. May God care for you." And, nodding hastily, Hans turned his face homeward and was gone.

"Come, boys," sighed Peter. "Now for our *tiffin*!"

Chapter 15

Homes

*I*t must not be supposed that our young Dutch-men had already forgotten the great skating race which was to take place on the twentieth. On the contrary, they had thought and spoken of it very often during the day. Even Ben, though he had felt more like a traveler than the rest, had never once, through all the sight-seeing, lost a certain vision of silver skates, which, for a week past, had haunted him night and day.

Like a true "John Bull," as Jacob had called him, he never doubted that his English fleetness, English strength, English everything, could at any time enable him, on the ice, to put all Holland to shame, and the rest of the world, too, for that matter. Ben certainly was a superb skater. He had enjoyed not half the opportunities for practicing that had fallen to his new comrades but he had improved his share to the utmost and was, besides, so strong of frame, so supple of limb, in short, such a tight, trim, quick, graceful fellow in every way that he had taken to skating as naturally as a chamois to leaping or an eagle to soaring.

Only to the heavy heart of poor Hans had the vision of the silver skates failed to appear during that starry winter night and the brighter sunlit day.

Even Gretel had seen them flitting before her as she sat beside her mother through those hours of weary watching—not as prizes to be won but as treasures passing hopelessly beyond her reach.

Rychie, Hilda and Katrinka—why, they had scarcely known any other thought than "The race! The race! It will come off on the twentieth!"

These three girls were friends. Though of nearly the same age, talent, and station, they were as different as girls could be.

Hilda van Gleck, you already know, was a warmhearted, noble girl of fourteen. Rychie Korbes was beautiful to look upon, far more sparkling and pretty than Hilda but not half so bright and sunny within. Clouds of pride, discontent, and envy had already gathered in her heart and were growing bigger and darker every day. Of course, these often relieved themselves very much after the manner of other clouds. But who saw the storms and the weeping? Only her maid or her father, mother, and little brother—those who loved her better than all. Like other clouds, too, hers often took queer shapes, and what was really but mist and vapory fancy assumed the appearance of monster wrongs and mountains of difficulty. To her mind the poor peasant girl Gretel was not a human being, a God-created creature like herself—she was only something that meant poverty, rags, and dirt. Such as Gretel had no right to feel, to hope; above all, they should never cross the paths of their betters—that is, not in a disagreeable way. They could toil and labor for them at a respectful distance, even admire them, if they would do it humbly, but nothing more. If they rebel, put them down; if they suffer, "Don't trouble me about it" was Rychie's secret motto. And yet how witty she was, how tastefully she dressed, how charmingly she sang; how much feeling she displayed (for pet kittens and rabbits), and how completely she could bewitch sensible, honest-minded lads like Lambert van Mounen and Ludwig van Holp!

Carl was too much like her, within, to be an earnest admirer, and perhaps he suspected the clouds. He, being deep and surly and always uncomfortably in earnest, of course preferred the lively Katrinka, whose nature was made of a hundred tinkling bells. She was a coquette in her infancy, a coquette in her childhood, and now a coquette in her school days. Without a thought of harm she coquetted with her studies, her duties, even her little troubles. They shouldn't know when they bothered her, not they. She coquetted with her mother, her pet lamb, her baby brother, even with her own golden curls—tossing them back as if she despised them. Everyone liked her, but who could love her? She was never in earnest. A pleasant face, a pleasant heart, a pleasant manner—these only satisfy for an hour. Poor happy Katrinka! She tinkled, tinkled so merrily through their early days, but life is so apt to coquette with them in turn, to put all their sweet bells out of tune or to silence them one by one!

How different were the homes of these three girls from the tumbling old cottage where Gretel dwelt. Rychie lived in a beautiful house near Amsterdam, where the carved sideboards were laden with services of silver and gold and where silken tapestries hung in folds from ceiling to floor.

Hilda's father owned the largest mansion in Broek. Its glittering roof of polished tiles and its boarded front, painted in half a dozen various colors, were the admiration of the neighborhood.

Katrinka's home, not a mile distant, was the finest of Dutch country seats. The garden was so stiffly laid out in little paths and patches that the birds might have mistaken it for a great Chinese puzzle with all the pieces spread out ready for use. But in summer it was beautiful; the flowers made the best of their stiff quarters, and, when the gardener was not watching, glowed and bent and twined about each other in the prettiest way imaginable. Such a tulip bed! Why, the queen of the fairies would never care for a grander city in which to hold her court! But Katrinka preferred the bed of pink and white hyacinths. She loved their freshness and fragrance and the lighthearted way in which their bell-shaped blossoms swung in the breeze.

Carl was both right and wrong when he said that Katrinka and Rychie were furious at the very idea of the peasant Gretel joining in the race. He had heard Rychie declare that it was "Disgraceful, shameful, too bad!" which in Dutch, as in English, is generally the strongest expression an indignant girl can use; and he had seen Katrinka nod her pretty head and heard her sweetly echo, "Shameful, too bad!" as nearly like Rychie as tinkling bells can be like the voice of real anger. That had satisfied him. He never suspected that had Hilda, not Rychie, first talked with Katrinka on the subject, the bells would have jingled as willing an echo. She would have said, "Certainly, let her join us," and would have skipped off thinking no more about it. But *now* Katrinka, with sweet emphasis, pronounced it a shame that a goose-girl, a forlorn little creature like Gretel, should be allowed to spoil the race.

Rychie, being rich and powerful (in a schoolgirl way), had other followers besides Katrinka who were induced to share her opinions because they were either too careless or too cowardly to think for themselves.

Poor little Gretel! Her home was sad and dark enough now. Raff Brinker lay moaning upon his rough bed, and his *vrouw*, forgetting and forgiving everything, bathed his forehead, his lips, weeping and praying that he might not die. Hans, as we know, had started in desperation for Leyden to search for Dr. Boekman and induce him, if possible, to come to their father at once. Gretel, filled with a strange dread, had done the work as well as she could, wiped the rough brick floor, brought peat to build up the slow fire, and melted ice for her mother's use. This accomplished, she seated herself upon a low stool near the bed and begged her mother to try and sleep awhile.

"You are so tired," she whispered. "Not once have you closed your eyes since that dreadful hour last night. See, I have straightened the willow bed in the corner and spread everything soft upon it I could find, so that the mother might lie in comfort. Here is your jacket. Take off that pretty dress. I'll fold it away very carefully and put it in the big chest before you go to sleep."

Dame Brinker shook her head without turning her eyes from her husband's face.

"I can watch, mother," urged Gretel, "and I'll wake you every time the father stirs. You are so pale, and your eyes are so red—oh, mother, *do!*"

The child pleaded in vain. Dame Brinker would not leave her post.

Gretel looked at her in troubled silence, wondering whether it were very wicked to care more for one parent than for the other, and sure—yes, quite sure—that she dreaded her father while she clung to her mother with a love that was almost idolatry.

Hans loves the father so well, she thought, why cannot I? Yet I could not help crying when I saw his hand bleed that day, last month, when he snatched the knife—and now, when he moans, how I ache, ache all over. Perhaps I love him, after all, and God will see I am not such a bad, wicked girl as I thought. Yes, I love the poor father—almost as Hans does—not quite, for Hans is stronger and does not fear him. Oh, will that moaning go on forever and ever! Poor mother, how patient she is; *she* never pouts, as I do, about the money that went so strangely. If he only could, just for one instant, open his eyes and look at us, as Hans does, and tell us where mother's guilders went, I would not care for the rest. Yes, I would care. I don't want the poor father to die, to be all blue and cold like Annie Bouman's little sister. I *know* I don't. Dear God, I don't want Father to die.

Her thoughts merged into a prayer. When it ended the poor child scarcely knew. Soon she found herself watching a little pulse of light at the side of the fire, beating faintly but steadily, showing that somewhere in the dark pile there was warmth and light that would overspread it at last. A large earthen cup filled with burning peat stood near the bedside; Gretel had placed it there to "stop the father's shivering," she said. She watched it as it sent a glow around the mother's form, tipping her faded skirt with light and shedding a sort of newness over the threadbare bodice. It was a relief to Gretel to see the lines in that weary face soften as the firelight flickered gently across it.

Next she counted the windowpanes, broken and patched as they were, and finally, after tracing every crack and seam in the walls, fixed her gaze upon a carved shelf made by Hans. The shelf hung as high as Gretel could reach. It held a large leather-covered Bible with brass clasps, a wedding present to Dame Brinker from the family at Heidelberg.

Ah, how handy Hans is! If he were here, he could turn the father some way so the moans would stop. Dear, dear! If this sickness lasts, we shall never skate anymore. I must send my new skates back to the beautiful lady. Hans and I will not see the race. And Gretel's eyes, which had been dry before, grew full of tears.

"Never cry, child," said her mother soothingly. "This sickness may not be as bad as we think. The father has lain this way before."

Gretel sobbed now.

"Oh, mother, it is not that alone—you do not know all. I am very, very bad and wicked!"

"*You*, Gretel! You, so patient and good!" and a bright puzzled look beamed for an instant upon the child. "Hush, lovey, you'll wake him."

Gretel hid her face in her mother's lap and tried not to cry.

Her little hand, so thin and brown, lay in the coarse palm of her mother's, creased with many a hard day's work. Rychie would have shuddered to touch either, yet they pressed warmly upon each other. Soon Gretel looked up with that dull, homely look, which, they say, poor children in shanties are apt to have, and said in a trembling voice, "The father tried to burn you—he did—I saw him, and he was *laughing!*"

"Hush, child!"

The mother's words came so suddenly and sharply that Raff Brinker, dead as he was to all that was passing around him, twitched slightly upon the bed.

Gretel said no more but plucked drearily at the jagged edge of a hole in her mother's holiday gown. It had been burned there. Well for Dame Brinker that the gown was woolen.

Chapter 16

Haarlem—the Boys Hear Voices

*R*efreshed and rested, our boys came forth from the coffeehouse just as the big clock in the square, after the manner of certain Holland timekeepers, was striking two with its half-hour bell for half past two.

The captain was absorbed in thought, at first, for Hans Brinker's sad story still echoed in his ears. Not until Ludwig rebuked him with a laughing "Wake up, grandfather!" did he reassume his position as gallant boy leader of his band.

"Ahem! This way, young gentlemen!"

They were walking through the city, not on a curbed sidewalk, for such a thing is rarely found in Holland, but on the brick pavement that lay on the borders of the cobblestone carriage-way without breaking its level expanse.

Haarlem, like Amsterdam, was gayer than usual, in honor of Saint Nicholas.

A strange figure was approaching them. It was a small man dressed in black, with a short cloak. He wore a wig and a cocked hat from which a long crepe streamer was flying.

"Who comes here?" cried Ben. "What a queer-looking object."

"That's the *aanspreeker*," said Lambert. "Someone is dead."

"Is that the way men dress in mourning in this country?"

"Oh, no! The *aanspreeker* attends funerals, and it is his business, when anyone dies, to notify all the friends and relatives."

"What a strange custom."

"Well," said Lambert, "we needn't feel very badly about this particular death, for I see another man has lately been born to the world to fill up the vacant place."

Ben stared. "How do you know that?"

"Don't you see that pretty red pincushion hanging on yonder door?" asked Lambert in return.

"Yes."

"Well, that's a boy."

"A boy! What do you mean?"

"I mean that here in Haarlem, whenever a boy is born, the parents have a red pincushion put out at the door. If our young friend had been a girl instead of a boy the cushion would have been white. In some places they have much more fanciful affairs, all trimmed with lace, and even among the very poorest houses you will see a bit of ribbon or even a string tied on the door latch—"

"Look!" screamed Ben. "There *is* a white cushion on the door of that double-jointed house with the funny roof."

"I don't see any house with a funny roof."

"Oh, of course not," said Ben. "I forget you're a native, but all the roofs are queer to me, for that matter. I mean the house next to that green building."

"True enough, there's a girl! I tell you what, captain," called out Lambert, slipping easily into Dutch, "we must get out of this street as soon as possible. It's full of babies! They'll set up a squall in a moment."

The captain laughed. "I shall take you to hear better music

than that," he said. "We are just in time to hear the organ of St. Bavon. The church is open today."

"What, the great Haarlem organ?" asked Ben. "That will be a treat indeed. I have often read of it, with its tremendous pipes, and its vox humana* that sounds like a giant singing."

"The same," answered Lambert van Mounen.

Peter was right. The church was open, though not for religious services. Someone was playing upon the organ. As the boys entered, a swell of sound rushed forth to meet them. It seemed to bear them, one by one, into the shadows of the building.

Louder and louder it grew until it became like the din and roar of some mighty tempest, or like the ocean surging upon the shore. In the midst of the tumult a tinkling bell was heard; another answered, then another, and the storm paused as if to listen. The bells grew bolder; they rang out loud and clear. Other deep-toned bells joined in; they were tolling in solemn concert—ding, dong! ding, dong! The storm broke forth again with redoubled fury, gathering its distant thunder. The boys looked at each other but did not speak. It was growing serious. What was that? *Who* screamed? *What* screamed—that terrible musical scream? Was it man or demon? Or was it some monster shut up behind that carved brass frame, behind those great silver columns—some despairing monster begging, screaming for freedom? It was the *vox humana*!

At last an answer came—soft, tender, loving, like a mother's song. The storm grew silent; hidden birds sprang forth filling the air with glad, ecstatic music, rising higher and higher until the last faint note was lost in the distance.

The vox humana was stilled, but in the glorious hymn of thanksgiving that now arose, one could almost hear the throb-

---

*An organ stop which produces an effect resembling the human voice.

bing of a human heart. What did it mean? That man's implor-
ing cry should in time be met with a deep content? That
gratitude would give us freedom? To Peter and Ben it seemed
that the angels were singing. Their eyes grew dim and their
souls dizzy with a strange joy. At last, as if borne upward by
invisible hands, they were floating away on the music, all
fatigue forgotten, and with no wish but to hear forever those
beautiful sounds, when suddenly Van Holp's sleeve was pulled
impatiently and a gruff voice beside him asked, "How long are
you going to stay here, captain, blinking at the ceiling like a
sick rabbit? It's high time we started."

"Hush!" whispered Peter, only half aroused.

"Come, man! Let's go," said Carl, giving the sleeve a second
pull.

Peter turned reluctantly. He would not detain the boys
against their will. All but Ben were casting rather reproachful
glances at him.

"Well, boys," he whispered, "we will go. Softly now."

"That's the greatest thing I've seen or heard since I've been
in Holland!" cried Ben enthusiastically, as soon as they reached
the open air. "It's glorious!"

Ludwig and Carl laughed slyly at the English boy's *wartaal*, or
gibberish. Jacob yawned, and Peter gave Ben a look that made
him instantly feel that he and Peter were not so very different
after all, though one hailed from Holland and the other from
England. And Lambert, the interpreter, responded with a brisk
"You may well say so. I believe there are one or two organs
nowadays that are said to be as fine, but for years and years this
organ of St. Bavon was the grandest in the world."

"Do you know how large it is?" asked Ben. "I noticed that
the church itself was prodigiously high and that the organ filled
the end of the great aisle almost from floor to roof."

"That's true," said Lambert, "and how superb the pipes

looked—just like grand columns of silver. They're only for show, you know. The *real* pipes are behind them, some big enough for a man to crawl through, and some smaller than a baby's whistle. Well, sir, for size, the church is higher than Westminster Abbey, to begin with, and, as you say, the organ makes a tremendous show even then. Father told me last night that it is one hundred and eight feet high, fifty feet wide, and has over five thousand pipes. It has sixty-four stops—if you know what they are, *I* don't—and three keyboards."

"Good for you!" said Ben. "You have a fine memory. My head is a perfect colander for figures. They slip through as fast as they're poured in. But other facts and historical events stay behind—that's some consolation."

"There we differ," returned Van Mounen. "I'm great on names and figures, but history, take it altogether, seems to me to be the most hopeless kind of jumble."

Meantime Carl and Ludwig were having a discussion concerning some square wooden monuments they had observed in the interior of the church. Ludwig declared that each bore the name of the person buried beneath, and Carl insisted that they had no names but only the heraldic arms of the deceased painted on a black ground, with the date of the death in gilt letters.

"I ought to know," said Carl, "for I walked across to the east side, to look for the cannonball Mother told me was embedded there. It was fired into the church, in the year fifteen hundred and something, by those rascally Spaniards, while the services were going on. There it was in the wall, sure enough, and while I was walking back, I noticed the monuments. I tell you, they haven't a sign of a name upon them."

"Ask Peter," said Ludwig, only half convinced.

"Carl is right," replied Peter, who, though conversing with Jacob, had overheard their dispute. "Well, Jacob, as I was saying, Handel, the great composer, chanced to visit Haarlem, and, of course, he at once hunted up this famous organ. He gained admittance and was playing upon it with all his might when the regular organist chanced to enter the building. The man stood awestruck. He was a good player himself, but he had never heard such music before. 'Who is there?' he cried. 'If it is not an angel or the devil, it must be Handel!' When he discovered that it *was* the great musician, he was still more mystified! 'But how is this?' he said. 'You have done impossible things—no ten fingers on earth can play the passages you have given. Human hands couldn't control all the keys and stops!' 'I know it,' said Handel coolly, 'and for that reason I was forced to strike some notes with the end of my nose.' Donder! just think how the old organist must have stared!"

"Hey! What?" exclaimed Jacob, startled when Peter's animated voice suddenly became silent.

"Haven't you heard me, you rascal?" was the indignant rejoinder.

"Oh, yes—no. The fact is, I heard you at first. I'm awake now, but I do believe I've been walking beside you half asleep," stammered Jacob, with such a doleful, bewildered look on his face that Peter could not help laughing.

Chapter 17

The Man with Four Heads

*A*fter leaving the church, the boys stopped nearby, in the open marketplace, to look at the bronze statue of Laurens Janzoon Coster, who is believed by the Dutch to have been the inventor of printing. This is disputed by those who award the same honor to Johannes Gutenberg of Mayence; while many maintain that Faustus, a servant of Coster, stole his master's wooden types on a Christmas Eve, when the latter was at church, and fled with his booty, and his secret, to Mayence. Coster was a native of Haarlem, and the Hollanders are naturally anxious to secure the credit of the invention for their illustrious townsman. Certain it is that the first book he printed is kept by the city in a silver case wrapped in silk and is shown with great caution as a most precious relic. It is said he first conceived the idea of printing from cutting his name upon the bark of a tree and afterward pressing a piece of paper upon the characters.

Of course, Lambert and his English friend fully discussed this subject. They also had a rather warm argument concerning another invention. Lambert declared that the honor of giving both the telescope and microscope to the world lay between Metius and Jansen, both Hollanders, while Ben as stoutly insisted that Roger Bacon, an English monk of the thirteenth century, "wrote out the whole thing, sir, perfect descriptions of microscopes and telescopes, too, long before either of those other fellows were born."

On one subject, however, they both agreed: that the art of curing and pickling herrings was discovered by William Beukles of Holland, and that the country did perfectly right in honoring him as a national benefactor, for its wealth and importance had been in a great measure due to its herring trade.

"It is astonishing," said Ben, "in what prodigious quantities those fish are found. I don't know how it is here, but on the coast of England, off Yarmouth, the herring shoals have been known to be six and seven feet deep with fish."

"That *is* prodigious, indeed," said Lambert, "but you know your word *herring* is derived from the German *heer*, an army, on account of a way the fish have of coming in large numbers."

Soon afterward, while passing a cobbler's shop, Ben exclaimed, "Halloo! Lambert, here is the name of one of your greatest men over a cobbler's stall! Boerhaave. If it were only Hermann Boerhaave instead of Hendrick, it would be complete."

Lambert knit his brows reflectively as he replied, "Boerhaave—Boerhaave. The name is perfectly familiar; I remember, too, he was born in 1668, but the rest is all gone, as usual. There have been so many famous Hollanders, you see, it is impossible for a fellow to know them all. What was he? Did he have two heads? Or was he one of your great, natural swimmers like Marco Polo?"

"He had *four* heads," answered Ben, laughing, "for he was a great physician, naturalist, botanist, and chemist. I am full of him just now, for I read his life a few weeks ago."

"Pour out a little, then," said Lambert, "only walk faster or we shall lose sight of the other boys."

"Well," resumed Ben, quickening his pace and looking with

great interest at everything going on in the crowded street, "this Dr. Boerhaave was a great *anspewker*."

"A great *what?*" roared Lambert.

"Oh, I beg pardon. I was thinking of that man over there with the cocked hat. He's an *anspewker*, isn't he?"

"Yes. He's an *aanspreeker*, if that is what you mean to say. But what about your friend with the four heads?"

"Well, as I was going to say, the doctor was left a penniless orphan at sixteen without education or friends—"

"Jolly beginning!" interposed Lambert.

"Now, don't interrupt. He was a poor friendless orphan at sixteen, but he was so persevering and industrious, so determined to gain knowledge, that he made his way, and in time became one of the most learned men of Europe. All the— What is that?"

"Where? What do you mean?"

"Why, that paper on the door opposite. Don't you see? Two or three persons are reading it. I have noticed several of these papers since I've been here."

"Oh, that's only a health bulletin. Somebody in the house is ill, and to prevent a steady knocking at the door, the family write an account of the patient's condition on a placard and hang it outside the door, for the benefit of inquiring friends—a very sensible custom, I'm sure. Nothing strange about it that I can see. Go on, please. You said 'All the,' and there you left me hanging."

"I was going to say," resumed Ben, "that all the—all the— how comically persons do dress here, to be sure! Just look at those men and women with their sugarloaf hats. And see this woman ahead of us with a straw bonnet like a scoop shovel tapering to a point in the back. Did you ever see anything so funny? And those tremendous wooden shoes, too—I declare, she's a beauty!"

"Oh, they are only back-country folk," said Lambert, rather impatiently. "You might as well let old Boerhaave drop or else shut your eyes."

"Ha! ha! Well, I was *going* to say—all the big men of his day sought out this great professor. Even Peter the Great, when he came over to Holland from Russia to learn shipbuilding, attended his lectures regularly. By that time Boerhaave was professor of medicine and chemistry and botany at the University of Leyden. He had grown to be very wealthy as a practicing physician, but he used to say that the poor were his best patients because God would be their paymaster. All Europe learned to love and honor him. In short, he became so famous that a certain mandarin of China addressed a letter to 'the illustrious Boerhaave, physician in Europe,' and the letter found its way to him without any difficulty."

"My goodness! That is what I call being a public character. The boys have stopped. How now, Captain van Holp, what next?"

"We propose to move on," said Van Holp. "There is nothing to see at this season in the Bosch. The Bosch is a noble wood, Benjamin, a grand park where they have most magnificent trees, protected by law. Do you understand?"

"Ya!" nodded Ben as the captain proceeded.

"Unless you all desire to visit the Museum of Natural History, we may go on the grand canal again. If we had more time, it would be pleasant to take Benjamin up the Blue Stairs."

"What are the Blue Stairs, Lambert?" asked Ben.

"They are the highest point of the Dunes. You have a grand view of the ocean from there, besides a fine chance to see how wonderful these dunes are. One can hardly believe that the wind could ever heap up sand in so remarkable a way. But we have to go through Bloemendal to get there—not a very pretty village and some distance from here. What do you say?"

"Oh, I am ready for anything. For my part, I would rather steer direct for Leyden, but we'll do as the captain says. Hey, Jacob?"

"Ya, dat ish goot," said Jacob, who felt decidedly more like taking another nap than ascending the Blue Stairs.

The captain was in favor of going to Leyden.

"It's four long miles from here. Full sixteen of your English miles, Benjamin. We have no time to lose if you wish to reach there before midnight. Decide quickly, boys—Blue Stairs or Leyden?"

"Leyden," they answered, and were out of Haarlem in a twinkling, admiring the lofty, towerlike windmills and pretty country seats as they left the city behind them.

"If you really wish to see Haarlem," said Lambert to Ben, after they had skated awhile in silence, "you should visit it in summer. It is the greatest place in the world for beautiful flowers. The walks around the city are superb; and the 'wood,' with its miles of noble elms, all in full feather, is something to remember. You need not smile, old fellow, at my saying 'full feather.' I was thinking of waving plumes and got my words mixed up a little. But a Dutch elm beats everything; it is the noblest tree on earth, Ben—if you except the English oak."

"Aye," said Ben solemnly, "*if* you except the English oak." And for some moments he could scarcely see the canal because Robby and Jenny kept bobbing in the air before his eyes.

Chapter 18

Friends in Need

*I*n the meantime, the other boys were listening to Peter's account of an incident which had occurred long ago* in a part of the city where stood an ancient castle, whose lord had tyrannized over the burghers of the town to such an extent that they surrounded his castle and laid siege to it. Just at the last extremity, when the haughty lord felt that he could hold out no longer and was preparing to sell his life as dearly as possible, his lady appeared on the ramparts and offered to surrender everything, provided she was permitted to bring out, and retain, as much of her most precious household goods as she could carry upon her back. The promise was given, and the lady came forth from the gateway bearing her husband upon her shoulders. The burghers' pledge preserved him from the fury of the troops but left them free to wreak their vengeance upon the castle.

"Do you *believe* that story, Captain Peter?" asked Carl in an incredulous tone.

"Of course, I do. It is historical. Why should I doubt it?"

"Simply because no woman could do it—and if she could, she wouldn't. That is *my* opinion."

---

*Sir Thomas Carr's tour through Holland.

"And *I* believe there are many who *would*. That is, to save anyone they really cared for," said Ludwig.

Jacob, who in spite of his fat and sleepiness was of rather a sentimental turn, had listened with deep interest.

"That is right, little fellow," he said, nodding his head approvingly. "I believe every word of it. I shall never marry a woman who would not be glad to do as much for *me.*"

"Heaven help her!" cried Carl, turning to gaze at the speaker. "Why, Poot, three *men* couldn't do it!"

"Perhaps not," said Jacob quietly, feeling that he had asked rather too much of the future Mrs. Poot. "But she must be *willing*, that is all."

"Aye," responded Peter's cheery voice, "willing heart makes nimble foot—and who knows, but it may make strong arms also."

"Pete," asked Ludwig, changing the subject, "did you tell me last night that the painter Wouwerman was born in Haarlem?"

"Yes, and Jacob Ruysdael and Berghem too. I like Berghem because he was always good-natured. They say he always sang while he painted, and though he died nearly two hundred years ago, there are traditions still afloat concerning his pleasant laugh. He was a great painter, and he had a wife as cross as Xantippe."

"They balanced each other finely," said Ludwig. "He was kind and she was cross. But, Peter, before I forget it, wasn't that picture of St. Hubert and the horse painted by Wouwerman? You remember, Father showed us an engraving from it last night."

"Yes, indeed. There is a story connected with that picture."

"Tell us!" cried two or three, drawing closer to Peter as they skated on.

"Wouwerman," began the captain oratorically, "was born in 1620, just four years before Berghem. He was a master of his art and especially excelled in painting horses. Strange as it may seem, people were so long finding out his merits that, even after he had arrived at the height of his excellence, he was obliged to sell his pictures for very paltry prices. The poor artist became completely discouraged, and, worst of all, was over head and ears in debt. One day he was talking over his troubles with his father-confessor, who was one of the few who recognized his genius. The priest determined to assist him and accordingly lent him six hundred guilders, advising him at the same time to demand a better price for his pictures. Wouwerman did so and in the meantime paid his debts. Matters brightened with him at once. Everybody appreciated the great artist who painted such costly pictures. He grew rich. The six hundred guilders were returned, and in gratitude Wouwerman sent also a work which he had painted, representing his benefactor as St. Hubert kneeling before his horse—the very picture, Ludwig, of which we were speaking last night."

"So! so!" exclaimed Ludwig, with deep interest. "I must remember to take another look at the engraving as soon as we get home."

At that same hour, while Ben was skating with his companions beside the Holland dike, Robby and Jenny stood in their pretty English schoolhouse, ready to join in the duties of their reading class.

"Commence! Master Robert Dobbs," said the teacher, "page 242. Now, sir, mind every stop."

And Robby, in a quick childish voice, roared forth at school-room pitch, "Lesson 62. The Hero of Haarlem. Many years ago, there lived in Haarlem, one of the principal cities of Holland, a sunny-haired boy of gentle disposition. His father was a *sluicer*, that is, a man whose business it was to open and close the sluices, or large oaken gates, that are placed at regular distances across the entrances of the canals to regulate the amount of water that shall flow into them.

"The sluicer raises the gates more or less according to the quantity of water required, and closes them carefully at night, in order to avoid all possible danger of an oversupply running into the canal, or the water would soon overflow it and inundate the surrounding country. As a great portion of Holland is lower than the level of the sea, the waters are kept from flooding the land only by means of strong dikes, or barriers, and by means of these sluices, which are often strained to the utmost by the pressure of the rising tides. Even the little children in Holland know that constant watchfulness is required to keep the rivers and ocean from overwhelming the country, and that a moment's neglect of the sluicer's duty may bring ruin and death to all."

"Very good," said the teacher. "Now, Susan."

"One lovely autumn afternoon, when the boy was about eight years old, he obtained his parents' consent to carry some cakes to a blind man who lived out in the country, on the other side of the dike. The little fellow started on his errand with a light heart, and having spent an hour with his grateful old friend, he bade him farewell and started on his homeward walk.

"Trudging stoutly along by the canal, he noticed how the autumn rains had swollen the waters. Even while humming his careless, childish song, he thought of his father's brave old gates and felt glad of their strength, for, thought he, 'If *they* gave way, where would Father and Mother be? These pretty fields would all be covered with the angry waters—Father always calls them the *angry* waters. I suppose he thinks they are mad at him for keeping them out so long.' And with these thoughts just flitting across his brain, the little fellow stooped to pick the pretty blue flowers that grew along his way. Sometimes he stopped to throw some feathery seed ball in the air and watch it as it floated away; sometimes he listened to the stealthy rustling of a rabbit, speeding through the grass, but oftener he smiled as he recalled the happy light he had seen arise on the weary, listening face of his blind old friend."

"Now, Henry," said the teacher, nodding to the next little reader.

"Suddenly the boy looked around him in dismay. He had not noticed that the sun was setting. Now he saw that his long shadow on the grass had vanished. It was growing dark, he was still some distance from home, and in a lonely ravine, where even the blue flowers had turned to gray. He quickened his footsteps and, with a beating heart, recalled many a nursery tale of children belated in dreary forests. Just as he was bracing himself for a run, he was startled by the sound of trickling water. Whence did it come? He looked up and saw a small hole in the dike through which a tiny stream was flowing. Any child in Holland will shudder at the thought of *a leak in the dike!* The boy understood the danger at a glance. That little hole, if the water were allowed to trickle through, would soon be a large one, and a terrible inundation would be the result.

"Quick as a flash, he saw his duty. Throwing away his flowers, the boy clambered up the heights until he reached the hole. His chubby little finger was thrust in, almost before he knew it. The flowing was stopped! Ah! he thought, with a chuckle of boyish delight, the angry waters must stay back now! Haarlem shall not be drowned while *I* am here!

"This was all very well at first, but the night was falling rapidly. Chill vapors filled the air. Our little hero began to tremble with cold and dread. He shouted loudly; he screamed, 'Come here! come here!' but no one came. The cold grew more intense, a numbness, commencing in the tired little finger, crept over his hand and arm, and soon his whole body was filled with pain. He shouted again, 'Will no one come? Mother!

Mother!' Alas, his mother, good, practical soul, had already locked the doors and had fully resolved to scold him on the morrow for spending the night with blind Jansen without her permission. He tried to whistle. Perhaps some straggling boy might heed the signal, but his teeth chattered so, it was impossible. Then he called on God for help. And the answer came, through a holy resolution: 'I will stay here till morning.' "

"Now, Jenny Dobbs," said the teacher. Jenny's eyes were glistening, but she took a long breath and commenced.

"The midnight moon looked down upon that small, solitary form, sitting upon a stone, halfway up the dike. His head was bent but he was not asleep, for every now and then one restless hand rubbed feebly the outstretched arm that seemed fastened to the dike—and often the pale, tearful face turned quickly at some real or fancied sounds.

"How can we know the sufferings of that long and fearful watch—what falterings of purpose, what childish terrors came over the boy as he thought of the warm little bed at home, of his parents, his brothers and sisters, then looked into the cold, dreary night! If he drew away that tiny finger, the angry waters, grown angrier still, would rush forth, and never stop until they had swept over the town. No, he would hold it there till daylight—if he lived! He was not very sure of living. What did this strange buzzing mean? And then the knives that seemed pricking and piercing him from head to foot? He was not certain now that he could draw his finger away, even if he wished to.

"At daybreak a clergyman, returning from the bedside of a sick parishioner, thought he heard groans as he walked along on the top of the dike. Bending, he saw, far down on the side, a child apparently writhing with pain.

" 'In the name of wonder, boy,' he exclaimed, 'what are you doing there?'

" 'I am keeping the water from running out' was the simple answer of the little hero. 'Tell them to come quick.'

"It is needless to add that they did and that—"

"Jenny Dobbs," said the teacher, rather impatiently, "if you cannot control your feelings so as to read distinctly, we will wait until you recover yourself."

"Yes, sir!" said Jenny, quite startled.

It was strange, but at that very moment, Ben, far over the sea, was saying to Lambert, "The noble little fellow! I have frequently met with an account of the incident, but I never knew, till now, that it was really true."

"True! Of course it is," said Lambert. "I have given you the story just as Mother told it to me, years ago. Why, there is not a child in Holland who does not know it. And, Ben, you may not think so, but that little boy represents the spirit of the whole country. Not a leak can show itself anywhere either in its politics, honor, or public safety, that a million fingers are not ready to stop it, at any cost."

"Whew!" cried Master Ben. "Big talking that!"

"It's *true* talk, anyway," rejoined Lambert, so very quietly that Ben wisely resolved to make no further comment.

Chapter 19

On the Canal

*T*he skating season had commenced unusually early; our boys were by no means alone upon the ice. The afternoon was so fine that men, women, and children, bent upon enjoying the holiday, had flocked to the grand canal from far and near. Saint Nicholas had evidently remembered the favorite pastime; shining new skates were everywhere to be seen. Whole families were skimming their way to Haarlem or Leyden or the neighboring villages. The ice seemed fairly alive. Ben noticed the erect, easy carriage of the women, and their picturesque variety of costume. There were the latest fashions, fresh from Paris, floating past dingy, moth-eaten garments that had seen service through two generations; coal-scuttle bonnets perched over freckled faces bright with holiday smiles; stiff muslin caps with wings at the sides, flapping beside cheeks rosy with health and contentment; furs, too, encircling the whitest of throats; and scanty garments fluttering below faces ruddy with exercise. In short, every quaint and comical mixture of dry goods and flesh that Holland could furnish seemed sent to enliven the scene.

There were belles from Leyden, and fishwives from the border villages; cheese women from Gouda, and prim matrons from beautiful country seats on the Haarlemmer Meer. Gray-headed skaters were constantly to be seen; wrinkled old women with baskets upon their heads and plump little toddlers on skates clutching at their mothers' gowns. Some women carried their babies upon their backs, firmly secured with a bright shawl. The effect was pretty and graceful as they darted by or sailed slowly past, now nodding to an acquaintance, now chirruping and throwing soft baby talk to the muffled little ones they carried.

Boys and girls were chasing each other and hiding behind the one-horse sleds that, loaded high with peat or timber, pursued their cautious way along the track marked out as "safe." Beautiful, queenly women were there, enjoyment sparkling in their quiet eyes. Sometimes a long file of young men, each grasping the coat of the one before him, flew by with electric speed; and sometimes the ice squeaked under the chair of some gorgeous old dowager, or rich burgomaster's lady, who, very red in the nose and sharp in the eyes, looked like a scare-thaw invented by old Father Winter for the protection of his skating grounds. The chair would be heavy with foot stoves and cushions, to say nothing of the old lady. Mounted upon shining runners, it slid along, pushed by the sleepiest of servants, who, looking neither to the right nor the left, bent himself to his task while she cast direful glances upon the screaming little rowdies who invariably acted as bodyguard.

As for the men, they were pictures of placid enjoyment. Some were attired in ordinary citizen's dress, but many looked odd enough with their short woolen coats, wide breeches, and big silver buckles. These seemed to Ben like little boys who had, by a miracle, sprung suddenly into manhood and were forced to wear garments that their astonished mothers had altered in a hurry. He noticed, too, that nearly all the men had pipes, as they passed him whizzing and smoking like so many locomotives. There was every variety of pipes from those of common clay to the most expensive meerschaums mounted in silver and gold. Some were carved into extraordinary and fantastic shapes, representing birds, flowers, heads, bugs, and dozens of other things; some resembled the "Dutchman's pipe" that grows in our American woods; some were red and many were of a pure snowy white; but the most respectable were those which were ripening into a shaded brown. The deeper and richer the brown, of course, the more honored the pipe, for it was a proof that the owner, if honestly shading it, was deliberately devoting his manhood to the effort. What pipe would not be proud to be the object of such a sacrifice!

For a while Ben skated on in silence. There was so much to engage his attention that he almost forgot his companions. Part of the time he had been watching the iceboats as they flew over the great Haarlemmer Meer (or lake), the frozen surface of which was now plainly visible from the canal. These boats had very large sails, much larger, in proportion, than those of ordinary vessels, and were set upon a triangular frame furnished with an iron "runner" at each corner—the widest part of the triangle crossing the bow, and its point stretching beyond the stern. They had rudders for guiding and brakes for arresting their progress and were of all sizes and kinds, from small, rough affairs managed by a boy, to large and beautiful ones filled with gay pleasure parties and manned by competent sailors, who, smoking their stumpy pipes, reefed and tacked and steered with great solemnity and precision.

Some of the boats were painted and gilded in gaudy style and flaunted gay pennons from their mastheads; others, white as snow, with every spotless sail rounded by the wind, looked like swans borne onward by a resistless current. It seemed to Ben as, following his fancy, he watched one of these in the distance, that he could almost hear its helpless, terrified cry, but he soon found that the sound arose from a nearer and less romantic cause—from an iceboat not fifty yards from him, using its brakes to avoid a collision with a peat sled.

It was a rare thing for these boats to be upon the canal, and their appearance generally caused no little excitement among skaters, especially among the timid; but today every iceboat in the country seemed afloat or rather aslide, and the canal had its full share.

Ben, though delighted at the sight, was often startled at the swift approach of the resistless, high-winged things threatening to dart in any and every possible direction. It required all his energies to keep out of the way of the passersby and to prevent those screaming little urchins from upsetting him with their sleds. Once he halted to watch some boys who were making a hole in the ice preparatory to using their fishing spears. Just as he concluded to start again, he found himself suddenly bumped into an old lady's lap. Her push-chair had come upon him from the rear. The old lady screamed; the servant who was propelling her gave a warning hiss. In another instant Ben found himself apologizing to empty air. The indignant old lady was far ahead.

This was a slight mishap compared with one that now threatened him. A huge iceboat, under full sail, came tearing down the canal, almost paralyzing Ben with the thought of instant destruction. It was close upon him! He saw its gilded prow, heard the schipper shout, felt the great boom fairly whiz over his head, was blind, deaf, and dumb, all in an instant, then opened his eyes to find himself spinning some yards behind its great, skatelike rudder. It had passed within an inch of his shoulder, but he was safe! Safe to see England again, safe to kiss the dear faces that for an instant had flashed before him one by one—Father, Mother, Robby, and Jenny—that great boom had dashed their images into his very soul. He knew now how much he loved them. Perhaps this knowledge made him face complacently the scowls of those on the canal who seemed to feel that a boy in danger was necessarily a *bad* boy needing instant reprimand.

Lambert chided him roundly.

"I thought it was all over with you, you careless fellow! Why don't you look where you are going? Not content with sitting on all the old ladies' laps, you must make a Juggernaut of every iceboat that comes along. We shall have to hand you over to the *aanspreekers* yet, if you don't look out!"

"Please don't," said Ben with mock humility, then, seeing how pale Lambert's lips were, added in a low tone, "I do believe I *thought* more in that one moment, Van Mounen, than in all the rest of my past life."

There was no reply, and, for a while, the two boys skated on in silence.

Soon a faint sound of distant bells reached their ears.

"Hark!" said Ben. "What is that?"

"The carillons," replied Lambert. "They are trying the bells in the chapel of yonder village. Ah! Ben, you should hear the chimes of the 'New Church' at Delft; they are superb—nearly five hundred sweet-toned bells, and one of the best carillon-neurs of Holland to play upon them. Hard work, though. They say the fellow often has to go to bed from positive exhaustion, after his performances. You see, the bells are attached to a kind of keyboard, something like they have on pianofortes; there is also a set of pedals for the feet. When a brisk tune is going on, the player looks like a kicking frog fastened to his seat with a skewer."

"For shame," said Ben indignantly.

Peter had, for the present, exhausted his stock of Haarlem anecdotes, and now, having nothing to do but to skate, he and his three companions were hastening to catch up with Lambert and Ben.

"That English lad is fleet enough," said Peter. "If he were a born Hollander, he could do no better. Generally these John Bulls make but a sorry figure on skates. Halloo! Here you are, Van Mounen. Why, we hardly hoped for the honor of meeting you again. Whom were you flying from in such haste?"

"Snails," retorted Lambert. "What kept you?"

"We have been talking, and besides, we halted once to give Poot a chance to rest."

"He begins to look rather worn-out," said Lambert in a low voice.

Just then a beautiful iceboat with reefed sail and flying streamers swept leisurely by. Its deck was filled with children muffled up to their chins. Looking at them from the ice you could see only smiling little faces embedded in bright-colored woolen wrappings. They were singing a chorus in honor of Saint Nicholas. The music, starting in the discord of a hundred childish voices, floated, as it rose, into exquisite harmony:

> "Friend of sailors and of children!
>   Double claim have we,
> As in youthful joy we're sailing,
>   O'er a frozen sea!
>   Nicholas! Saint Nicholas!
>   Let us sing to thee!
>
> While through wintry air we're rushing,
>   As our voices blend,
> Are you near us? Do you hear us,
>   Nicholas, our friend?
>   Nicholas! Saint Nicholas!
>   Love can never end!

Sunny sparkles, bright before us,
   Chase away the cold!
Hearts where sunny thoughts are welcome,
   Never can grow old.
           Nicholas! Saint Nicholas!
             Never can grow old!

Pretty gift and loving lesson,
   Festival and glee,
Bid us thank thee as we're sailing
   O'er the frozen sea.
           Nicholas! Saint Nicholas!
             So we sing to thee!"

Chapter 20

Jacob Poot Changes the Plan

*T*he last note died away in the distance. Our boys, who in their vain efforts to keep up with the boat had felt that they were skating backward, turned to look at one another.

"How beautiful that was!" exclaimed Van Mounen.

"Just like a dream!" said Ludwig.

Jacob drew close to Ben, giving his usual approving nod, as he spoke. "Dat ish goot. Dat ish te pest vay. *I* shay petter to take to Leyden mit a poat!"

"Take a boat!" exclaimed Ben in dismay. "Why, man, our plan was to *skate*, not to be carried like little children."

"Tuyfels!" retorted Jacob, "dat ish no little—no papies—to go for poat!"

The boys laughed but exchanged uneasy glances. It would be great fun to jump on an iceboat, if they had a chance, but to abandon so shamefully their grand undertaking—who could think of such a thing?

An animated discussion arose at once.

Captain Peter brought his party to a halt.

"Boys," he said, "it strikes me that we should consult Jacob's wishes in this matter. He started the excursion, you know."

"Pooh!" sneered Carl, throwing a contemptuous glance at Jacob. "Who's tired? We can rest all night at Leyden."

Ludwig and Lambert looked anxious and disappointed. It was no slight thing to lose the credit of having skated all the way from Broek to The Hague and back again, but both agreed that Jacob should decide the question.

Good-natured, tired Jacob! He read the popular sentiment at a glance.

"Oh, no," he said in Dutch. "I was joking. We will skate, of course."

The boys gave a delighted shout and started on again with renewed vigor.

All but Jacob. He tried his best not to seem fatigued and, by not saying a word, saved his breath and energy for the great business of skating. But in vain. Before long, the stout body grew heavier and heavier—the tottering limbs weaker and weaker. Worse than all, the blood, anxious to get as far as possible from the ice, mounted to the puffy, good-natured cheeks, and made the roots of his thin yellow hair glow into a fiery red.

This kind of work is apt to summon vertigo, of whom good Hans Andersen writes—the same who hurls daring young hunters from the mountains or spins them from the sharpest heights of the glaciers or catches them as they tread the stepping-stones of the mountain torrent.

Vertigo came, unseen, to Jacob. After tormenting him awhile, with one touch sending a chill from head to foot, with the next scorching every vein with fever, she made the canal rock and tremble beneath him, the white sails bow and spin as they passed, then cast him heavily upon the ice.

"Halloo!" cried Van Mounen. "There goes Poot!"

Ben sprang hastily forward.

"Jacob! Jacob, are you hurt?"

Peter and Carl were lifting him. The face was white enough now. It seemed like a dead face—even the good-natured look was gone.

A crowd collected. Peter unbuttoned the poor boy's jacket, loosened his red tippet, and blew between the parted lips.

"Stand off, good people!" he cried. "Give him air!"

"Lay him down," called a woman from the crowd.

"Stand him upon his feet," shouted another.

"Give him wine," growled a stout fellow who was driving a loaded sled.

"Yes, yes, give him wine!" echoed everybody.

Ludwig and Lambert shouted in concert, "Wine! Wine! Who has wine?"

A sleepy-eyed Dutchman began to fumble mysteriously under the heaviest of blue jackets, saying as he did so, "Not so much noise, young masters, not so much noise! The boy was a fool to faint like a girl."

"Wine, quick!" cried Peter, who, with Ben's help, was rubbing Jacob from head to foot.

Ludwig stretched forth his hand imploringly toward the Dutchman, who, with an air of great importance, was still fumbling beneath the jacket.

"*Do* hurry! He will die! Has anyone else any wine?"

"He *is* dead!" said an awful voice from among the bystanders.

This startled the Dutchman.

"Have a care!" he said, reluctantly drawing forth a small blue flask. "This is schnapps. A little is enough."

A little *was* enough. The paleness gave way to a faint flush. Jacob opened his eyes, and, half bewildered, half ashamed, feebly tried to free himself from those who were supporting him.

·   ·   ·

There was no alternative, now, for our party but to have their exhausted comrade carried, in some way, to Leyden. As for expecting him to skate anymore that day, the thing was impossible. In truth, by this time each boy began to entertain secret yearnings toward iceboats, and to avow a Spartan resolve not to desert Jacob. Fortunately a gentle, steady breeze was setting southward. If some accommodating *schipper** would but come along, matters would not be quite so bad after all.

Peter hailed the first sail that appeared. The men in the stern would not even look at him. Three drays on runners came along, but they were already loaded to the utmost. Then an iceboat, a beautiful, tempting little one, whizzed past like an arrow. The boys had just time to stare eagerly at it when it was gone. In despair they resolved to prop up Jacob with their strong arms, as well as they could, and take him to the nearest village.

At that moment a very shabby iceboat came in sight. With but little hope of success Peter hailed it, at the same time taking off his hat and flourishing it in the air.

The sail was lowered, then came the scraping sound of the brake, and a voice called from the deck, "What now?"

"Will you take us on?" cried Peter, hurrying with his companions as fast as he could, for the boat was "bringing to" some distance ahead. "Will you take us on?"

"We'll pay for the ride!" shouted Carl.

The man on board scarcely noticed him except to mutter something about its not being a *trekschuit*. Still looking toward Peter, he asked, "How many?"

"Six."

"Well, it's Nicholas's Day—up with you! Young gentleman sick?" He nodded toward Jacob.

---

*Skipper. Master of a small trading vessel—a pleasure boat or iceboat.

"Yes—broken down. Skated all the way from Broek," answered Peter. "Do you go to Leyden?"

"That's as the wind says. It's blowing that way now. Scramble up!"

Poor Jacob! If that willing Mrs. Poot had only appeared just then, her services would have been invaluable. It was as much as the boys could do to hoist him into the boat. All were in at last. The *schipper*, puffing away at his pipe, let out the sail, lifted the brake, and sat in the stern with folded arms.

"Whew! How fast we go!" cried Ben. "This is something! Feel better, Jacob?"

"Much petter, I tanks you."

"Oh, you'll be as good as new in ten minutes. This makes a fellow feel like a bird."

Jacob nodded and blinked his eyes.

"Don't go to sleep, Jacob, it's too cold. You might never wake up, you know. Persons often freeze to death in that way."

"I no sleep," said Jacob confidently, and in two minutes he was snoring.

Carl and Ludwig laughed.

"We must wake him!" cried Ben. "It is dangerous, I tell you. Jacob! Ja-a-c—"

Captain Peter interfered, for three of the boys were helping Ben for the fun of the thing.

"Nonsense! Don't shake him! Let him alone, boys. One never snores like that when one's freezing. Cover him up with something. Here, this cloak will do. Hey, *schipper*?" And he looked toward the stern for permission to use it.

The man nodded.

"There," said Peter, tenderly adjusting the garment, "let him sleep. He will be frisky as a lamb when he wakes. How far are we from Leyden, *schipper*?"

"Not more'n a couple of pipes," replied a voice, rising from smoke like the genii in fairy tales (puff! puff!). "Likely not more'n one an' a half"—puff! puff!—"if this wind holds." Puff! puff! puff!

"What is the man saying, Lambert" asked Ben, who was holding his mittened hands against his cheeks to ward off the cutting air.

"He says we're about two pipes from Leyden. Half the boors here on the canal measure distances by the time it takes them to finish a pipe."

"How ridiculous."

"See here, Benjamin Dobbs," retorted Lambert, growing unaccountably indignant at Ben's quiet smile. "See here, you've a way of calling every other thing you see on *this* side of the German ocean 'ridiculous.' It may suit *you*, this word, but it doesn't suit *me*. When you want anything ridiculous, just remember your English custom of making the Lord Mayor of London, at his installation, count the nails in a horseshoe to prove *his learning*."

"Who told you we had any such custom as that?" cried Ben, looking grave in an instant.

"Why, I *know* it, no use of anyone telling me. It's in all the books—and it's true. It strikes me," continued Lambert, laughing in spite of himself, "that you have been kept in happy ignorance of a good many ridiculous things on *your* side of the map."

"Humph!" exclaimed Ben, trying not to smile. "I'll inquire into that Lord Mayor business when I get home. There must be some mistake. B-r-r-roooo! How fast we're going. This is glorious!"

It was a grand sail, or ride, I scarce know which to call it. Perhaps *fly* would be the best word, for the boys felt very much as Sinbad did when, tied to the roc's leg, he darted through the clouds; or as Bellerophon felt when he shot through the air on the back of his winged horse Pegasus.

Sailing, riding, or flying, whichever it was, everything was rushing past, backward, and before they had time to draw a long breath, Leyden itself, with its high-peaked roofs, flew halfway to meet them.

When the city came in sight, it was high time to waken the sleeper. That feat accomplished, Peter's prophecy came to pass. Master Jacob was quite restored and in excellent spirits.

The *schipper* made a feeble remonstrance when Peter, with hearty thanks, endeavored to slip some silver pieces into his tough brown palm.

"Ye see, young master," said he, drawing away his hand, "the regular line o' trade's *one* thing, and a favor's another."

"I know it," said Peter, "but those boys and girls of yours will want sweets when you get home. Buy them some in the name of Saint Nicholas."

The man grinned. "Aye, true enough, I've young 'uns in plenty, a clean boatload of them. You are a sharp young master at guessing."

This time the knotty hand hitched forward again, quite carelessly, it seemed, but its palm was upward. Peter hastily dropped in the money and moved away.

The sail soon came tumbling down. Scrape, scrape went the brake, scattering an ice shower round the boat.

"Good-bye, *schipper*!" shouted the boys, seizing their skates and leaping from the deck one by one. "Many thanks to you!"

"Good-bye! good-b— Hold! Here! Stop! I want my coat."

Ben was carefully assisting his cousin over the side of the boat.

"What is the man shouting about? Oh, I know, you have his wrapper around your shoulders!"

"Dat ish true," answered Jacob, half jumping, half tumbling down upon the framework, "dat ish vot make him sho heavy."

"Made *you* so heavy, you mean, Poot?"

"Ya, made you sho heavy—dat ish true," said Jacob innocently as he worked himself free from the big wrapper. "Dere, now you hands it mit him straits way and tells him I voz much tanks for dat."

"Ho! for an inn!" cried Peter as they stepped into the city. "Be brisk, my fine fellows!"

Chapter 21

Mynheer Kleef and His Bill of Fare

*T*he boys soon found an unpretentious establishment near the Breedstraat (Broad Street) with a funnily painted lion over the door. This was the Roode Leeuw, or Red Lion, kept by one Huygens Kleef, a stout Dutchman with short legs and a very long pipe.

By this time they were in a ravenous condition. The *tiffin*, taken at Haarlem, had served only to give them an appetite, and this had been heightened by their exercise and swift sail upon the canal.

"Come, mine host! Give us what you can!" cried Peter rather pompously.

"I can give you anything—everything," answered Mynheer Kleef, performing a difficult bow.

"Well, give us sausage and pudding."

"Ah, *mynheer*, the sausage is all gone. There is no pudding."

"Salmagundi, then, and plenty of it."

"That is out also, young master."

"Eggs, and be quick."

"Winter eggs are *very* poor eating," answered the innkeeper, puckering his lips and lifting his eyebrows.

"No eggs? Well—caviar."

The Dutchman raised his fat hands. "Caviar! That is made of gold! Who has caviar to sell?"

Peter had sometimes eaten it at home; he knew that it was made of the roe of the sturgeon and certain other large fish, but he had no idea of its cost.

"Well, mine host, what have you?"

"What have I? Everything. I have rye bread, sauerkraut, potato salad, and the fattest herring in Leyden."

"What do you say, boys?" asked the captain. "Will that do?"

"Yes," cried the famished youths, "if he'll only be quick."

Mynheer moved off like one walking in his sleep, but soon opened his eyes wide at the miraculous manner in which his herring were made to disappear. Next came, or rather went, potato salad, rye bread and coffee—then Utrecht water flavored with orange, and, finally, slices of dry gingerbread. This last delicacy was not on the regular bill of fare, but Mynheer Kleef, driven to extremes, solemnly produced it from his own private stores and gave only a placid blink when his voracious young travelers started up, declaring they had eaten enough.

"I should think so!" he exclaimed internally, but his smooth face gave no sign.

Softly rubbing his hands, he asked, "Will your worships have beds?"

"Will your worships have beds?" mocked Carl. "What do you mean? Do we look sleepy?"

"Not at all, master. But I would cause them to be warmed and aired. None sleep under damp sheets at the Red Lion."

"Ah, I understand. Shall we come back here to sleep, captain?"

Peter was accustomed to finer lodgings, but this was a frolic.

"Why not?" he replied. "We can fare excellently here."

"Your worship speaks only the truth," said *mynheer* with great deference.

"How fine to be called 'your worship,' " laughed Ludwig, aside to Lambert, while Peter replied, "Well, mine host, you may get the rooms ready by nine."

"I have one beautiful chamber, with three beds, that will hold all of your worships," said Mynheer Kleef coaxingly.

"That will do."

"Whew!" whistled Carl when they reached the street.

Ludwig started. "What now?"

"Nothing, only Mynheer Kleef of the Red Lion little thinks how we shall make things spin in that same room tonight. We'll set the bolsters flying!"

"Order!" cried the captain. "Now, boys, I must seek this great Dr. Boekman before I sleep. If he is in Leyden, it will be no great task to find him, for he always puts up at the Golden Eagle when he comes here. I wonder that you did not all go to bed at once. Still, as you are awake, what say you to walking with Ben up by the Museum or the Stadhuis?"

"Agreed," said Ludwig and Lambert, but Jacob preferred to go with Peter. In vain Ben tried to persuade him to remain at the inn and rest. He declared that he never felt "petter," and wished of all things to take a look at the city, for it was his first "stop mit Leyden."

"Oh, it will not harm him," said Lambert. "How long the day has been—and what glorious sport we have had. It hardly seems possible that we left Broek only this morning."

Jacob yawned.

"I have enjoyed it well," he said, "but it seems to me at least a week since we started."

Carl laughed and muttered something about "twenty naps."

"Here we are at the corner. Remember, we all meet at the Red Lion at eight," said the captain as he and Jacob walked away.

Chapter 22

The Red Lion Becomes Dangerous

*T*he boys were glad to find a blazing fire awaiting them upon their return to the Red Lion. Carl and his party were there first. Soon afterward Peter and Jacob came in. They had inquired in vain concerning Dr. Boekman. All they could ascertain was that he had been seen in Haarlem that morning.

"As for his being in Leyden," the landlord of the Golden Eagle had said to Peter, "the thing is impossible. He always lodges here when in town. By this time there would be a crowd at my door waiting to consult him. Bah! People make such fools of themselves!"

"He is called a great surgeon," said Peter.

"Yes, the greatest in Holland. But what of that? What of being the greatest pill choker and knife slasher in the world? The man is a bear. Only last month on this very spot, he called me *a pig,* before three customers!"

"No!" exclaimed Peter, trying to look surprised and indignant.

"Yes, master—*a pig,*" repeated the landlord, puffing at his pipe with in injured air. "Bah! If he did not pay fine prices and bring customers to my house, I would sooner see him in the Vleit Canal than give him lodging."

Perhaps mine host felt that he was speaking too openly to a stranger, or it may be he saw a smile lurking in Peter's face, for he added sharply, "Come, now, what more do you wish? Supper? Beds?"

"No, *mynheer,* I am but searching for Dr. Boekman."

"Go find him. He is not in Leyden."

Peter was not to be put off so easily. After receiving a few more rough words he succeeded in obtaining permission to leave a note for the famous surgeon, or rather, he *bought* from his amiable landlord the privilege of writing it there, and a promise that it should be promptly delivered when Dr. Boekman arrived. This accomplished, Peter and Jacob returned to the Red Lion.

This inn had once been a fine house, the home of a rich burgher, but having grown old and shabby, it had passed through many hands, until finally it had fallen into the possession of Mynheer Kleef. He was fond of saying as he looked up at its dingy, broken walls, "Mend it and paint it, and there's not a prettier house in Leyden." It stood six stories high from the street. The first three were of equal breadth but of various heights, the last three were in the great, high roof, and grew smaller and smaller like a set of double steps until the top one was lost in a point. The roof was built of short, shining tiles, and the windows, with their little panes, seemed to be scattered irregularly over the face of the building, without the slightest attention to outward effect. But the public room on the ground floor was the landlord's joy and pride. He never said, "Mend it and paint it," there, for everything was in the highest condition of Dutch neatness and order. If you will but open your mind's eye, you may look into the apartment.

Imagine a large, bare room, with a floor that seemed to be

made of squares cut out of glazed earthen pie dishes, first a yellow piece, then a red, until the whole looked like a vast checkerboard. Fancy a dozen high-backed wooden chairs standing around, then a great hollow chimney place all aglow with its blazing fire, reflected a hundred times in the polished steel firedogs; a tiled hearth, tiled sides, tiled top, with a Dutch sentence upon it; and over all, high above one's head, a narrow mantelshelf, filled with shining brass candlesticks, pipe lighters, and tinderboxes. Then see, in one end of the room, three pine tables; in the other, a closet and a deal dresser. The latter is filled with mugs, dishes, pipes, tankards, earthen and glass bottles, and is guarded at one end by a brass-hooped keg standing upon long legs. Everything dim with tobacco smoke but otherwise clean as soap and sand can make it.

Next, picture two sleepy, shabby-looking men, in wooden shoes, seated near the glowing fireplace, hugging their knees and smoking short, stumpy pipes; Mynheer Kleef walking softly and heavily about, clad in leather knee breeches, felt shoes, and a green jacket wider than it is long; then throw a heap of skates in the corner and put six tired well-dressed boys, in various attitudes, upon the wooden chairs, and you will see the coffee room of the Red Lion just as it appeared at nine o'clock on the evening of December 6, 184–. For supper, gingerbread again; slices of Dutch sausage, rye bread sprinkled with anise seed, pickles, a bottle of Utrecht water, and a pot of very mysterious coffee. The boys were ravenous enough to take all they could get and pronounce it excellent. Ben made wry faces, but Jacob declared he had never eaten a better meal. After they had laughed and talked awhile, and counted their money by way of settling a discussion that arose concerning their expenses, the captain marched his company off to bed, led on by a greasy pioneer boy who carried skates and a candlestick instead of an ax.

One of the ill-favored men by the fire had shuffled toward the dresser and was ordering a mug of beer, just as Ludwig, who brought up the rear, was stepping from the apartment. "I don't like that fellow's eye," he whispered to Carl. "He looks like a pirate or something of that kind."

"Looks like a granny!" answered Carl in sleepy disdain.

Ludwig laughed uneasily.

"Granny or no granny," he whispered, "I tell you he looks just like one of those men in the *voetspoelen.*"

"Pooh!" sneered Carl, "I knew it. That picture was too much for you. Look sharp now, and see if yon fellow with the candle doesn't look like the other villain."

"No, indeed, his face is as honest as a Gouda cheese. But, I say, Carl, that really was a horrid picture."

"Humph! What did you stare at it so long for?"

"I couldn't help it."

By this time the boys had reached the "beautiful room with three beds in it." A dumpy little maiden with long earrings met them at the doorway, dropped them a curtsy, and passed out. She carried a long-handled thing that resembled a frying pan with a cover.

"I am glad to see that," said Van Mounen to Ben.

"What?"

"Why, the warming pan. It's full of hot ashes; she's been heating our beds."

"Oh, a warming pan, eh! Much obliged to her, I'm sure," said Ben, too sleepy to make any further comment.

Meantime, Ludwig still talked of the picture that had made such a strong impression upon him. He had seen it in a shop window during their walk. It was a poorly painted thing, representing two men tied back to back, standing on shipboard, surrounded by a group of seamen who were preparing to cast them together into the sea. This mode of putting prisoners to death was called *voetspoelen,* or feet washing, and was practiced by the Dutch upon the pirates of Dunkirk in 1605; and again by the Spaniards upon the Dutch, in the horrible massacre that followed the siege of Haarlem. Bad as the painting was, the expression upon the pirates' faces was well given. Sullen and despairing as they seemed, they wore such a cruel, malignant aspect that Ludwig had felt a secret satisfaction in contemplating their helpless condition. He might have forgotten the scene by this time but for that ill-looking man by the fire. Now, while he capered about, boylike, and threw himself with an antic into his bed, he inwardly hoped that the *voetspoelen* would not haunt his dreams.

It was a cold, cheerless room; a fire had been newly kindled in the burnished stove and seemed to shiver even while it was trying to burn. The windows, with their funny little panes, were bare and shiny, and the cold waxed floor looked like a sheet of yellow ice. Three rush-bottomed chairs stood stiffly against the wall, alternating with three narrow wooden bedsteads that made the room look like the deserted ward of a hospital. At any other time the boys would have found it quite impossible to sleep in pairs, especially in such narrow quarters, but tonight they lost all fear of being crowded and longed only to lay their weary bodies upon the featherbeds that lay lightly upon each cot. Had the boys been in Germany instead of Holland, they might have been covered, also, by a bed of down or feathers. This peculiar form of luxury was at that time adopted only by wealthy or eccentric Hollanders.

Ludwig, as we have seen, had not quite lost his friskiness, but the other boys, after one or two feeble attempts at pillow firing, composed themselves for the night with the greatest dignity. Nothing like fatigue for making boys behave themselves!

"Good night, boys!" said Peter's voice from under the covers.

"Good night," called back everybody but Jacob, who already lay snoring beside the captain.

"I say," shouted Carl after a moment, "don't sneeze, anybody. Ludwig's in a fright!"

"No such thing," retorted Ludwig in a smothered voice. Then there was a little whispered dispute, which was ended by Carl, saying, "For *my* part, I don't know what fear is. But you really are a timid fellow, Ludwig."

Ludwig grunted sleepily but made no further reply.

It was the middle of the night. The fire had shivered itself to death, and, in place of its gleams, little squares of moonlight lay upon the floor, slowly, slowly shifting their way across the room. Something else was moving also, but they did not see it. Sleeping boys keep but a poor lookout. During the early hours of the night, Jacob Poot had been gradually but surely winding himself with all the bed covers. He now lay like a monster chrysalis beside the half-frozen Peter, who, accordingly, was skating with all his might over the coldest, bleakest of dreamland icebergs.

Something else, I say, besides the moonlight, was moving across the bare, polished floor—moving not quite so slowly but quite as stealthily.

Wake up, Ludwig! The *voetspoelen* pirate is growing real!

No. Ludwig does not waken, but he moans in his sleep.

Does not Carl hear it—Carl the brave, the fearless?

No. Carl is dreaming of the race.

And Jacob? Van Mounen? Ben?

Not they. They, too, are dreaming of the race, and Katrinka is singing through their dreams—laughing, flitting past them; now and then a wave from the great organ surges through their midst.

Still the thing moves, slowly, slowly.

Peter! Captain Peter, there is danger!

*   *   *

Peter heard no call, but in his dream, he slid a few thousand feet from one iceberg to another, and the shock awoke him.

Whew! How cold he was! He gave a hopeless, desperate tug at the chrysalis in vain. Sheet, blanket, and spread were firmly wound about Jacob's inanimate form. Peter looked drowsily toward the window.

Clear moonlight, he thought. We shall have pleasant weather tomorrow. Halloo! What's that?

He saw the moving thing, or rather something black, crouching upon the floor, for it had halted as Peter stirred.

He watched in silence.

Soon it moved again, nearer and nearer. It was a man crawling upon hands and feet!

The captain's first impulse was to call out, but he took an instant to consider matters.

The creeper had a shining knife in one hand. This was ugly, but Peter was naturally self-possessed. When the head turned, Peter's eyes were closed as if in sleep, but at other times, nothing could be keener, sharper, than the captain's gaze.

Closer, closer crept the robber. His back was very near Peter now. The knife was laid softly upon the floor. One careful arm reached forth stealthily to drag the clothes from the chair by the captain's bed—the robbery had commenced.

Now was Peter's time! Holding his breath, he sprang up and leapt with all his strength upon the robber's back, stunning the rascal with the force of the blow. To seize the knife was but a second's work. The robber began to struggle, but Peter sat like a giant astride the prostrate form.

"If you stir," said the brave boy in as terrible a voice as he could command, "stir but one inch, I will plunge this knife into your neck. Boys! Boys! Wake up!" he shouted, still pressing down the black head and holding the knife at pricking distance. "Give us a hand! I've got him!"

The chrysalis rolled over, but made no other sign.

"Up, boys!" cried Peter, never budging. "Ludwig! Lambert! Thunder! Are you all dead?"

Dead? Not they! Van Mounen and Ben were on their feet in an instant.

"Hey? What now?" they shouted.

"I've got a robber here," said Peter coolly. "Lie still, you scoundrel, or I'll slice your head off! Now, boys, cut out your bed cord—plenty of time. He's a dead man if he stirs."

Peter felt that he weighed a thousand pounds. So he did, with that knife in his hand.

The man growled and swore but dared not move.

Ludwig was up by this time. He had a great jackknife, the pride of his heart, in his breeches pocket. It could do good service now. They bared the bedstead in a moment. It was laced backward and forward with a rope.

"I'll cut it," cried Ludwig, sawing away at the knot. "Hold him tight, Peter!"

"What fellow? Donder!"

"Hurrah for Poot!" cried all the boys as Jacob, sliding quickly to the floor, bedclothes and all, took in the state of affairs at a glance and sat heavily beside Peter on the robber's back.

Oh, didn't the fellow groan then!

"No use in holding him down any longer, boys," said Peter, rising, but bending as he did so to draw a pistol from his man's belt. "You see, I've been keeping guard over this pretty little weapon for the last ten minutes. It's cocked, and the least wriggle might have set it off. No danger now. I must dress myself. You and I, Lambert, will go for the police. I'd no idea it was so cold."

"Where is Carl?" asked one of the boys.

They looked at one another. Carl certainly was not among them.

"Oh!" cried Ludwig, frightened at last, "where is he? Perhaps he's had a fight with the robber and got killed."

"Not a bit of it," said Peter quietly as he buttoned his stout jacket. "Look under the beds."

They did so. Carl was not there.

Just then they heard a commotion on the stairway. Ben hastened to open the door. The landlord almost tumbled in; he was armed with a big blunderbuss. Two or three lodgers followed; then the daughter, with an upraised frying pan in one hand and a candle in the other; and, behind her, looking pale and frightened, the gallant Carl!

"There's your man, mine host," said Peter, nodding toward the prisoner.

Mine host raised his blunderbuss, the girl screamed, and Jacob, more nimble than usual, rolled quickly from the robber's back.

"Don't fire," cried Peter, "he is tied, hand and foot. Let's roll him over and see what he looks like."

Carl stepped briskly forward, with a blustering, "Yes. *We'll* turn him over in a way he won't like. Lucky we've caught him!"

"Ha! ha!" laughed Ludwig. "Where were you, Master Carl?"

"Where was I?" retorted Carl angrily. "Why, I went to give the alarm, to be sure!"

All the boys exchanged glances, but they were too happy and elated to say anything ill-natured. Carl certainly was bold enough now. He took the lead while three others aided him in turning the helpless man.

While the robber lay faceup, scowling and muttering, Ludwig took the candlestick from the girl's hand.

"I must have a good look at the beauty," he said, drawing

closer, but the words were no sooner spoken than he turned pale and started so violently that he almost dropped the candle.

"The *voetspoelen!*" he cried. "Why, boys, it's the man who sat by the fire!"

"Of course it is," answered Peter. "We counted our money before him like simpletons. But what have we to do with *voetspoelen,* brother Ludwig? A month in jail is punishment enough."

The landlord's daughter had left the room. She now ran in, holding up a pair of huge wooden shoes. "See, father," she cried, "here are his great ugly boats. It's the man that we put in the next room after the young masters went to bed. Ah! It was wrong to send the poor young gentlemen up here so far out of sight and sound."

"The scoundrel!" hissed the landlord. "He has disgraced my house. I go for the police at once!"

In less than fifteen minutes two drowsy-looking officers were in the room. After telling Mynheer Kleef that he must appear early in the morning with the boys and make his complaint before a magistrate, they marched off with their prisoner.

One would think the captain and his band could have slept no more that night, but the mooring has not yet been found that can prevent youth and an easy conscience from drifting down the river of dreams. The boys were too much fatigued to let so slight a thing as capturing a robber bind them to wakefulness. They were soon in bed again, floating away to strange scenes made of familiar things. Ludwig and Carl had spread their bedding upon the floor. One had already forgotten the *voetspoelen,* the race—everything, but Carl was wide-awake. He heard the carillons ringing out their solemn nightly music and the watchman's noisy clapper putting in discord at the quarter hours; he saw the moonshine glide away from the window and the red morning light come pouring in, and all the while he kept thinking, Pooh! What a goose I have made of myself!

Carl Schummel, alone, with none to look or to listen, was not quite so grand a fellow as Carl Schummel strutting about in his boots.

Chapter 23

Before the Court

*Y*ou may believe the landlord's daughter bestirred herself to prepare a good meal for the boys next morning. *Mynheer* had a Chinese gong that could make more noise than a dozen breakfast bells. Its hideous reveille, clanging through the house, generally startled the drowsiest lodgers into activity, but the maiden would not allow it to be sounded this morning.

"Let the brave young gentlemen sleep," she said to the greasy kitchen boy. "They shall be warmly fed when they waken."

It was ten o'clock when Captain Peter and his band came straggling down one by one.

"A pretty hour," said mine host gruffly. "It is high time we were before the court. Fine business, this, for a respectable inn. You will testify truly, young masters, that you found most excellent fare and lodging at the Red Lion?"

"Of course we will," answered Carl saucily, "and pleasant company, too, though they visit at rather unseasonable hours."

A stare and a "humph!" was all the answer *mynheer* made to this, but the daughter was more communicative. Shaking her earrings at Carl, she said sharply, "Not so very pleasant, either, master traveler, if you could judge by the way *you* ran away from it!"

"Impertinent creature!" hissed Carl under his breath as he began busily to examine his skate straps. Meantime the kitchen boy, listening outside at the crack of the door, doubled himself with silent laughter.

After breakfast the boys went to the police court, accompanied by Huygens Kleef and his daughter. *Mynheer's* testimony was principally to the effect that such a thing as a robber at the Red Lion had been unheard of until last night, and as for the Red Lion, it was a most respectable inn, as respectable as any house in Leyden. Each boy, in turn, told all he knew of the affair and identified the prisoner in the box as the same man who entered their room in the dead of night. Ludwig was surprised to find that the robber was a man of ordinary size—especially after he had described him, under oath, to the court as a tremendous fellow with great, square shoulders and legs of prodigious weight. Jacob swore that he was awakened by the robber kicking and thrashing upon the floor, and immediately afterward, Peter and the rest (feeling sorry that they had not explained the matter to their sleepy comrade) testified that the man had not moved a muscle from the moment the point of the dagger touched his throat, until, bound from head to foot, he was rolled over for inspection. The landlord's daughter made one boy blush, and all the court smile, by declaring, "If it hadn't been for that handsome young gentleman there"—pointing to Peter—"they might have all been murdered in their beds; for the dreadful man had a great, shining knife most as long as Your Honor's arm," and *she* believed, "the handsome young gentleman had struggled hard enough to get it away from him, but he was too modest, bless him to say so."

Finally, after a little questioning and cross-questioning from the public prosecutor, the witnesses were dismissed, and the robber was handed over to the consideration of the criminal court.

"The scoundrel!" said Carl savagely when the boys reached the street. "He ought to be sent to jail at once. If I had been in your place, Peter, I certainly should have killed him outright!"

"He was fortunate, then, in falling into gentler hands," was Peter's quiet reply. "It appears he has been arrested before under a charge of housebreaking. He did not succeed in robbing this time, but he broke the door fastenings, and that I believe makes a burglary in the eye of the law. He was armed with a knife, too, and that makes it worse for him, poor fellow!"

"Poor fellow!" mimicked Carl. "One would think he was your brother!"

"So he is my brother, and yours, too, Carl Schummel, for that matter," answered Peter, looking into Carl's eye. "We cannot say what we might have become under other circumstances. We have been bolstered up from evil, since the hour we were born. A happy home and good parents might have made that man a fine fellow instead of what he is. God grant the law may cure and not crush him!"

"Amen to that!" said Lambert heartily while Ludwig van Holp looked at his brother in such a bright, proud way that Jacob Poot, who was an only son, wished from his heart that the little form buried in the old church at home had lived to grow up beside him.

"Humph!" said Carl, "it's very well to be saintly and forgiving, and all that sort of thing, but I'm naturally hard. All these fine ideas seem to rattle off me like hailstones—and it's nobody's business, either, if they do."

Peter recognized a touch of good feeling in this clumsy concession. Holding out his hand, he said in a frank, hearty tone, "Come, lad, shake hands, and let us be good friends even if we don't exactly agree on all questions."

"We do agree better than you think," sulked Carl, as he returned Peter's grasp.

"All right," responded Peter briskly. "Now, Van Mounen, we await Benjamin's wishes. Where would he like to go?"

"To the Egyptian Museum," answered Lambert after holding a brief consultation with Ben.

"That is on the Breedstraat. To the museum let it be. Come, boys!"

Chapter 24

The Beleaguered Cities

"*T*his open square before us," said Lambert as he and Ben walked on together, "is pretty in summer, with its shady trees. They call it the Ruine. Years ago it was covered with houses, and the Rapenburg Canal, here, ran through the street. Well, one day a barge loaded with forty thousand pounds of gunpowder, bound for Delft, was lying alongside, and the bargemen took a notion to cook their dinner on the deck, and before anyone knew it, sir, the whole thing blew up, killing lots of persons and scattering about three hundred houses to the winds."

"What?" exclaimed Ben. "Did the explosion destroy three hundred houses?"

"Yes, sir, my father was in Leyden at the time. He says it was terrible. The explosion occurred just at noon and was like a volcano. All this part of the town was on fire in an instant, buildings tumbling down and men, women, and children groaning under the ruins. The king himself came to the city and acted nobly, Father says, staying out in the streets all night, encouraging the survivors in their efforts to arrest the fire and rescue as many as possible from under the heaps of stone and rubbish. Through his means a collection for the benefit of the sufferers was raised throughout the kingdom, besides a hundred thousand guilders paid out of the treasury. Father was only nineteen years old then. It was in 1807, I believe, but he remembers it perfectly. A friend of his, Professor Luzac, was among the killed. They have a tablet erected to his memory, in Saint Peter's Church, farther on—the queerest thing you ever saw—with an image of the professor carved upon it, representing him just as he looked when he was found after the explosion."

"What a strange idea! Isn't Boerhaave's monument in Saint Peter's also?"

"I cannot remember. Perhaps Peter knows."

The captain delighted Ben by saying that the monument was there and that he thought they might be able to see it during the day.

"Lambert," continued Peter, "ask Ben if he saw Van der Werf's portrait at the town hall last night?"

"No," said Lambert, "I can answer for him. It was too late to go in. I say, boys, it is really wonderful how much Ben knows. Why, he has told me a volume of Dutch history already. I'll wager he has the siege of Leyden at his tongue's end."

"His tongue must burn, then," interposed Ludwig, "for if Bilderdyk's account is true, it was a pretty hot affair."

Ben was looking at them with an inquiring smile.

"We are speaking of the siege of Leyden," explained Lambert.

"Oh, yes," said Ben eagerly, "I had forgotten all about it. This was the very place. Let's give old Van der Werf three cheers. Hur—"

Van Mounen uttered a hasty "Hush!" and explained that, patriotic as the Dutch were, the police would soon have something to say if a party of boys cheered in the street at midday.

"What? Not cheer Van der Werf?" cried Ben indignantly. "One of the greatest chaps in history? Only think! Didn't he hold out against those murderous Spaniards for months and months? There was the town, surrounded on all sides by the enemy; great black forts sending fire and death into the very heart of the city—but no surrender! Every man a hero—women, and children, too, brave and fierce as lions, provisions giving out, the very grass from between the paving stones gone—till people were glad to eat horses and cats and dogs and rats. Then came the plague—hundreds dying in the streets—but no surrender! Then when they could bear no more, when the people, brave as they were, crowded about Van der Werf in the public square begging him to give up, what did the noble old burgomaster say? 'I have sworn to defend this city, and with God's help, *I mean to do it!* If my body can satisfy your hunger, take it, and divide it among you, but expect no surrender so long as I am alive.' Hurrah! Hur—"

Ben was getting uproarious. Lambert playfully clapped his hand over his friend's mouth. The result was one of those quick India-rubber scuffles fearful to behold but delightful to human nature in its polliwog state.

"Vat wash te matter, Pen?" asked Jacob, hurrying forward.

"Oh! nothing at all," panted Ben, "except that Van Mounen was afraid of starting an English riot in this orderly town. He stopped my cheering for old Van der—"

"Ya! ya—it ish no goot to sheer—to make te noise for dat. You vill shee old Van der Does's likeness mit te Stadhuis."

"See old Van der Does? I thought it was Van der Werf's picture they had there."

"Ya," responded Jacob, "Van der Werf—vell, vot of it! Both ish just ash goot—"

"Yes, Van der Does was a noble old Dutchman, but he was not Van der Werf. I know he defended the city like a brick, and—"

"Now vot for you shay dat, Penchamin? He no defend te

citty mit breek, he fight like goot soltyer mit his guns. You like make te fun mit effrysinks Tutch."

"No! No! No! I said he defended the city *like* a brick. That is very high praise, I would have you understand. We English call even the Duke of Wellington a brick."

Jacob looked puzzled, but his indignation was already on the ebb.

"Vell, it ish no matter. I no tink, before, soltyer mean breek, but it ish no matter."

Ben laughed good-naturedly, and seeing that his cousin was tired of talking in English, he turned to his friend of the two languages.

"Van Mounen, they say the very carrier pigeons that brought news of relief to the besieged city are somewhere here in Leyden. I really should like to see them. Just think of it! At the very height of the trouble, if the wind didn't turn and blow in the waters and drown hundreds of the Spaniards and enable the Dutch boats to sail in right over the land with men and provisions to the very gates of the city. The pigeons, you know, did great service, in bearing letters to and fro. I have read somewhere that they were reverently cared for from that day, and when they died, they were stuffed and placed for safekeeping in the town hall. We must be sure to have a look at them."

Van Mounen laughed. "On that principle, Ben, I suppose when you go to Rome, you'll expect to see the identical goose who saved the capitol. But it will be easy enough to see the pigeons. They are in the same building with Van der Werf's portrait. Which was the greatest defense, Ben, the siege of Leyden or the siege of Haarlem?"

"Well," replied Ben thoughtfully, "Van der Werf is one of my heroes. We all have our historical pets, you know, but I really think the siege of Haarlem brought out a braver, more heroic resistance even, than the Leyden one; besides, they set the Leyden sufferers an example of courage and fortitude, for their turn came first."

"I don't know much about the Haarlem siege," said Lambert, "except that it was in 1573. Who beat?"

"The Spaniards," said Ben. "The Dutch had stood out for months. Not a man would yield, nor a woman, either, for that matter. They shouldered arms and fought gallantly beside their husbands and fathers. Three hundred of them did duty under Kanau Hesselaer, a great woman, and brave as Joan of Arc. All this time the city was surrounded by the Spaniards under Frederic of Toledo, son of that beauty, the Duke of Alva. Cut off from all possible help from without, there seemed to be no hope for the inhabitants, but they shouted defiance over the city walls. They even threw bread into the enemy's camps to show that they were not afraid of starvation. Up to the last they held out bravely, waiting for the help that never could come—growing bolder and bolder until their provisions were exhausted. Then it was terrible. In time hundreds of famished creatures fell dead in the streets, and the living had scarcely strength to bury them. At last they made the desperate resolution that, rather than perish by lingering torture, the strongest would form in a square, placing the weakest in the center, and rush in a body to their death, with the faint chance of being able to fight their way through the enemy. The Spaniards received a hint of this, and believing there was nothing the Dutch would not dare to do, they concluded to offer terms."

"High time, I should think."

"Yes, with falsehood and treachery they soon obtained an entrance into the city, promising protection and forgiveness to all except those whom the citizens themselves would acknowledge as deserving of death."

"You don't say so!" said Lambert, quite interested. "That ended the business, I suppose."

"Not a bit of it," returned Ben, "for the Duke of Alva had already given his son orders to show mercy to none."

"Ah! There was where the great Haarlem massacre came in. I remember now. You can't wonder that the Hollanders dislike Spain when you read of the way they were butchered by Alva and his hosts, though I admit that our side sometimes retaliated terribly. But as I have told you before, I have a very indistinct idea of historical matters. Everything is utter confusion—from the flood to the battle of Waterloo. One thing is plain, however, the Duke of Alva was about the worst specimen of a man that ever lived."

"That gives only a faint idea of him," said Ben, "but I hate to think of such a wretch. What if he *had* brains and military skill and all that sort of thing! Give me such men as Van der Werf, and— What now?"

"Why," said Van Mounen, who was looking up and down the street in a bewildered way. "We've walked right past the museum, and I don't see the boys. Let us go back."

Chapter 25

Leyden

*T*he boys met at the museum and were soon engaged in examining its extensive collection of curiosities, receiving a new insight into Egyptian life, ancient and modern. Ben and Lambert had often visited the British Museum, but that did not prevent them from being surprised at the richness of the Leyden collection. There were household utensils, wearing apparel, weapons, musical instruments, sarcophagi, and mummies of men, women, and cats, ibexes, and other creatures. They saw a massive gold armlet that had been worn by an Egyptian king at a time when some of these same mummies, perhaps, were nimbly treading the streets of Thebes; and jewels and trinkets such as Pharaoh's daughter wore, and the children of Israel borrowed when they departed out of Egypt.

There were other interesting relics, from Rome and Greece, and some curious Roman pottery which had been discovered in digging near The Hague—relics of the days when the countrymen of Julius Caesar had settled there. Where have they not settled? I for one would hardly be astonished if relics of the ancient Romans should someday be found deep under the grass growing around the Bunker Hill monument.

When the boys left this museum, they went to another and

saw a wonderful collection of fossil animals, skeletons, birds, minerals, precious stones, and other natural specimens, but as they were not learned men, they could only walk about and stare, enjoy the little knowledge of natural history they possessed, and wish with all their hearts they had acquired more. Even the skeleton of the mouse puzzled Jacob. What wonder? He was not used to seeing the cat-fearing little creatures running about in their bones—and how could he ever have imagined their necks to be so queer?

Besides the Museum of Natural History, there was Saint Peter's Church to be visited, containing Professor Luzac's memorial, and Boerhaave's monument of white and black marble, with its urn and carved symbols of the four ages of life, and its medallion of Boerhaave, adorned with his favorite motto, *Simplex sigillum veri*. They also obtained admittance to a tea garden, which in summer was a favorite resort of the citizens and, passing naked oaks and fruit trees, ascended a high mound which stood in the center. This was the site of a round tower now in ruins, said by some to have been built by Hengist the Anglo-Saxon king, and by others to have been the castle of one of the ancient counts of Holland.

As the boys walked about on the top of its stone wall, they could get but a poor view of the surrounding city. The tower stood higher when, more than two centuries ago, the inhabitants of beleaguered Leyden shouted to the watcher on its top their wild, despairing cries, "Is there any help? Are the waters rising? What do you see?"

And for months he could only answer, "No help. I see around us nothing but the enemy."

Ben pushed these thoughts away and, resolutely looking down into the bare tea garden, filled it in imagination with gay summer groups. He tried to forget old battle clouds and picture only curling wreaths of tobacco smoke, rising from among men, women, and children enjoying their tea and coffee in the open air. But a tragedy came in spite of him.

Poot was bending over the edge of the high wall. It would be just like him to grow dizzy and tumble off. Ben turned impatiently away. If the fellow, with his weak head, knew no better than to be venturesome, why, let him tumble. Horror! What meant that heavy, crashing sound?

Ben could not stir. He could only gasp. "Jacob!"

"Jacob!" cried another startled voice and another. Ready to faint, Ben managed to turn his head. He saw a crowd of boys on the edge of the wall opposite, but Jacob was not there!

"Good heavens!" he cried, springing forward, "where is my cousin?"

The crowd parted. It was only four boys, after all. There sat Jacob in their midst, holding his sides and laughing heartily.

"Did I frighten you all?" he said in his native Dutch. "Well, I will tell you how it was. There was a big stone lying on the wall and I put my—my foot out just to push it a little, you see, and the first thing I knew, down went the stone all the way to the bottom and left me sitting here on top with both my feet in the air. If I had not thrown myself back at that moment, I certainly should have rolled over after the stone. Well, it is no matter. Help me up, boys."

"You're hurt!" said Ben, seeing a shade of seriousness pass over his cousin's face as they lifted him to his feet.

Jacob tried to laugh again. "Oh, no—I feels little hurt ven I stant up, but it ish no matter."

The monument to Van der Werf in the Hooglandsche Kerk was not accessible that day, but the boys spent a few pleasant moments in the Stadhuis, or town hall, a long irregular structure somewhat in the Gothic style, uncouth in architecture but picturesque from age. Its little steeple, tuneful with bells, seemed to have been borrowed from some other building and hastily clapped on as a finishing touch.

Ascending the grand staircase, the boys soon found themselves in rather a gloomy apartment, containing the masterpiece of Lucas van Leyden, or Hugens, a Dutch artist born three hundred and seventy years ago, who painted well when he was ten years of age and became distinguished in art when only fifteen. This picture, called the *Last Judgment*, considering the remote age in which it was painted, is truly a remarkable production. The boys, however, were less interested in tracing out the merits of the work than they were in the fact of its being a triptych—that is, painted on three divisions, the two outer ones swung on hinges so as to close, when required, over the main portion.

The historical pictures of Harel de Moor and other famous Dutch artists interested them for a while, and Ben had to be almost pulled away from the dingy old portrait of Van der Werf.

The town hall, as well as the Egyptian Museum, is on the Breedstraat, the longest and finest street in Leyden. It has no canal running through it, and the houses, painted in every variety of color, have a picturesque effect as they stand with their gable ends to the street; some are very tall with half of their height in their steplike roofs; others crouch before the public edifices and churches. Being clean, spacious, well-shaded, and adorned with many elegant mansions, it compares favorably with the finer portions of Amsterdam. It is kept scrupulously neat. Many of the gutters are covered with boards that open like trapdoors, and it is supplied with pumps surmounted with shining brass ornaments kept scoured and bright at the public cost. The city is intersected by numerous water roads formed by the river Rhine, there grown sluggish, fatigued by its long travel, but more than one hundred and fifty stone bridges reunite the dissevered streets. The same world-renowed river, degraded from the beautiful, free-flowing Rhine, serves as a moat around the rampart that surrounds Leyden and is crossed by drawbridges at the imposing gateways that give access to the city. Fine broad promenades, shaded by noble trees, border the canals and add to the retired appearance of the houses behind, heightening the effect of scholastic seclusion that seems to pervade the place.

Ben, as he scanned the buildings on the Rapenburg Canal, was somewhat disappointed in the appearance of the great University of Leyden. But when he recalled its history—how, attended with all the pomp of a grand civic display, it had been founded by the Prince of Orange as a tribute to the citizens for the bravery displayed during the siege; when he remembered the great men in religion, learning, and science who had once studied there and thought of the hundreds of students now sharing the benefits of its classes and its valuable scientific museums—he was quite willing to forego architectural beauty, though he could not help feeling that no amount of it could have been misplaced on such an institution.

Peter and Jacob regarded the building with an even deeper, more practical interest, for they were to enter it as students in the course of a few months.

"Poor Don Quixote would have run a hopeless tilt in this part of the world," said Ben after Lambert had been pointing out some of the oddities and beauties of the suburbs. "It is all windmills. You remember his terrific contest with one, I suppose."

"No," said Lambert bluntly.

"Well, I don't, either, that is, not definitely. But there was something of that kind in his adventures, and if there wasn't, there should have been. Look at them, how frantically they whirl their great arms—just the thing to excite the crazy knight to mortal combat. It bewilders one to look at them. Help me to count all those we can see, Van Mounen. I want a big item for my notebook." And after a careful reckoning, superintended by all the party, Master Ben wrote in pencil, "Saw, Dec., 184–, ninety-eight windmills within full view of Leyden."

He would have been glad to visit the old brick mill in which the painter Rembrandt was born, but he abandoned the project upon learning that it would take them out of their way. Few boys as hungry as Ben was by this time would hesitate long between Rembrandt's home a mile off and *tiffin* close by. Ben chose the latter.

After *tiffin*, they rested awhile, and then took another, which, for form's sake, they called dinner. After dinner the boys sat warming themselves, at the inn; all but Peter, who occupied the time in another fruitless search for Dr. Boekman.

This over, the party once more prepared for skating. They were thirteen miles from The Hague and not as fresh as when they had left Broek early on the previous day, but they were in good spirits and the ice was excellent.

Chapter 26

The Palace and the Wood

*A*s the boys skated onward, they saw a number of fine country seats, all decorated and surrounded according to the Dutchest of Dutch taste, but impressive to look upon, with their great, formal houses, elaborate gardens, square hedges, and wide ditches—some crossed by a bridge, having a gate in the middle to be carefully locked at night. These ditches, everywhere traversing the landscape, had long ago lost their summer film and now shone under the sunlight like trailing ribbons of glass.

The boys traveled bravely, all the while performing the surprising feat of producing gingerbread from their pockets and causing it to vanish instantly.

Twelve miles were passed. A few more long strokes would take them to The Hague, when Van Mounen proposed that they should vary their course by walking into the city through the Bosch.

"Agreed!" cried one and all—and their skates were off in a twinkling.

The Bosch is a grand park of wood, nearly two miles long, containing the celebrated House in the Wood—*Huis in't Bosch*—sometimes used as a royal residence.

This building, though plain outside for a palace, is elegantly furnished within and finely frescoed—that is, the walls and ceilings are covered with groups and designs painted directly upon them while the plaster was fresh. Some of the rooms are tapestried with Chinese silk, beautifully embroidered. One contains a number of family portraits, among them a group of royal children who in time were orphaned by a certain ax, which figures very frequently in European history. These children were painted many times by the Dutch artist Van Dyck, who was court painter to their father, Charles the First of England. Beautiful children they were. What a deal of trouble the English nation would have been spared had they been as perfect in heart and soul as they were in form!

The park surrounding the palace is charming, especially in summer, for flowers and birds make it bright as fairyland. Long rows of magnificent oaks rear their proud heads, conscious that no profaning hand will ever bring them low. In fact, the Wood has for ages been held as an almost sacred spot. Children are never allowed to meddle with its smallest twig. The ax of the woodman has never resounded there. Even war and riot have passed it reverently, pausing for a moment in their devastating way. Philip of Spain, while he ordered Dutchmen to be mowed down by hundreds, issued a mandate that not a bough of the beautiful Wood should be touched. And once, when in a time of great necessity the State was about to sacrifice it to assist in filling a nearly exhausted treasury, the people rushed to the rescue, and nobly contributed the required amount rather than that the Bosch should fall.

What wonder, then, that the oaks have a grand, fearless air? Birds from all Holland have told them how, elsewhere, trees are cropped and bobbed into shape—but *they* are untouched. Year after year they expand in unclipped luxuriance and beauty; their wide-spreading foliage, alive with song, casts a cool shade over lawn and pathway or bows to its image in the sunny ponds.

Meanwhile, as if to reward the citizens for allowing her to have her way for once, Nature departs from the invariable level, wearing gracefully the ornaments that have been reverently bestowed upon her. So the lawn slopes in a velvety green; the paths wind in and out; flower beds glow and send forth perfume; and ponds and sky look at each other in mutual admiration.

Even on that winter day the Bosch was beautiful. Its trees were bare, but beneath them still lay the ponds, every ripple smoothed into glass. The blue sky was bright overhead, and as it looked down through the thicket of boughs, it saw another blue sky, not nearly so bright, looking up from the dim thicket under the ice.

Never had the sunset appeared more beautiful to Peter than when he saw it exchanging farewell glances with the windows and shining roofs of the city before him. Never had The Hague itself seemed more inviting. He was no longer Peter van Holp, going to visit a great city, nor a fine young gentleman bent on sight-seeing; he was a knight, an adventurer, travel-soiled and weary, a Hop-o'-my-Thumb grown large, a Fortunatus approaching the enchanted castle where luxury and ease awaited him, for his own sister's house was not half a mile away.

"At last, boys," he cried in high glee, "we may hope for a royal resting place—good beds, warm rooms, and something fit to eat. I never realized before what a luxury such things are. Our lodgings at the Red Lion have made us appreciate our own homes."

Chapter 27

The Merchant Prince
and the Sister-Princess

*W*ell might Peter feel that his sister's house was like an enchanted castle. Large and elegant as it was, a spell of quiet hung over it. The very lion crouching at its gate seemed to have been turned into stone through magic. Within, it was guarded by genii, in the shape of red-faced servants, who sprang silently forth at the summons of bell or knocker. There was a cat also, who appeared as knowing as any Puss-in-Boots, and a brass gnome in the hall whose business it was to stand with outstretched arms ready to receive sticks and umbrellas. Safe within the walls bloomed a Garden of Delight, where the flowers firmly believed it was summer, and a sparkling fountain was laughing merrily to itself because Jack Frost could not find it. There was a Sleeping Beauty, too, just at the time of the boys' arrival, but when Peter, like a true prince, flew lightly up the stairs and kissed her eyelids, the enchantment was broken. The princess became his own good sister, and the fairy castle just one of the finest, most comfortable houses of The Hague.

As may well be believed, the boys received the heartiest of welcomes. After they had conversed awhile with their lively hostess, one of the genii summoned them to a grand repast in a red-curtained room, where floor and ceiling shone like polished ivory, and the mirrors suddenly blossomed into rosy-cheeked boys as far as the eye could reach.

They had caviar now, and salmagundi, and sausage and cheese, besides salad and fruit and biscuit and cake. How the boys could partake of such a medley was a mystery to Ben, for the salad was sour and the cake was sweet; the fruit was dainty and the salmagundi heavy with onions and fish. But, while he was wondering, he made a hearty meal, and was soon absorbed in deciding which he really preferred, the coffee or the anisette cordial. It was delightful too—this taking one's food from dishes of frosted silver and liqueur glasses from which Titania herself might have sipped. The young gentleman afterward wrote to his mother that, pretty and choice as things were at home, he had never known what cut glass, china, and silver services were until he visited The Hague.

Of course, Peter's sister soon heard of all the boys' adventures. How they had skated over forty miles and seen rare sights on the way; how they had lost their purse and found it again. How one of the party had fallen and given them an excuse for a grand sail in an iceboat; how, above all, they had caught a robber and so, for a second time, saved their slippery purse.

"And now, Peter," said the lady when the story was finished, "you must write at once to tell the good people of Broek that your adventures have reached their height, that you and your fellow travelers have all been taken prisoners."

The boys looked startled.

"Indeed, I shall do no such thing," laughed Peter. "We must leave tomorrow at noon."

But the sister had already decided differently, and a Holland lady is not to be easily turned from her purpose. In short, she held forth such strong temptations and was so bright and cheerful and said so many coaxing and unanswerable things, in both English and Dutch, that the boys were all delighted when it was settled that they should remain at The Hague for at least two days.

Next the grand skating race was talked over; Mevrouw van Gend gladly promised to be present on the occasion. "I shall witness your triumph, Peter," she said, "for you are the fastest skater I ever knew."

Peter blushed and gave a slight cough as Carl answered for him.

"Ah, mervouw, he is swift, but all the Broek boys are fine skaters—even the ragpickers." And he thought bitterly of poor Hans.

The lady laughed. "That will make the race all the more exciting," she said. "But I shall wish each of you to be the winner."

At this moment her husband Mynheer van Gend came in, and the enchantment falling upon the boys was complete.

The invisible fairies of the household at once clustered about them, whispering that Jasper van Gend had a heart as young and fresh as their own, and if he loved anything in this world more than industry, it was sunshine and frolic. They also hinted something about his having a heart full of love and a head full of wisdom and finally gave the boys to understand that when mynheer said a thing, he meant it.

Therefore his frank "Well, now, this is pleasant," as he shook hands with them all, made the boys feel quite at home and as happy as squirrels.

There were fine paintings in the drawing room and exquisite statuary, and portfolios filled with rare Dutch engravings, besides many beautiful and curious things from China and Japan. The boys felt that it would require a month to examine all the treasures of the apartment.

Ben noticed with pleasure English books lying upon the table. He saw also over the carved upright piano, life-size portraits of William of Orange and his English queen, a sight that, for a time, brought England and Holland side by side in his heart. William and Mary have left a halo around the English throne to this day, he the truest patriot that ever served an adopted country, she the noblest wife that ever sat upon a British throne, up to the time of Victoria and Albert the Good. As Ben looked at the pictures he remembered accounts he had read of King William's visit to The Hague in the winter of 1691. He who sang the Battle of Ivry had not yet told the glowing story of that day, but Ben knew enough of it to fancy that he could almost hear the shouts of the delighted populace as he looked from the portraits to the street, which at this moment was aglow with a bonfire, kindled in a neighboring square.

That royal visit was one never to be forgotten. For two years William of Orange had been monarch of a foreign land, his head working faithfully for England, but his whole heart yearning for Holland. Now, when he sought its shores once more, the entire nation bade him welcome. Multitudes flocked to The Hague to meet him—"many thousands came sliding or skating along the frozen canals from Amsterdam, Rotterdam, Leyden, Haarlem, Delft."* All day long the festivities of the capital were kept up, the streets were gorgeous with banners, evergreen arches, trophies, and mottoes of welcome and emblems of industry. William saw the deeds of his ancestors and scenes of his own past life depicted on banners and tapestries along the streets. At night superb fireworks were displayed upon the ice. Its glassy surface was like a mirror. Sparkling fountains of light sprang up from below to meet the glittering cascades leaping upon it. Then a feathery fire of crimson and green shook

---

*Macaulay's *History of England*.

millions of rubies and emeralds into the ruddy depths of the ice—and all this time the people were shouting, "God bless William of Orange. Long live the king!" They were half mad with joy and enthusiasm. William, their own prince, their stadtholder, had become the ruler of three kingdoms; he had been victorious in council and in war, and now, in his hour of greatest triumph, had come as a simple guest to visit them. The king heard their shouts with a beating heart. It is a great thing to be beloved by one's country. His English courtiers complimented him upon his reception. "Yes," said he, "but the shouting is nothing to what it would have been if Mary had been with me!"

While Ben was looking at the portraits, Mynheer van Gend was giving the boys an account of a recent visit to Antwerp. As it was the birthplace of Quentin Matsys, the blacksmith who for love of an artist's daughter studied until he became a great painter, the boys asked their host if he had seen any of Matsys' works.

"Yes, indeed," he replied, "and excellent they are. His famous triptych in a chapel of the Antwerp cathedral, with the Descent from the Cross on the center panel, is especially fine, but I confess I was more interested in his well."

"What well, *mynheer*?" asked Ludwig.

"One in the heart of the city, near this same cathedral, whose lofty steeple is of such delicate workmanship that the French emperor said it reminded him of Mechlin lace. The well is covered with a Gothic canopy surmounted by the figure of a knight in full armor. It is all of metal and proves that Matsys was an artist at the forge as well as at the easel; indeed, his great fame is mainly derived from his miraculous skill as an artificer in iron."

Next, *mynheer* showed the boys some exquisite Berlin castings, which he had purchased in Antwerp. They were *iron jewelry,* and very delicate—beautiful medallions designed from rare paintings, bordered with fine tracery and openwork—worthy, he said, of being worn by the fairest lady of the land. Consequently the necklace was handed with a bow and a smile to the blushing Mevrouw van Gend.

Something in the lady's aspect, as she bent her bright young face over the gift, caused *mynheer* to add earnestly, "I can read your thoughts, sweetheart."

She looked up in playful defiance.

"Ah, now I am sure of them! You were thinking of those noblehearted women, but for whom Prussia might have fallen. I know it by that proud light in your eye."

"The proud light in my eye plays me false, then," she answered. "I had no such grand matter in my mind. To confess the simple truth, I was only thinking how lovely this necklace would be with my blue brocade."

"So, so!" exclaimed the rather crestfallen spouse.

"But I *can* think of the other, Jasper, and it will add a deeper value to your gift. You remember the incident, do you not, Peter? How when the French were invading Prussia and for lack of means the country was unable to defend itself against the enemy, the women turned the scale by pouring their plate and jewels into the public treasury—"

Aha! thought *mynheer* as he met his *vrouw*'s kindling glance. The proud light is there now, in earnest.

Peter remarked maliciously that the women had still proved true to their vanity on that occasion, for jewelry they would have. If gold or silver were wanted by the kingdom, they would relinquish it and use iron, but they could not do without their ornaments.

"What of that?" said the *vrouw,* kindling again. "It is no sin to love beautiful things if you adapt your material to circumstances. All *I* have to say is, the women saved their country and, indirectly, introduced a very important branch of manufacture. Is not that so, Jasper?"

"Of course it is, sweetheart," said *mynheer*, "but Peter needs no word of mine to convince him that all the world over women have never been found wanting in their country's hour of trial, though"—(bowing to *mevrouw*)—"his own countrywomen stand foremost in the records of female patriotism and devotion."

Then, turning to Ben, the host talked with him in English of the fine old Belgian city. Among other things he told the origin of its name. Ben had been taught that Antwerp was derived from *ae'nt werf* (on the wharf), but Mynheer van Gend gave him a far more interesting derivation.

It appears that about three thousand years ago, a great giant, named Antigonus, lived on the river Scheld, on the site of the present city of Antwerp. This giant claimed half the merchandise of all navigators who passed his castle. Of course, some were inclined to oppose this simple regulation. In such cases Antigonus, by way of teaching them to practice better manners next time, cut off and threw into the river the right hands of the merchants. Thus handwerpen (or hand-throwing), changed to Antwerp, came to be the name of the place. The escutcheon or arms of the city has two hands upon it; what better proof than this could one have of the truth of the story, especially when one wishes to believe it!

The giant was finally conquered and thrown into the Scheld by a hero called Brabo, who, in turn, gave a name to the district known as Brabant. Since then the Dutch merchants have traveled the river in peace; but I, for one, thank old Antigonus for giving the city so romantic an origin.

When Mynheer van Gend had related in two languages this story of Antwerp, he was tempted to tell other legends—some in English, some in Dutch; and so the moments, borne upon the swift shoulders of gnomes and giants, glided rapidly away toward bedtime.

It was hard to break up so pleasant a party, but the Van Gend household moved with the regularity of clockwork. There was no lingering at the threshold when the cordial "Good night!" was spoken. Even while our boys were mounting the stairs, the invisible household fairies again clustered around them, whispering that system and regularity had been chief builders of the master's prosperity.

Beautiful chambers with three beds in them were not to be found in this mansion. Some of the rooms contained two, but each visitor slept alone. Before morning, the motto of the party evidently was, "Every boy his own chrysalis," and Peter, at least, was not sorry to have it so.

Tired as he was, Ben, after noting a curious bell rope in the corner, began to examine his bedclothes. Each article filled him with astonishment—the exquisitely fine pillow spread trimmed with costly lace and embroidered with a gorgeous crest and initial, the *dekbed* cover (a great silk bag, large as the bed, stuffed with swan's down), and the pink satin quilts, embroidered with garlands of flowers. He could scarcely sleep for thinking what a queer little bed it was, so comfortable and pretty, too, with all its queerness. In the morning he examined the top coverlet with care, for he wished to send home a description of it in his next letter. It was a beautiful Japanese spread, marvelous in texture as well as in its variety of brilliant coloring, and worth, as Ben afterward learned, not less than three hundred dollars.

The floor was of polished wooden mosaic, nearly covered with a rich carpet bordered with thick black fringe. Another room displayed a margin of satinwood around the carpet. Hung with tapestry, its walls of crimson silk were topped with a gilded cornice which shot down gleams of light far into the polished floor.

Over the doorway of the room in which Jacob and Ben slept was a bronze stork that, with outstretched neck, held a lamp to light the guests into the apartment. Between the two narrow beds of carved whitewood and ebony stood the household treasure of the Van Gends, a massive oaken chair upon which the Prince of Orange had once sat during a council meeting. Opposite stood a quaintly carved clothespress, waxed and polished to the utmost and filled with precious stores of linen; beside it a table holding a large Bible, whose great golden clasps looked poor compared with its solid, ribbed binding made to outlast six generations.

There was a ship model on the mantelshelf, and over it hung an old portrait of Peter the Great, who, you know, once gave the dockyard cats of Holland a fine chance to look at a king, which is one of the special prerogatives of cats. Peter, though czar of Russia, was not too proud to work as a common ship-wright in the dockyards of Saardam and Amsterdam, that he might be able to introduce among his countrymen Dutch improvements in shipbuilding. It was this willingness to be thorough in even the smallest beginnings that earned for him the title of Peter the Great.

Peter the little (comparatively speaking) was up first, the next morning; knowing the punctual habits of his brother-in-law, he took good care that none of the boys should oversleep themselves. A hard task he found it to wake Jacob Poot, but after pulling that young gentleman out of bed, and, with Ben's help, dragging him about the room for a while, he succeeded in arousing him.

While Jacob was dressing and moaning within him because the felt slippers, provided him as a guest, were too tight for his swollen feet, Peter wrote to inform their friends at Broek of the

safe arrival of his party at The Hague. He also begged his
mother to send word to Hans Brinker that Dr. Boekman had
not yet reached Leyden but that a letter containing Hans's
message had been left at the hotel where the doctor always
lodged during his visits to the city. "Tell him also," wrote
Peter, "that I shall call there again, as I pass through Leyden.
The poor boy seemed to feel sure that 'the *meester*' would
hasten to save his father, but we, who know the gruff old
gentleman better, may be confident he will do no such thing. It
would be a kindness to send a visiting physician from Amsterdam to the cottage at once, if Jufvrouw* Brinker will consent to
receive any but the great king of the *meesters*, as Dr. Boekman
certainly is.

"You know, mother," added Peter, "that I have always considered Sister van Gend's house as rather quiet and lonely, but I
assure you, it is not so now. Sister says our presence has warmed
it for the whole winter. Brother van Gend is very kind to us all.
He says we make him wish that he had a houseful of boys of his
own. He has promised to let us ride on his noble black horses.
They are gentle as kittens, he says, if one has but a firm touch
at the rein. Ben, according to Jacob's account, is a glorious
rider, and your son Peter is not a very bad hand at the business;
so we two are to go out together this morning mounted like
knights of old. After we return, Brother van Gend says he will
lend Jacob his English pony and obtain three extra horses; and
all of the party are to trot about the city in a grand cavalcade,
led on by him. He will ride the black horse which Father sent
him from Friesland. My sister's pretty roan with the long white
tail is lame, and she will ride none other; else she would

---

*In Holland, women of the lower grades of society do not take the title of
Mrs. (or *mevrouw*) when they marry, as with us. They assume their husband's
name but are still called Miss (*jufvrouw*, pronounced *yuffrow*).

accompany us. I could scarcely close my eyes last night after
Sister told me of the plan. Only the thought of poor Hans
Brinker and his sick father checked me, but for that I could
have sung for joy. Ludwig has given us a name already—the
Broek Cavalry. We flatter ourselves that we shall make an
imposing appearance, especially in single file. . . ."

The Broek Cavalry were not disappointed. Mynheer van
Gend readily procured good horses; and all the boys could ride,
though none were as perfect horsemen (or horseboys) as Peter
and Ben. They saw The Hague to their hearts' content, and
The Hague saw them—expressing its approbation loudly, through
the mouths of small boys and cart dogs; silently, through bright
eyes that, not looking very deeply into things, shone as they
looked at the handsome Carl and twinkled with fun as a certain
portly youth with shaking cheeks rode past bumpetty, bumpetty,
bump!

On their return, the boys pronounced the great porcelain
stove in the family sitting room a decidedly useful piece of
furniture, for they could gather around it and get warm without
burning their noses or bringing on chilblains. It was so very
large that, though hot nowhere, it seemed to send out warmth
by the houseful. Its pure white sides and polished brass rings
made it a pretty object to look upon, notwithstanding the fact
that our ungrateful Ben, while growing thoroughly warm and
comfortable beside it, concocted a satirical sentence for his
next letter, to the effect that a stove in Holland must, of
course, resemble a great tower of snow or it wouldn't be in
keeping with the oddity of the country.

To describe all the boys saw and did on that day and the next
would render this little book a formidable volume indeed. They
visited the brass cannon foundry, saw the liquid fire poured into
molds, and watched the smiths who, half naked, stood in the
shadow, like demons playing with flame. They admired the

grand public buildings and massive private houses, the elegant streets, and noble Bosch—pride of all beauty-loving Holland-ers. The palace with its brilliant mosaic floors, its frescoed ceilings and gorgeous ornaments, filled Ben with delight; he was surprised that some of the churches were so very plain—elaborate sometimes in external architecture but bare and bleak within with their blank, whitewashed walls.

If there were no printed record, the churches of Holland would almost tell her story. I will not enter into the subject here, except to say that Ben—who had read of her struggles and wrongs and of the terrible retribution she from time to time dealt forth—could scarcely tread a Holland town without mentally leaping horror-stricken over the bloody stepping-stones of its history. He could not forget Philip of Spain nor the Duke of Alva even while rejoicing in the prosperity that followed the Liberation. He looked into the meekest of Dutch eyes for some-thing of the fire that once lit the haggard faces of those desperate, lawless men who, wearing with pride the title of "Beggars," which their oppressors had mockingly cast upon them, became the terror of land and sea. In Haarlem he had wondered that the air did not still resound with the cries of Alva's three thousand victims. In Leyden his heart had swelled in sympathy as he thought of the long procession of scarred and famished creatures who after the siege, with Adrian van der Werf at their head, tottered to the great church to sing a glorious anthem because Leyden was free! He remembered that this was even before they had tasted the bread brought by the Dutch ships. They would praise God first, then eat. Thousands of trembling voices were raised in glad thanksgiving. For a moment it swelled higher and higher, then suddenly changed to sobbing—not one of all the multitude could sing another note. But who shall say that the anthem, even to its very end, was not heard in heaven!

Here, in The Hague, other thoughts came to Ben—of how Holland in later years unwillingly put her head under the French yoke, and how, galled and lashed past endurance, she had resolutely jerked it out again. He liked her for that. What nation of any spirit, thought he, could be expected to stand such work, paying all her wealth into a foreign treasury and yielding up the flower of her youth under foreign conscription. It was not so very long ago, either, since English guns had been heard booming close by in the German Ocean; well—all the fighting was over at last. Holland was a snug little monarchy now in her own right, and Ben, for one, was glad of it. Arrived at this charitable conclusion, he was prepared to enjoy to the utmost all the wonders of her capital; he quite delighted Mynheer van Gend with his hearty and intelligent interest—so, in fact, did all the boys, for a merrier, more observant party never went sight-seeing.

Chapter 28

Through the Hague

*T*he picture gallery in the Maurits Huis,* one of the finest in the world, seemed only to have flashed by the boys during a two-hour visit, so much was there to admire and examine. As for the royal cabinet of curiosities in the same building, they felt that they had but glanced at it, though they were there nearly half a day. It seemed to them that Japan had poured all her treasures within its walls. For a long period Holland, always foremost in commerce, was the only nation allowed to have any intercourse with Japan. One can well forego a journey to that country if he can but visit the museum at The Hague.

Room after room is filled with collections from the Hermit Empire—costumes peculiar to various ranks and pursuits, articles of ornament, household utensils, weapons, armor, and surgical instruments. There is also an ingenious Japanese model of the Island of Desina, the Dutch factory in Japan. It appears almost as the island itself would if seen through a reversed opera glass and makes one feel like a Gulliver coming unexpectedly upon a Japanese Lilliput. There you see hundreds of people in native costumes, standing, kneeling, stooping, reaching—all at

*A building erected by Prince Maurice of Nassau.

work, or pretending to be—and their dwellings, even their very furniture, spread out before you, plain as day. In another room a huge tortoiseshell dollhouse, fitted up in Dutch style and inhabited by dignified Dutch dolls, stands ready to tell you at a glance how people live in Holland.

Gretel, Hilda, Katrinka, even the proud Rychie Korbes would have been delighted with this, but Peter and his gallant band passed it by without a glance. The war implements had the honor of detaining them for an hour; such clubs, such murderous krits, or daggers, such firearms, and, above all, such wonderful Japanese swords, quite capable of performing the accredited Japanese feat of cutting a man in two at a single stroke!

There were Chinese and other Oriental curiosities in the collection. Native historical relics, too, upon which our young Dutchmen gazed very soberly, though they were secretly proud to show them to Ben.

There was a model of the cabin at Saardam in which Peter the Great lived during his short career as a shipbuilder. Also, wallets and bowls—once carried by the "Beggar" Confederates who, uniting under the Prince of Orange, had freed Holland from the tyranny of Spain; the sword of Admiral van Speyk, who about ten years before had perished in voluntarily blowing up his own ship; and Van Tromp's armor with the marks of bullets upon it. Jacob looked around, hoping to see the broom which the plucky admiral fastened to his masthead, but it was not there. The waistcoat which William Third* of England wore during the last days of his life, possessed great interest for Ben, and one and all gazed with a mixture of reverence and horror-worship at the identical clothing worn by William the Silent*

---

*William, Prince of Orange, who became king of England, was a great-grandson of William the Silent, Prince of Orange, who was murdered by Geraerts (or Gerard) July 10, 1584.

when he was murdered at Delft by Balthazar Geraerts. A tawny leather doublet and plain surcoat of gray cloth, a soft felt hat, and a high neck-ruff from which hung one of the "Beggars' " medals—these were not in themselves very princely objects, though the doublet had a tragic interest from its dark stains and bullet holes. Ben could readily believe, as he looked upon the garments, that the Silent Prince, true to his greatness of character, had been exceedingly simple in his attire. His aristocratic prejudices were, however, decidedly shocked when Lambert told him of the way in which William's bride first entered The Hague.

"The beautiful Louisa de Coligny, whose father and former husband both had fallen at the Massacre of St. Bartholomew, was coming to be fourth wife to the Prince, and of course," said Lambert, "we Hollanders were too gallant to allow the lady to enter the town on foot. No, sir, we sent—or rather my ancestors did—a clean, open post-wagon to meet her, with a plank across it for her to sit upon!"

"Very gallant indeed!" exclaimed Ben, with almost a sneer in his polite laugh. "And she the daughter of an admiral of France."

"Was she? Upon my word, I had nearly forgotten that. But, you see, Holland had very plain ways in the good old time; in fact, we are a very simple, frugal people to this day. The Van Gend establishment is a decided exception, you know."

"A very agreeable exception, I think," said Ben.

"Certainly, certainly. But, between you and me, Mynheer van Gend, though he has wrought his own fortunes, can afford to be magnificent and yet be frugal."

"Exactly so," said Ben profoundly, at the same time stroking his upper lip and chin, which latterly he believed had been showing delightful and unmistakable signs of coming dignities.

While tramping on foot through the city, Ben often longed

for a good English sidewalk. Here, as in the other towns, there was no curb, no raised pavement for foot travelers, but the streets were clean and even, and all vehicles were kept scrupulously within a certain tract. Strange to say, there were nearly as many sleds as wagons to be seen, though there was not a particle of snow. The sleds went scraping over the bricks or cobblestones, some provided with an apparatus in front for sprinkling water, to diminish the friction, and some rendered less musical by means of a dripping oil rag, which the driver occasionally applied to the runners.

Ben was surprised at the noiseless way in which Dutch laborers do their work. Even around the warehouses and docks there was no bustle, no shouting from one to another. A certain twitch of the pipe, or turn of the head, or, at most, a raising of the hand, seemed to be all the signal necessary. Entire loads of cheeses or herrings are pitched from cart or canalboat into the warehouses without a word; but the passerby must take his chance of being pelted, for a Dutchman seldom looks before or behind him while engaged at work.

Poor Jacob Poot, who seemed destined to bear all the mishaps of the journey, was knocked nearly breathless by a great cheese, which a fat Dutchman was throwing to a fellow laborer, but he recovered himself and passed on without the least indignation. Ben professed great sympathy on the occasion, but Jacob insisted that it was "notting."

"Then why did you screw your face so when it hit you?"

"What for screw mine face?" repeated Jacob soberly. "Vy, it vash de—de—"

"The what?" insisted Ben maliciously.

"Vy, de-de-vat you call dis, vat you taste mit de nose?"

Ben laughed. "Oh, you mean the smell."

"Yesh. Dat ish it," said Jacob eagerly. "It wash de shmell. I draw mine face for dat!"

"Ha! ha!" roared Ben. "That's a good one. A Dutch boy smell a cheese. You can never make me believe *that!*"

"Vell, it ish no matter," replied Jacob, trudging on beside Ben in perfect good humor. "Vait till you hit mit cheese—dat ish all."

Soon he added pathetically, "Penchamin, I no likes be call Tutch—dat ish no goot. I bees a Hollander."

Just as Ben was apologizing, Lambert hailed him.

"Hold up! Ben, here is the fish market. There is not much to be seen at this season. But we can take a look at the storks if you wish."

Ben knew that storks were held in peculiar reverence in Holland and that the bird figured upon the arms of the capital. He had noticed cart wheels placed upon the roofs of Dutch cottages to entice storks to settle upon them; he had seen their huge nests, too, on many a thatched gable roof from Broek to The Hague. But it was winter now. The nests were empty. No greedy birdlings opened their mouths—or rather their heads—at the approach of a great white-winged thing, with outstretched neck and legs, bearing a dangling something for their breakfast. The long-bills were far away, picking up food on African shores, and before they would return in the spring, Ben's visit to the land of dikes would be over.

Therefore he pressed eagerly forward, as Van Mounen led the way through the fish market, anxious to see if storks in Holland were anything like the melancholy specimens he had seen in the Zoological Gardens of London.

It was the same old story. A tamed bird is a sad bird, say what you will. These storks lived in a sort of kennel, chained by the feet like felons, though supposed to be honored by being kept at the public expense. In summer they were allowed to walk about the market, where the fish stalls were like so many free dining saloons to them. Untasted delicacies in the form of raw fish and butcher's offal lay about their kennels now, but the city guests preferred to stand upon one leg, curving back their long neck and leaning their head sidewise, in a blinking reverie. How gladly they would have changed their petted state for the busy life of some hardworking stork mother or father, bringing up a troublesome family on the roof of a rickety old building where flapping windmills frightened them half to death every time they ventured forth on a frolic.

Ben soon made up his mind, and rightly, too, that The Hague with its fine streets and public parks, shaded with elms, was a magnificent city. The prevailing costume was like that of London or Paris, and his British ears were many a time cheered by the music of British words. The shops were different in many respects from those on Oxford Street and the Strand, but they often were illumined by a printed announcement that English was "spoken within." Others proclaimed themselves to have London stout for sale, and one actually promised to regale its customers with English roast beef.

Over every possible shop door was the never-failing placard, TABAK TE KOOP (tobacco to be sold). Instead of colored glass globes in the windows, or high jars of leeches, the drugstores had a gaping Turk's head at the entrance—or, if the establishment were particularly fine, a wooden mandarin entire, indulging in a full yawn.

Some of these queer faces amused Ben exceedingly; they seemed to have just swallowed a dose of physic, but Van Mounen declared he could not see anything funny about them. A druggist showed his sense by putting a *Gaper* before his door, so that his place would be known at once as an *apotheek* and that was all there was to it.

Another thing attracted Ben—the milkmen's carts. These were small affairs, filled with shiny brass kettles, or stone jars, and drawn by dogs. The milkman walked meekly beside his cart, keeping his dog in order and delivering the milk to customers. Certain fish dealers had dogcarts, also, and when a herring dog chanced to meet a milk dog, he invariably put on airs and growled as he passed him. Sometimes a milk dog would recognize an acquaintance before another milk cart across the street, and then how the kettles would rattle, especially if they were empty! Each dog would give a bound and, never caring for his master's whistle, insist upon meeting the other halfway. Sometimes they contented themselves with an inquisitive sniff, but generally the smaller dog made an affectionate snap snap at the larger one's ear, or a friendly tussle was engaged in by way of exercise. Then woe to the milk kettles, and woe to the dogs!

The whipping over, each dog, expressing his feelings as best he could, would trot leisurely back to his work.

If some of these animals were eccentric in their ways, others were remarkably well behaved. In fact, there was a school for dogs in the city, established expressly for training them. Ben probably saw some of its graduates. Many a time he noticed a span of barkers trotting along the street with all the dignity of horses, obeying the slightest hint of the men walking briskly beside them. Sometimes, when their load was delivered, the dealer would jump in the cart and have a fine drive to his home beyond the gates of the city; and sometimes, I regret to say, a patient *vrouw* would trudge beside the cart with fish basket upon her head and a child in her arms—while her lord enjoyed his drive, carrying no heavier burden than a stumpy clay pipe, the smoke of which mounted lovingly into her face.

Chapter 29

A Day of Rest

*T*he sight-seeing came to an end at last, and so did our boys' visit to The Hague. They had spent three happy days and nights with the Van Gends, and, strange to say, had not once, in all that time, put on skates. The third day had indeed been one of rest. The noise and bustle of the city was hushed; sweet Sunday bells sent blessed, tranquil thoughts into their hearts. Ben felt, as he listened to their familiar music, that the Christian world is one, after all, however divided by sects and differences it may be. As the clock speaks everyone's native language in whatever land it may strike the hour, so church bells are never foreign if our hearts but listen.

Led on by those clear voices, our party, with Mevrouw van Gend and her husband, trod the quiet but crowded streets, until they came to a fine old church in the southern part of the city.

The interior was large and, notwithstanding its great stained windows, seemed dimly lighted, though the walls were white and dashes of red and purple sunshine lay brightly upon pillar and pew.

Ben saw a few old women moving softly through the aisles, each bearing a high pile of foot stoves which she distributed among the congregation by skillfully slipping out the under one, until none were left. It puzzled him that *mynheer* should settle himself with the boys in a comfortable side pew, after seating his *vrouw* in the body of the church, which was filled with chairs exclusively appropriated to the women. But Ben was learning only a common custom of the country.

The pews of the nobility and the dignitaries of the city were circular in form, each surrounding a column. Elaborately carved, they formed a massive base to their great pillars standing out in bold relief against the blank, white walls beyond. These columns, lofty and well proportioned, were nicked and defaced from violence done to them long ago; yet it seemed quite fitting that, before they were lost in the deep arches overhead, their softened outlines should leaf out as they did into richness and beauty.

Soon Ben lowered his gaze to the marble floor. It was a pavement of gravestones. Nearly all the large slabs, of which it was composed, marked the resting places of the dead. An armorial design engraved upon each stone, with inscription and date, told whose form was sleeping beneath, and sometimes three of a family were lying one above the other in the same sepulcher.

He could not but think of the solemn funeral procession winding by torchlight through those lofty aisles and bearing its silent burden toward a dark opening whence the slab had been lifted, in readiness for its coming. It was something to feel that his sister Mabel, who died in her flower, was lying in a sunny churchyard where a brook rippled and sparkled in the daylight and waving trees whispered together all night long; where flowers might nestle close to the headstone, and moon and stars shed their peace upon it, and morning birds sing sweetly overhead.

Then he looked up from the pavement and rested his eyes upon the carved oaken pulpit, exquisitely beautiful in design and workmanship. He could not see the minister—though, not long before, he had watched him slowly ascending its winding stair—a mild-faced man wearing a ruff about his neck and a short cloak reaching nearly to the knee.

Meantime the great church had been silently filling. Its pews were somber with men and its center radiant with women in their fresh Sunday attire. Suddenly a soft rustling spread through the building. All eyes were turned toward the minister now appearing above the pulpit.

Although the sermon was spoken slowly, Ben could understand little of what was said; but when the hymn came, he joined in with all his heart. A thousand voices lifted in love and praise offered a grander language that he could readily comprehend.

Once he was startled, during a pause in the service, by seeing a little bag suddenly shaken before him. It had a tinkling bell at its side and was attached to a long stick carried by one of the deacons of the church. Not relying solely upon the mute appeal of the poor boxes fastened to the columns near the entrance, this more direct method was resorted to, of awaking the sympathies of the charitable.

Fortunately Ben had provided himself with a few stivers, or the musical bag must have tinkled before him in vain.

More than once, a dark look rose on our English boy's face that morning. He longed to stand up and harangue the people concerning a peculiarity that filled him with pain. Some of the men wore their hats during the service or took them off whenever the humor prompted, and many put theirs on in the church as soon as they arose to leave. No wonder Ben's sense of propriety was wounded; and yet a higher sense would have been exercised had he tried to feel willing that Hollanders should follow the customs of their country. But his

English heart said over and over again, "It is outrageous! It is sinful!"

There is an angel called Charity who often would save our hearts a great deal of trouble if we would but let her in.

Chapter 30

Homeward Bound

*O*n Monday morning, bright and early, our boys bade farewell to their kind entertainers and started on their homeward journey.

Peter lingered awhile at the lion-guarded door, for he and his sister had many parting words to say.

As Ben saw them bidding each other good-bye, he could not help feeling that kisses as well as clocks were wonderfully alike everywhere. The English kiss that his sister Jenny gave when he left home had said the same to him that the Vrouw van Gend's Dutch kiss said to Peter. Ludwig had taken his share of the farewell in the most matter-of-fact manner possible, and though he loved his sister well, had winced a little at her making such a child of him as to put an extra kiss "for mother" upon his forehead.

He was already upon the canal with Carl and Jacob. Were they thinking about sisters or kisses? Not a bit of it. They were so happy to be on skates once more, so impatient to dart at once into the very heart of Broek that they spun and wheeled about like crazy fellows, relieving themselves, meantime, by muttering something about "Peter and donder," not worth translating.

Even Lambert and Ben, who had been waiting at the street corner, began to grow impatient.

The captain joined them at last; they were soon on the canal with the rest.

"Hurry up, Peter," growled Ludwig. "We're freezing by inches— there! I knew you'd be the last after all to get on your skates!"

"Did you?" said his brother, looking up with an air of deep interest. "Clever boy!"

Ludwig laughed but tried to look cross as he said, "I'm in earnest. We must get home sometime this year."

"Now, boys," cried Peter, springing up as he fastened the last buckle. "There's a clear way before us! We will imagine it's the grand race. Ready! One, two, three, start!"

I assure you very little was said for the first half hour. They were six Mercuries skimming the ice. In plain English they went like lightning—no, that is imaginary too. The fact is, one cannot decide what to say when half a dozen boys are whizzing past at such a rate. I can only tell you that each did his best, flying, with bent body and eager eyes, in and out among the placid skaters on the canal, until the very guard shouted to them to "Hold up!" This only served to send them onward with a two-boy power that startled all beholders.

But the laws of inertia are stronger even than canal guards.

After a while Jacob slackened his speed, then Ludwig, then Lambert, then Carl.

They soon halted to take a long breath and finally found themselves standing in a group gazing after Peter and Ben, who were still racing in the distance as if their lives were at stake.

"It is very evident," said Lambert as he and his three companions started up again, "that neither of them will give up until he can't help it."

"What foolishness!" growled Carl, "to tire themselves at the beginning of the journey. But they're racing in earnest—that's certain. Halloo! Peter's flagging!"

"Not so!" cried Ludwig. "Catch him being beaten!"

"Ha! ha!" sneered Carl. "I tell you, boy, Benjamin is ahead."

Now, if Ludwig disliked anything in this world, it was to be called a boy—probably because he was nothing else. He grew indignant at once.

"Humph, what are *you*, I wonder. There, sir! *Now* look and see if Peter isn't ahead!"

"*I* think he *is*," interposed Lambert, "but I can't quite tell at this distance."

"*I* think he isn't!" retorted Carl.

Jacob was growing anxious—he always abhorred an argument—so he said in a coaxing tone, "Don't quarrel—don't quarrel!"

"Don't quarrel!" mocked Carl, looking back at Jacob as he skated. "Who's quarreling? Poot, you're a goose!"

"I can't help that," was Jacob's meek reply. "See! they are nearing the turn of the canal."

"*Now* we can see!" cried Ludwig in great excitement. "Peter will make it first, I know."

"He can't—for Ben is ahead!" insisted Carl. "*Gunst!* That iceboat will run over him. No! He is clear! They're a couple of geese, anyhow. Hurrah! they're at the turn. Who's ahead?"

"Peter!" cried Ludwig joyfully.

"Good for the captain!" shouted Lambert and Jacob.

And Carl condescended to mutter, "It *is* Peter after all. I thought, all the time, that head fellow was Ben."

This turn in the canal had evidently been their goal, for the two racers came to a sudden halt after passing it.

Carl said something about being "glad that they had sense enough to stop and rest," and the four boys skated on in silence to overtake their companions.

All the while Carl was secretly wishing that he had kept on with Peter and Ben, as he felt sure he could easily have come out winner. He was a very rapid, though by no means a graceful, skater.

Ben was looking at Peter with mingled vexation, admiration, and surprise as the boys drew near.

They heard him saying in English, "You're a perfect bird on the ice, Peter van Holp. The first fellow that ever beat me in a fair race, I can tell you!"

Peter, who understood the language better than he could speak it, returned a laughing bow at Ben's compliment but made no further reply. Possibly he was scant of breath at the time.

"Now, Penchamin, vat you do mit yourself? Get so hot as a fire brick—dat ish no goot," was Jacob's plaintive comment.

"Nonsense!" answered Ben. "This frosty air will cool me soon enough. I am not tired."

"You are beaten, though, my boy," said Lambert in English, "and fairly too. How will it be, I wonder, on the day of the grand race?"

Ben flushed and gave a proud, defiant laugh, as if to say, "This was mere pastime. I'm *determined* to beat then, come what will!"

Chapter 31

Boys and Girls

*B*y the time the boys reached the village of Voorhout, which stands near the grand canal, about halfway between The Hague and Haarlem, they were forced to hold a council. The wind, though moderate at first, had grown stronger and stronger, until at last they could hardly skate against it. The weather vanes throughout the country had evidently entered into a conspiracy.

"No use trying to face such a blow as this," said Ludwig. "It cuts its way down a man's throat like a knife."

"Keep your mouth shut, then," grunted the affable Carl, who was strong-chested as a young ox. "I'm for keeping on."

"In this case," interposed Peter, "we must consult the weakest of the party rather than the strongest."

The captain's principle was all right, but its application was not flattering to Master Ludwig. Shrugging his shoulders, he retorted, "Who's weak? Not I, for one, but the wind's stronger than any of us. I hope you'll condescend to admit that!"

"Ha! ha!" laughed Van Mounen, who could barely keep his feet. "So it is."

Just then the weather vanes telegraphed to each other by a peculiar twitch—and, in an instant, the gust came. It nearly threw the strong-chested Carl; it almost strangled Jacob and quite upset Ludwig.

"This settles the question," shouted Peter. "Off with your skates! We'll go into Voorhout."

At Voorhout they found a little inn with a big yard. The yard was well bricked, and, better than all, was provided with a complete set of skittles, so our boys soon turned the detention into a frolic. The wind was troublesome even in that sheltered quarter, but they were on good standing ground and did not mind it.

First a hearty dinner—then the game. With pins as long as their arms and balls as big as their heads, plenty of strength left for rolling, and a clean sweep of sixty yards for the strokes—no wonder they were happy.

That night Captain Peter and his men slept soundly. No prowling robber came to disturb them, and, as they were distributed in separate rooms, they did not even have a bolster battle in the morning.

Such a breakfast they ate! The landlord looked frightened. When he had asked them where they "belonged," he made up his mind that the Broek people starved their children. It was a shame. "Such fine young gentlemen too!"

Fortunately the wind had tired itself out and fallen asleep in the great sea cradle beyond the dunes. There were signs of snow; otherwise the weather was fine.

It was mere child's play for the well-rested boys to skate to Leyden. Here they halted awhile, for Peter had an errand at the Golden Eagle.

He left the city with a lightened heart; Dr. Boekman had been at the hotel, read the note containing Hans's message, and departed for Broek.

"I cannot say it was your letter sent him off so soon,"

explained the landlord. "Some rich lady in Broek was taken bad very sudden, and he was sent for in haste."

Peter turned pale.

"What was the name?" he asked.

"Indeed, it went in one ear and out the other, for all I hindered it. Plague to people who can't see a traveler in comfortable lodgings, but they must whisk him off before one can breathe."

"A lady in Broek, did you say?"

"Yes." Very gruffly. "Any other business, young master?"

"No, mine host, except that I and my comrades here would like a bite of something and a drink of hot coffee."

"Ah," said the landlord sweetly, "a bite you shall have, and coffee, too, the finest in Leyden. Walk up to the stove, my masters—now I think again—that was a widow lady from Rotterdam, I think they said, visiting at one Van Stoepel's if I mistake not."

"Ah!" said Peter, greatly relieved. "They live in the white house by the Schlossen Mill. Now, *mynheer,* the coffee, please!"

What a goose I was, thought he, as the party left the Golden Eagle, to feel so sure it was my mother. But she may be somebody's mother, poor woman, for all that. Who can she be? I wonder.

There were not many upon the canal that day, between Leyden and Haarlem. However, as the boys neared Amsterdam, they found themselves once more in the midst of a moving throng. The big *ysbreeker** had been at work for the first time that season, but there was any amount of skating ground left yet.

---

*Icebreaker. A heavy machine armed with iron spikes for breaking the ice as it is dragged along. Some of the small ones are worked by men, but the large ones are drawn by horses, sixty or seventy of which are sometimes attached to one *ysbreeker.*

"Three cheers for home!" cried Van Mounen as they came in sight of the great Western Dock (Westelijk Dok). "Hurrah! Hurrah!" shouted one and all. "Hurrah! Hurrah!"

This trick of cheering was an importation among our party. Lambert van Mounen had brought it from England. As they always gave it in English, it was considered quite an exploit and, when circumstances permitted, always enthusiastically performed, to the sore dismay of their quiet-loving countrymen.

Therefore, their arrival at Amsterdam created a great sensation, especially among the small boys on the wharfs.

The Y was crossed. They were on the Broek Canal.

Lambert's home was reached first.

"Good-bye, boys!" he cried as he left them. "We've had the greatest frolic ever known in Holland."

"So we have. Good-bye, Van Mounen!" answered the boys. "Good-bye!"

Peter hailed him. "I say, Van Mounen, the classes begin tomorrow!"

"I know it. Our holiday is over. Good-bye, again."

"Good-bye!"

Broek came in sight. Such meetings! Katrinka was on the canal! Carl was delighted. Hilda was there! Peter felt rested in an instant. Rychie was there! Ludwig and Jacob nearly knocked each other over in their eagerness to shake hands with her.

Dutch girls are modest and generally quiet, but they have very glad eyes. For a few moments it was hard to decide whether Hilda, Rychie, or Katrinka felt the most happy.

Annie Bouman was also on the canal, looking even prettier than the other maidens in her graceful peasant's costume. But she did not mingle with Rychie's party; neither did she look unusually happy.

The one she liked most to see was not among the newcomers. Indeed, he was not upon the canal at all. She had not been near Broek before, since the Eve of Saint Nicholas, for she was staying with her sick grandmother in Amsterdam and had been granted a brief resting spell, as the grandmother called it, because she had been such a faithful little nurse night and day.

Annie had devoted her resting spell to skating with all her might toward Broek and back again, in the hope of meeting her mother or some of her family on the canal, or, it might be, Gretel Brinker. Not one of them had she seen, and she must hurry back without ever catching a glimpse of her mother's cottage, for the poor helpless grandmother, she knew, was by this time moaning for someone to turn her upon her cot.

Where can Gretel be? thought Annie as she flew over the ice; she can almost always steal a few moments from her work at this time of day. Poor Gretel! What a dreadful thing it must be to have a dull father! I should be woefully afraid of him, I know—so strong and yet so strange!

Annie had not heard of his illness. Dame Brinker and her affairs received but little notice from the people of the place.

If Gretel had not been known as a goose girl, she might have had more friends among the peasantry of the neighborhood. As it was, Annie Bouman was the only one who did not feel ashamed to avow herself by word and deed the companion of Gretel and Hans.

When the neighbors' children laughed at her for keeping such poor company, she would simply flush when Hans was ridiculed, or laugh in a careless, disdainful way, but to hear little Gretel abused always awakened her wrath.

"Goose girl, indeed!" she would say. "I can tell you any of you are fitter for the work than she. My father often said last summer that it troubled him to see such a bright-eyed, patient little maiden tending geese. Humph! She would not harm them, as you would, Janzoon Kolp, and she would not tread upon them as you might, Kate Wouters."

This would be pretty sure to start a laugh at the clumsy, ill-natured Kate's expense, and Annie would walk loftily away from the group of young gossips. Perhaps some memory of Gretel's assailants crossed her mind as she skated rapidly toward Amsterdam, for her eyes sparkled ominously, and she more than once gave her pretty head a defiant toss. When that mood passed, such a bright, rosy, affectionate look illuminated her face that more than one weary working man turned to gaze after her and to wish that he had a glad, contented lass like that for a daughter.

There were five joyous households in Broek that night.

The boys were back safe and sound, and they found all well at home. Even the sick lady at neighbor Van Stoepel's was out of danger.

But the next morning! Ah, how stupidly school bells will ding-dong, ding-dong, when one is tired.

Ludwig was sure he had never listened to anything so odious. Even Peter felt pathetic on the occasion. Carl said it was a shame for a fellow to have to turn out when his bones were splitting. And Jacob soberly bade Ben "Goot-pye!" and walked off with his satchel as if it weighed a hundred pounds.

Chapter 32

The Crisis

While the boys are nursing their fatigue we will take a peep into the Brinker cottage.

Can it be that Gretel and her mother have not stirred since we saw them last? That the sick man upon the bed has not even turned over? It was four days ago, and there is the sad group just as it was before. No, not precisely the same, for Raff Brinker is paler; his fever is gone, though he knows nothing of what is passing. Then they were alone in the bare, clean room. Now there is another group in an opposite corner.

Dr. Boekman is there, talking in a low tone with a stout young man who listens intently. The stout young man is his student and assistant. Hans is there also. He stands near the window, respectfully waiting until he shall be accosted.

"You see, Vollenhoven," said Dr. Boekman, "it is a clear case of—" And here the doctor went off into a queer jumble of Latin and Dutch that I cannot conveniently translate.

After a while, as Vollenhoven looked at him rather blankly, the learned man condescended to speak to him in simpler phrase.

"It is probably like Rip Donderdunck's case," he explained in a low, mumbling tone. "He fell from the top of Voppelploot's windmill. After the accident the man was stupid and finally became idiotic. In time he lay helpless like yon fellow on the bed, moaned, too, like him, and kept constantly lifting his hand to his head. My learned friend Von Choppem performed an operation upon this Donderdunck and discovered under the skull a small dark sac, which pressed upon the brain. This had been the cause of the trouble. My friend Von Choppem removed it—a splendid operation! You see, according to Celsus—" And here the doctor again went off into Latin.

"Did the man live?" asked the assistant respectfully.

Dr. Boekman scowled. "That is of no consequence. I believe he died, but why not fix your mind on the grand features of the case? Consider a moment how—" And he plunged into Latin mysteries more deeply than ever.

"But, *mynheer,*" gently persisted the student, who knew that the doctor would not rise to the surface for hours unless pulled at once from his favorite depths. "*Mynheer,* you have other engagements today, three legs in Amsterdam, you remember, and an eye in Broek, and that tumor up the canal."

"The tumor can wait," said the doctor reflectively. "That is another beautiful case—a beautiful case! The woman has not lifted her head from her shoulder for two months—magnificent tumor, sir!"

The doctor by this time was speaking aloud. He had quite forgotten where he was.

Vollenhoven made another attempt.

"This poor fellow on the bed, *mynheer.* Do you think you can save him?"

"Ah, indeed, certainly," stammered the doctor, suddenly perceiving that he had been talking rather off the point. "Certainly, that is—I hope so."

"If anyone in Holland can, *mynheer,*" murmured the assistant with honest bluntness, "it is yourself."

The doctor looked displeased, growled out a tender request for the student to talk less, and beckoned Hans to draw near.

This strange man had a great horror of speaking to women, especially on surgical matters. "One can never tell," he said, "at what moment the creatures will scream or faint." Therefore he explained Raff Brinker's case to Hans and told him what he believed should be done to save the patient.

Hans listened attentively, growing red and pale by turns and throwing quick, anxious glances toward the bed.

"It may *kill* the father—did you say, *mynheer*?" he exclaimed at last in a trembling whisper.

"It may, my boy. But I have a strong belief that it will cure and not kill. Ah! If boys were not such dunces, I could lay the whole matter before you, but it would be of no use."

Hans looked blank at this compliment.

"It would be of no use," repeated Dr. Boekman indignantly. "A great operation is proposed, but one might as well do it with a hatchet. The only question asked is, 'Will it kill?'"

"The question is *everything* to us, *mynheer*," said Hans, with tearful dignity.

Dr. Boekman looked at him in sudden dismay.

"Ah! Exactly so. You are right, boy, I am a fool. Good boy. One does not wish one's father killed—of course not. I am a fool."

"Will he die, *mynheer*, if this sickness goes on?"

"Humph! This is no new illness. The same thing growing worse every instant—pressure on the brain—will take him off soon like *that*," said the doctor, snapping his fingers.

"And the operation *may* save him," pursued Hans. "How soon, *mynheer*, can we know?"

Dr. Boekman grew impatient.

"In a day, perhaps, an hour. Talk with your mother, boy, and let her decide. My time is short."

Hans approached his mother; at first, when she looked up at him, he could not utter a syllable; then, turning his eyes away, he said in a firm voice, "I must speak with the mother alone."

Quick little Gretel, who could not quite understand what was passing, threw rather an indignant look at Hans and walked away.

"Come back, Gretel, and sit down," said Hans sorrowfully.

She obeyed.

Dame Brinker and her boy stood by the window while the doctor and his assistant, bending over the bedside, conversed together in a low tone. There was no danger of disturbing the patient. He appeared like one blind and deaf. Only his faint, piteous moans showed him to be a living man. Hans was talking earnestly, and in a low voice, for he did not wish his sister to hear.

With dry, parted lips, Dame Brinker leaned toward him, searching his face, as if suspecting a meaning beyond his words. Once she gave a quick, frightened sob that made Gretel start but, after that, listened calmly.

When Hans ceased to speak, his mother turned, gave one long, agonized look at her husband, lying there so pale and unconscious, and threw herself on her knees beside the bed.

Poor little Gretel! What did all this mean? She looked with questioning eyes at Hans; he was standing, but his head was bent as if in prayer—at the doctor. He was gently feeling her father's head and looked like one examining some curious stone—at the assistant. The man coughed and turned away—at her mother. Ah, little Gretel, that was the best you could do—to kneel beside her and twine your warm, young arms about her neck, to weep and implore God to listen.

When the mother arose, Dr. Boekman, with a show of trouble in his eyes, asked gruffly, "Well, *jufvrouw,* shall it be done?"

"Will it pain him, *mynheer?*" she asked in a trembling voice.

"I cannot say. Probably not. Shall it be done?"

"It may *cure* him, you said, and—*mynheer*, did you tell my boy that—perhaps—perhaps . . ." She could not finish.

"Yes, *jufvrouw*, I said the patient might sink under the operation, but we will hope it may prove otherwise." He looked at his watch. The assistant moved impatiently toward the window. "Come, *jufvrouw*, time presses. Yes or no?"

Hans wound his arm about his mother. It was not his usual way. He even leaned his head against her shoulder.

"The *meester* awaits an answer," he whispered.

Dame Brinker had long been the head of her house in every sense. Many a time she had been very stern with Hans, ruling him with a strong hand and rejoicing in her motherly discipline. *Now* she felt so weak, so helpless. It was something to feel that firm embrace. There was strength even in the touch of that yellow hair.

She turned to her boy imploringly.

"Oh, Hans! What shall I say?"

"Say what God tells thee, Mother," answered Hans, bowing his head.

One quick, questioning prayer to Heaven rose from the mother's heart.

The answer came.

She turned toward Dr. Boekman.

"It is right, *mynheer*. I consent."

"Humph!" grunted the doctor, as if to say, "You've been long enough about it." Then he conferred a moment with his assistant, who listened with great outward deference but was inwardly rejoicing at the grand joke he would have to tell his fellow students. He had actually seen a tear in "old Boekman's" eye.

Meanwhile Gretel looked on in trembling silence, but when

she saw the doctor open a leather case and take out one sharp, gleaming instrument after another, she sprang forward.

"Oh, Mother! The poor father meant no wrong. Are they going to *murder* him?"

"I do not know, child," screamed Dame Brinker, looking fiercely at Gretel. "I do not know."

"This will not do, *jufvrouw*," said Dr. Boekman sternly, and at the same time he cast a quick, penetrating look at Hans. "You and the girl must leave the room. The boy may stay."

Dame Brinker drew herself up in an instant. Her eyes flashed. Her whole countenance was changed. She looked like one who had never wept, never felt a moment's weakness. Her voice was low but decided. "I stay with my husband, *mynheer.*"

Dr. Boekman looked astonished. His orders were seldom disregarded in this style. For an instant his eye met hers.

"You may remain, *jufvrouw*," he said in an altered voice.

Gretel had already disappeared.

In one corner of the cottage was a small closet where her rough, boxlike bed was fastened against the wall. None would think of the trembling little creature crouching there in the dark.

Dr. Boekman took off his heavy coat, filled an earthen basin with water, and placed it near the bed. Then, turning to Hans, he asked, "Can I depend upon you, boy?"

"You can, *mynheer.*"

"I believe you. Stand at the head, here—your mother may sit at your right—so." And he placed a chair near the cot.

"Remember, *jufvrouw*, there must be no cries, no fainting."

Dame Brinker answered him with a look.

He was satisfied.

"Now, Vollenhoven."

Oh, that case with the terrible instruments! The assistant lifted them. Gretel, who had been peering with brimming eyes through the crack of the closet door, could remain silent no longer.

She rushed frantically across the apartment, seized her hood, and ran from the cottage.

Chapter 33

Gretel and Hilda

*I*t was recess hour. At the first stroke of the schoolhouse bell, the canal seemed to give a tremendous shout and grow suddenly alive with boys and girls. The sly thing, shining so quietly under the noonday sun, was a kaleidoscope at heart and only needed a shake from that great clapper to start it into dazzling changes.

Dozens of gaily clad children were skating in and out among each other, and all their pent-up merriment of the morning was relieving itself in song and shout and laughter. There was nothing to check the flow of frolic. Not a thought of schoolbooks came out with them into the sunshine. Latin, arithmetic, grammar—all were locked up for an hour in the dingy schoolroom. The teacher might be a noun if he wished, and a proper one at that, but *they* meant to enjoy themselves. As long as the skating was as perfect as this, it made no difference whether Holland were on the North Pole or the equator; and, as for philosophy, how could they bother themselves about inertia and gravitation and such things when it was as much as they could do to keep from getting knocked over in the commotion.

In the height of the fun one of the children called out, "What is that?"

"What? Where?" cried a dozen voices.

"Why, don't you see? That dark thing over there by the idiot's cottage."

"I don't see anything," said one.

"I do," shouted another. "It's a dog."

"Where's any dog?" put in a squeaky voice that we have heard before. "It's no such thing—it's a heap of rags."

"Pooh! Voost," retorted another gruffly, "that's about as near the fact as you ever get. It's the goose girl, Gretel, looking for rats."

"Well, what of it?" squeaked Voost. "Isn't *she* a bundle of rags, I'd like to know?"

"Ha! ha! Pretty good for you, Voost! You'll get a medal for wit yet, if you keep on."

"You'd get something else if her brother Hans were here. I'll warrant you would!" said a muffled-up little fellow with a cold in his head.

As Hans was *not* there, Voost could afford to scout the insinuation.

"Who cares for *him*, little sneezer? I'd fight a dozen like him any day, and you in the bargain."

"You would! would you? I'd like to catch you at it," and, by way of proving his words, the sneezer skated off at the top of his speed.

Just then a general chase after three of the biggest boys of the school was proposed—and friend and foe, frolicsome as ever, were soon united in a common cause.

Only one of all that happy throng remembered the dark little form by the idiot's cottage. Poor, frightened Gretel! She was not thinking of them, though their merry laughter floated lightly toward her, making her feel like one in a dream.

How loud the moans were behind the darkened window! What if those strange men were really killing her father!

The thought made her spring to her feet with a cry of horror!

"Ah, no!" She sobbed, sinking upon the frozen mound of earth where she had been sitting. Mother is there, and Hans. They will care for him. But how pale they were. And even Hans was crying!

Why did the cross old *meester* keep *him* and send me away, she thought. I could have clung to the mother and kissed her. That always makes her stroke my hair and speak gentle, even after she has scolded me. How quiet it is now! Oh, if the father should die, and Hans, and the mother, what *would* I do? And Gretel, shivering with cold, buried her face in her arms and cried as if her heart would break.

The poor child had been tasked beyond her strength during the past four days. Through all, she had been her mother's willing little handmaiden, soothing, helping, and cheering the half-widowed woman by day and watching and praying beside her all the long night. She knew that something terrible and mysterious was taking place at this moment, something that had been too terrible and mysterious for even kind, good Hans to tell.

Then new thoughts came. Why had not Hans told her? It was a shame. It was *her* father as well as his. She was no baby. She had once taken a sharp knife from the father's hand. She had even drawn him away from the mother on that awful night when Hans, as big as he was, could not help her. Why, then, must she be treated like one who could do nothing? Oh, how very still it was—how bitter, bitter cold! If Annie Bouman had only stayed home instead of going to Amsterdam, it wouldn't be so lonely. How cold her feet were growing! Was it the moaning that made her feel as if she were floating in the air?

This would not do—the mother might need her help at any moment!

Rousing herself with an effort, Gretel sat upright, rubbing

her eyes and wondering—wondering that the sky was so bright and blue, wondering at the stillness in the cottage, more than all, at the laughter rising and falling in the distance.

Soon she sank down again, the strange medley of thought growing more and more confused in her bewildered brain.

What a strange lip the *meester* had! How the stork's nest upon the roof seemed to rustle and whisper down to her! How bright those knives were in the leather case—brighter perhaps than the silver skates. If she had but worn her new jacket, she would not shiver so. The new jacket was pretty—the only pretty thing she had ever worn. God had taken care of her father so long. He would do it still, if those two men would but go away. Ah, now the *meesters* were on the roof, they were clambering to the top—no—it was her mother and Hans—or the storks. It was so dark, who could tell? And the mound rocking, swinging in that strange way. How sweetly the birds were singing. They must be winter birds, for the air was thick with icicles—not one bird but twenty. Oh! hear them, Mother. Wake me, Mother, for the race. I am so tired with crying, and crying—

A firm hand was laid upon her shoulder.

"Get up, little girl!" cried a kind voice. "This will not do, for you to lie here and freeze."

Gretel slowly raised her head. She was so sleepy that it seemed nothing strange to her that Hilda van Gleck should be leaning over her, looking with kind, beautiful eyes into her face. She had often dreamed it before.

But she had never dreamed that Hilda was shaking her roughly, almost dragging her by main force; never dreamed that she heard her saying, "Gretel! Gretel Brinker! you *must* wake!"

This was real. Gretel looked up. Still the lovely, delicate young lady was shaking, rubbing, fairly pounding her. It must be a dream. No, there was the cottage—and the stork's nest and the *meester's* coach by the canal. She could see them now quite plainly. Her hands were tingling, her feet throbbing. Hilda was forcing her to walk.

At last Gretel began to feel like herself again.

"I have been asleep," she faltered, rubbing her eyes with both hands and looking very much ashamed.

"Yes, indeed, entirely too much asleep"—laughed Hilda, whose lips were very pale—"but you are well enough now. Lean upon me, Gretel. There, keep moving, you will soon be warm enough to go by the fire. Now let me take you into the cottage."

"Oh, no! no! no! *jufvrouw*, not in there! The *meester* is there. He sent me away!"

Hilda was puzzled, but she wisely forbore to ask at present for an explanation. "Very well, Gretel, try to walk faster. I saw you upon the mound, some time ago, but I thought you were playing. That is right, keep moving."

All this time the kindhearted girl had been forcing Gretel to walk up and down, supporting her with one arm and, with the other, striving as well as she could to take off her own warm sacque.

Suddenly Gretel suspected her intention.

"Oh, *jufvrouw! jufvrouw!*" she cried imploringly. "*Please* never think of such a thing as *that*. Oh! please keep it on. I am burning all over, *jufvrouw*! I really am burning. Not burning exactly, but pins and needles pricking all over me. Oh, *jufvrouw*, don't!"

The poor child's dismay was so genuine that Hilda hastened to reassure her.

"Very well, Gretel, move your arms then—so. Why, your cheeks are as pink as roses, already. I think the *meester* would let you in now, he certainly would. Is your father so very ill?"

"Ah, *jufvrouw*," cried Gretel, weeping afresh, "he is dying, I think. There are two *meesters* in with him at this moment, and the mother has scarce spoken today. Can you hear him moan, *jufvrouw*?" she added with sudden terror. "The air buzzes so I cannot hear. He may be dead! Oh, I do wish I could hear him!"

Hilda listened. The cottage was very near, but not a sound could be heard.

Something told her that Gretel was right. She ran to the window.

"You cannot see there, my lady," sobbed Gretel eagerly. "The mother has oiled paper hanging inside. But at the other one, in the south end of the cottage, you can look in where the paper is torn."

Hilda, in her anxiety, ran around, past the corner where the low roof was fringed with its loosened thatch.

A sudden thought checked her.

"It is not right for me to peep into another's house in this way," she said to herself. Then, softly calling to Gretel, she added in a whisper, "You may look—perhaps he is only sleeping."

Gretel tried to walk briskly toward the spot, but her limbs were trembling. Hilda hastened to her support.

"You are sick, yourself, I fear," she said kindly.

"No, not sick, *jufvrouw*, but my heart cries all the time now, even when my eyes are as dry as yours. Why, *jufvrouw*, your eyes are not dry! Are you crying for *us*! Oh, *jufvrouw*, if God sees you! Oh! I know father will get better now." And the little creature, even while reaching to look through the tiny window, kissed Hilda's hand again and again.

The sash was sadly patched and broken, a torn piece of paper hung halfway down across it. Gretel's face was pressed to the window.

"Can you see anything?" whispered Hilda at last.

"Yes—the father lies very still, his head is bandaged, and all their eyes are fastened upon him. Oh, *jufvrouw*!" almost screamed Gretel, as she started back and, by a quick, dexterous movement, shook off her heavy wooden shoes. "I *must* go in to my mother! Will you come with me?"

"Not now, the bell is ringing. I shall come again soon. Good-bye!"

Gretel scarcely heard the words. She remembered for many a day afterward the bright, pitying smile on Hilda's face as she turned away.

Chapter 34

The Awakening

*A*n angel could not have entered the cottage more noiselessly. Gretel, not daring to look at anyone, slid softly to her mother's side.

The room was very still. She could hear the old doctor breathe. She could almost hear the sparks as they fell into the ashes on the hearth. The mother's hand was very cold, but a burning spot glowed on her cheek, and her eyes were like a deer's—so bright, so sad, so eager.

At last there was a movement upon the bed, very slight, but enough to cause them all to start. Dr. Boekman leaned eagerly forward.

Another movement. The large hand, so white and soft for a poor man's hand, twitched, then raised itself steadily toward the forehead.

It felt the bandage, not in a restless, crazy way but with a questioning movement that caused even Dr. Boekman to hold his breath.

Then the eyes opened slowly.

"Steady! Steady!" said a voice that sounded very strange to Gretel. "Shift that mat higher, boys! Now throw on the clay. The waters are rising fast. No time to—"

Dame Brinker sprang forward like a young panther.

She seized his hands and, leaning over him, cried, "Raff! Raff, boy, speak to me!"

"Is it you, Meitje?" he asked faintly. "I have been asleep, hurt, I think. Where is little Hans?"

"Here I am, Father!" shouted Hans, half mad with joy. But the doctor held him back.

"He knows us!" screamed Dame Brinker. "Great God! He knows us! Gretel! Gretel! Come, see your father!"

In vain Dr. Boekman commanded "Silence!" and tried to force them from the bedside. He could not keep them off.

Hans and his mother laughed and cried together as they hung over the newly awakened man. Gretel made no sound but gazed at them all with glad, startled eyes. Her father was speaking in a faint voice.

"Is the baby asleep, Meitje?"

"The baby!" echoed Dame Brinker. "Oh, Gretel! That is *you!* And he calls Hans 'little Hans.' Ten years asleep! Oh, *mynheer,* you have saved us all. He has known nothing for ten years! Children, why don't you thank the *meester?*"

The good woman was beside herself with joy. Dr. Boekman said nothing, but as his eye met hers, he pointed upward. She understood. So did Hans and Gretel.

With one accord they knelt by the cot, side by side. Dame Brinker felt for her husband's hand even while she was praying. Dr. Boekman's head was bowed; the assistant stood by the hearth with his back toward them.

"Why do you pray?" murmured the father, looking feebly from the bed as they rose. "Is it God's day?"

It was not Sunday, but his *vrouw* bowed her head—she could not speak.

"Then we should have a chapter," said Raff Brinker, speaking slowly and with difficulty. "I do not know how it is. I am very, very weak. Mayhap the minister will read to us."

Gretel lifted the big Dutch Bible from its carved shelf. Dr. Boekman, rather dismayed at being called a minister, coughed and handed the volume to his assistant.

"Read," he muttered. "These people must be kept quiet or the man will die yet."

When the chapter was finished, Dame Brinker motioned mysteriously to the rest by way of telling them that her husband was asleep.

"Now, *jufvrouw*," said the doctor in a subdued tone as he drew on his thick woolen mittens, "there must be perfect quiet. You understand. This is truly a most remarkable case. I shall come again tomorrow. Give the patient no food today," and, bowing hastily, he left the cottage, followed by his assistant.

His grand coach was not far away; the driver had kept the horses moving slowly up and down by the canal nearly all the time the doctor had been in the cottage.

Hans went out also.

"May God bless you, *mynheer*!" he said, blushing and trembling. "I can never repay you, but if—"

"Yes, you can," interrupted the doctor crossly. "You can use your wits when the patient wakes again. This clacking and sniveling is enough to kill a well man, let alone one lying on the edge of his grave. If you want your father to get well, keep 'em quiet."

So saying, Dr. Boekman, without another word, stalked off to meet his coach, leaving Hans standing there with eyes and mouth wide open.

Hilda was reprimanded severely that day for returning late to school after recess and for imperfect recitations.

She had remained near the cottage until she heard Dame

Brinker laugh, until she had heard Hans say, "Here I am, Father!" And then she had gone back to her lessons. What wonder that she missed them! How could she get a long string of Latin verbs by heart when her heart did not care a fig for them but would keep saying to itself, "Oh, I am so glad! I am so glad!"

Chapter 35

Bones and Tongues

*B*ones are strange things. One would suppose that they knew nothing at all about school affairs, but they do. Even Jacob Poot's bones, buried as they were in flesh, were sharp in the matter of study hours.

Early on the morning of his return they ached through and through, giving Jacob a twinge at every stroke of the school bell, as if to say, "Stop that clapper! There's trouble in it." After school, on the contrary, they were quiet and comfortable; in fact, they seemed to be taking a nap among their cushions.

The other boys' bones behaved in a similar manner, but that is not so remarkable. Being nearer the daylight than Jacob's, they might be expected to be more learned in the ways of the world. Master Ludwig's, especially, were like beauty, only skin deep; they were the most knowing bones you ever heard of! Just put before him, ever so quietly, a grammar book with a long lesson marked in it, and immediately the sly bone over his eyes would set up such an aching! Request him to go to the garret for your foot stove, instantly the bones would remind him that he was "too tired." Ask him to go to the confectioner's, a mile away, and *presto*! not a bone would remember that it ever had been used before.

Bearing all this in mind, you will not wonder when I tell you that our five boys were among the happiest of the happy throng pouring forth from the schoolhouse that day.

Peter was in excellent spirits. He had heard through Hilda of Dame Brinker's laugh and of Hans's joyous words, and he needed no further proof that Raff Brinker was a cured man. In fact, the news had gone forth in every direction, for miles around. Persons who had never before cared for the Brinkers, or even mentioned them, except with a contemptuous sneer or a shrug of pretended pity, now became singularly familiar with every point of their history. There was no end to the number of ridiculous stories that were flying about.

Hilda, in the excitement of the moment, had stopped to exchange a word with the doctor's coachman as he stood by the horses, pommeling his chest and clapping his hands. Her kind heart was overflowing. She could not help pausing to tell the cold, tired-looking man that she thought the doctor would be out soon; she even hinted to him that she suspected—only suspected—that a wonderful cure had been performed, an idiot brought to his senses. Nay, she was *sure* of it, for she had heard his widow laugh—no, not his widow, of course, but his wife, for the man was as much alive as anybody, and, for all she knew, sitting up and talking like a lawyer.

All this was very indiscreet. Hilda, in an impenitent sort of way, felt it to be so.

But it is always so delightful to impart pleasant or surprising news!

She went tripping along by the canal, quite resolved to repeat the sin, ad infinitum, and tell nearly every girl and boy in the school.

Meantime, Janzoon Kolp came skating by. Of course, in two seconds, he was striking slippery attitudes and shouting saucy things to the coachman, who stared at him in indolent disdain.

This, to Janzoon, was equivalent to an invitation to draw nearer. The coachman was now upon his box, gathering up the reins and grumbling at his horses.

Janzoon accosted him.

"I say. What's going on at the idiot's cottage? Is your boss in there?"

Coachman nodded mysteriously.

"Whew!" whistled Janzoon, drawing closer. "Old Brinker dead?"

The driver grew big with importance and silent in proportion.

"See here, old pincushion, I'd run home yonder and get you a chunk of gingerbread if I thought you could open your mouth."

Old pincushion was human—long hours of waiting had made him ravenously hungry. At Janzoon's hint, his countenance showed signs of a collapse.

"That's right, old fellow," pursued his tempter. "Hurry up! What news—old Brinker dead?"

"No, cured! Got his wits," said the coachman, shooting forth his words, one at a time, like so many bullets.

Like bullets (figuratively speaking) they hit Janzoon Kolp. He jumped as if he had been shot.

"*Goede Gunst!* You don't say so!"

The man pressed his lips together and looked significantly toward Master Kolp's shabby residence.

Just then Janzoon saw a group of boys in the distance. Hailing them in a rowdy style, common to boys of his stamp all over the world, whether in Africa, Japan, Amsterdam, or Paris, he scampered toward them, forgetting coachman, gingerbread, everything but the wonderful news.

Therefore, by sundown it was well known throughout the neighboring country that Dr. Boekman, chancing to stop at the cottage, had given the idiot Brinker a tremendous dose of medicine, as brown as gingerbread. It had taken six men to hold him while it was poured down. The idiot had immediately sprung to his feet, in full possession of all his faculties, knocked over the doctor or thrashed him (there was admitted to be a slight uncertainty as to which of these penalties was inflicted), then sat down and addressed him for all the world like a lawyer. After that he had turned and spoken beautifully to his wife and children. Dame Brinker had laughed herself into violent hysterics. Hans had said, "Here I am, Father, your own dear son!" And Gretel had said, "Here I am, Father, your own dear Gretel!" And the doctor had afterward been seen leaning back in his carriage looking just as white as a corpse.

Chapter 36

A New Alarm

*W*hen Dr. Boekman called the next day at the Brinker cottage, he could not help noticing the cheerful, comfortable aspect of the place. An atmosphere of happiness breathed upon him as he opened the door. Dame Brinker sat complacently knitting beside the bed, her husband was enjoying a tranquil slumber, and Gretel was noiselessly kneading rye bread on the table in the corner.

The doctor did not remain long. He asked a few simple questions, appeared satisfied with the answers, and after feeling his patient's pulse, said, "Ah, very weak yet, *jufvrouw*. Very weak, indeed. He must have nourishment. You may begin to feed the patient. Ahem! Not too much, but what you do give him, let it be strong and of the best."

"Black bread we have, *mynheer*, and porridge," replied Dame Brinker cheerily. "They have always agreed with him well."

"Tut! tut!" said the doctor, frowning. "Nothing of the kind. He must have the juice of fresh meat, white bread, dried and toasted, good Malaga wine, and—ahem! The man looks cold. Give him more covering, something light and warm. Where is the boy?"

"Hans, *mynheer*, has gone into Broek to look for work. He will be back soon. Will the *meester* please be seated?"

Whether the hard, polished stool offered by Dame Brinker did not look particularly tempting, or whether the dame herself frightened him, partly because she was a woman and partly because an anxious, distressed look had suddenly appeared in her face, I cannot say. Certain it is that our eccentric doctor looked hurriedly about him, muttered something about "an extraordinary case," bowed, and disappeared before Dame Brinker had time to say another word.

Strange that the visit of their good benefactor should have left a cloud, yet so it was. Gretel frowned, an anxious childish frown, and kneaded her bread dough violently without looking up. Dame Brinker hurried to her husband's bedside, leaned over him, and fell into silent but passionate weeping.

In a moment Hans entered.

"Why, Mother," he whispered in alarm, "what ails thee? Is the father worse?"

She turned her quivering face toward him, making no attempt to conceal her distress.

"Yes. He is starving—perishing. The *meester* said it."

Hans turned pale.

"What does this mean, Mother? We must feed him at once. Here, Gretel, give me the porridge."

"Nay!" cried his mother distractedly, yet without raising her voice, "it may kill him. Our poor fare is too heavy for him. Oh, Hans, he will die—the father will *die* if we use him this way. He must have meat and sweet wine and a *dekbed*. Oh, what shall I do, what shall I do?" she sobbed, wringing her hands. "There is not a stiver in the house."

Gretel pouted. It was the only way she could express sympathy just then. Her tears fell one by one into the dough.

"Did the *meester* say he *must* have these things, Mother?" asked Hans.

"Yes, he did."

"Well, Mother, don't cry, *he shall have them.* I shall bring meat and wine before night. Take the cover from my bed. I can sleep in the straw."

"Yes, Hans, but it is heavy, scant as it is. The *meester* said he must have something light and warm. He will perish. Our peat is giving out, Hans. The father has wasted it sorely, throwing it on when I was not looking, dear man."

"Never mind, Mother," whispered Hans cheerfully. "We can cut down the willow tree and burn it, if need be, but I'll bring home something tonight. There *must* be work in Amsterdam, though there's none in Broek. Never fear, Mother, the worst trouble of all is past. We can brave anything now that the father is himself again."

"Aye!" sobbed Dame Brinker, hastily drying her eyes. "That is true indeed."

"Of course it is. Look at him, Mother, how softly he sleeps. Do you think God would let him starve, just after giving him back to us. Why, Mother, I'm as *sure* of getting all the father needs as if my pocket was bursting with gold. There, now, don't fret." And, hurriedly kissing her, Hans caught up his skates and slipped from the cottage.

Poor Hans! Disappointed in his morning's errand, half sickened with this new trouble, he wore a brave look and tried to whistle as he tramped resolutely off with the firm intention of mending matters.

Want had never before pressed as sorely upon the Brinker family. Their stock of peat was nearly exhausted, and all the flour in the cottage was in Gretel's dough. They had scarcely cared to eat during the past few days, scarcely realized their condition. Dame Brinker had felt so sure that she and the children could earn money before the worst came that she had given herself up to the joy of her husband's recovery. She had not even told Hans that the few pieces of silver in the old mitten were quite gone.

Hans reproached himself, now, that he had not hailed the doctor when he saw him enter his coach and drive rapidly away in the direction of Amsterdam.

Perhaps there is some mistake, he thought. The *meester* surely would have known that meat and sweet wine were not at our command; and yet the father looks very weak—he certainly does. I *must* get work. If Mynheer van Holp were back from Rotterdam, I could get plenty to do. But Master Peter told me to let him know if he could do aught to serve us. I shall go to him at once. Oh, if it were but summer!

All this time Hans was hastening toward the canal. Soon his skates were on, and he was skimming rapidly toward the residence of Mynheer van Holp.

"The father must have meat and wine at once," he muttered, "but how can I earn the money in time to buy them today? There is no other way but to go, as I *promised*, to Master Peter. What would a gift of meat and wine be to him? When the father is once fed, I can rush down to Amsterdam and earn the morrow's supply."

Then came other thoughts—thoughts that made his heart thump heavily and his cheeks burn with a new shame. It is *begging*, to say the least. Not one of the Brinkers has ever been a beggar. Shall I be the first? Shall my poor father just coming back into life, learn that his family have asked for charity—he, always so wise and thrifty? "No," cried Hans aloud, "better a thousand times to part with the watch."

I can at least borrow money on it in Amsterdam! he thought, turning around. That will be no disgrace. I can find work at once and get it back again. Nay, perhaps I can even *speak to the father about it!*

This last thought almost made the lad dance for joy. Why not, indeed, speak to the father? He was a rational being now. He may wake, thought Hans, quite bright and rested—may tell us the watch is of no consequence, to sell it of course! Huzza! And Hans almost flew over the ice.

A few moments more and the skates were again swinging from his arm. He was running toward the cottage.

His mother met him at the door.

"Oh, Hans!" she cried, her face radiant with joy, "the young lady has been here with her maid. She brought everything— meat, jelly, wine, and bread—a whole basketful! Then the *meester* sent a man from town with more wine and a fine bed and blankets for the father. Oh, he will get well now! God bless them!"

"God bless them!" echoed Hans, and for the first time that day his eyes filled with tears.

Chapter 37

The Father's Return

*T*hat evening Raff Brinker felt so much better that he insisted upon sitting up awhile on the rough high-backed chair by the fire. For a few moments there was quite a commotion in the little cottage. Hans was all-important on the occasion, for his father was a heavy man and needed something firm to lean upon. The dame, though none of your fragile ladies, was in such a state of alarm and excitement at the bold step they were taking in lifting him without the *meester*'s orders that she came near pulling her husband over, even while she believed herself to be his main prop and support.

"Steady, *vrouw*, steady," panted Raff. "Have I grown old and feeble, or is it the fever makes me thus helpless?"

"Hear the man!"—Dame Brinker laughed—"talking like any other Christian. Why, you're only weak from the fever, Raff. Here's the chair, all fixed snug and warm. Now, sit thee down—hi-di-didy—there we are!"

With these words Dame Brinker let her half of the burden settle slowly into the chair. Hans prudently did the same.

Meanwhile Gretel flew about generally, bringing every possible thing to her mother to tuck behind the father's back and spread over his knees. Then she twitched the carved bench under his feet, and Hans kicked the fire to make it brighter.

The father was sitting up at last. What wonder that he looked about him like one bewildered. "Little Hans" had just been almost carrying him. "The baby" was over four feet long and was demurely brushing up the hearth with a bundle of willow wisps. Meitje, the *vrouw*, winsome and fair as ever, had gained at least fifty pounds in what seemed to him a few hours. She also had some new lines in her face that puzzled him. The only familiar things in the room were the pine table that he had made before he was married, the Bible upon the shelf, and the cupboard in the corner.

Ah! Raff Brinker, it was only natural that your eyes should fill with hot tears even while looking at the joyful faces of your loved ones. Ten years dropped from a man's life are no small loss; ten years of manhood, of household happiness and care; ten years of honest labor, of conscious enjoyment of sunshine and outdoor beauty, ten years of grateful life—one day looking forward to all this; the next, waking to find them passed and a blank. What wonder the scalding tears dropped one by one upon your cheek!

Tender little Gretel! The prayer of her life was answered through those tears. She *loved* her father from that moment. Hans and his mother glanced silently at each other when they saw her spring toward him and throw her arms about his neck.

"Father, *dear* Father," she whispered, pressing her cheek close to his, "don't cry. We are all here."

"God bless thee," sobbed Raff, kissing her again and again. "I had forgotten that!"

Soon he looked up again and spoke in a cheerful voice. "I should know her, *vrouw*," he said, holding the sweet young face between his hands and gazing at it as though he were watching it grow. "I should know her. The same blue eyes and the lips and, ah! me, the little song she could sing almost before she could stand. But that was long ago," he added with a sigh, still looking at her dreamily. "Long ago; it's all gone now."

"Not so, indeed," cried Dame Brinker eagerly. "Do you think I would let her forget it? Gretel, child, sing the old song thou hast known so long!"

Raff Brinker's hands fell wearily and his eyes closed, but it was something to see the smile playing about his mouth as Gretel's voice floated about him like incense.

It was a simple air; she had never known the words.

With loving instinct she softened every note until Raff almost fancied that his two-year-old baby was once more beside him.

As soon as the song was finished Hans mounted a wooden stool and began to rummage in the cupboard.

"Have a care, Hans," said Dame Brinker, who through all her poverty was ever a tidy housewife. "Have a care, the wine is there at your right and the white bread beyond it."

"Never fear, Mother," answered Hans, reaching far back on an upper shelf. "I shall do no mischief."

Jumping down, he walked toward his father and placed an oblong block of pine wood in his hands. One of its ends was rounded off, and some deep cuts had been made on the top.

"Do you know what it is, Father?" asked Hans.

Raff Brinker's face brightened. "Indeed, I do, boy! It is the boat I was making you yest—alack, not yesterday but years ago."

"I have kept it ever since, Father. It can be finished when your hand grows strong again."

"Yes, but not for you, my lad. I must wait for the grandchildren. Why, you are nearly a man. Have you helped your mother, boy, through all these years?"

"Aye and bravely," put in Dame Brinker.

"Let me see," muttered the father, looking in a puzzled way at them all, "how long is it since the night when the waters were coming in? 'Tis the last I remember."

"We have told thee true, Raff. It was ten years last Pinxter week."

"Ten years—and I fell then, you say? Has the fever been on me ever since?"

Dame Brinker scarce knew how to reply. Should she tell him all? Tell him that he had been an idiot, almost a lunatic? The doctor had charged her on no account to worry or excite his patient.

Hans and Gretel looked astonished.

"Like enough, Raff," she said, nodding her head and raising her eyebrows, "when a heavy man like thee falls on his head, it's hard to say what will come—but thou'rt well *now*, Raff. Thank the good Lord!"

The newly awakened man bowed his head.

"Aye, well enough, mine *vrouw*," he said after a moment's silence, "but my brain turns somehow like a spinning wheel. It will not be right till I get on the dikes again. When shall I be at work, think you?"

"Hear the man!" cried Dame Brinker, delighted yet frightened, too, for that matter. "We must get him on the bed, Hans. Work, indeed!"

They tried to raise him from the chair, but he was not ready yet.

"Be off with ye!" he said with something like his old smile (Gretel had never seen it before). "Does a man want to be lifted about like a log? I tell you before three suns I shall be on the dikes again. Ah! There'll be some stout fellows to greet me.

Jan Kamphuisen and young Hoogsvliet. They have been good friends to thee, Hans, I'll warrant."

Hans looked at his mother. Young Hoogsvliet had been dead five years. Jan Kamphuisen was in the jail at Amsterdam.

"Aye, they'd have done their share, no doubt," said Dame Brinker, parrying the inquiry, "had we asked them. But what with working and studying, Hans has been busy enough without seeking comrades."

"Working and studying," echoed Raff, in a musing tone. "Can the youngsters read and cipher, Meitje?"

"You should hear them!" she answered proudly. "They can run through a book while I mop the floor. Hans there is as happy over a page of big words as a rabbit in a cabbage patch; as for ciphering—"

"Here, lad, help a bit," interrupted Raff Brinker. "I must get me on the bed again."

Chapter 38

The Thousand Guilders

*N*one seeing the humble supper eaten in the Brinker cottage that night would have dreamed of the dainty fare hidden away nearby. Hans and Gretel looked rather wistfully toward the cupboard as they drank their cupful of water and ate their scanty share of black bread; but even in thought they did not rob their father.

"He relished his supper well," said Dame Brinker, nodding sidewise toward the bed, "and fell asleep the next moment. Ah, the dear man will be feeble for many a day. He wanted sore to sit up again, but while I made show of humoring him and getting ready, he dropped off. Remember that, my girl, when you have a man of your own (and many a day may it be before that comes to pass), remember you can never rule by differing; 'humble wife is husband's boss.' Tut! tut! Never swallow such a mouthful as that again, child. Why, I could make a meal off two such pieces. What's in thee, Hans? One would think there were cobwebs on the wall."

"Oh, no, Mother, I was only thinking—"

"Thinking about what? Ah, no use asking," she added in a changed tone. "I was thinking of the same a while ago. Well, well, it's no blame if we *did* look to hear something by this time about the thousand guilders but not a word—no—it's plain enough he knows naught about them."

Hans looked up anxiously, dreading that his mother should grow agitated, as usual, when speaking of the lost money, but she was silently nibbling her bread and looking with a doleful stare toward the window.

"Thousand guilders," echoed a faint voice from the bed. "Ah, I am sure they have been of good use to you, *vrouw*, through the long years while your man was idle."

The poor woman started up. These words quite destroyed the hope that of late had been glowing within her.

"Are you awake, Raff?" she faltered.

"Yes, Meitje, and I feel much better. Our money was well saved, *vrouw*, I was saying. Did it last through all these ten years?"

"I—I—have not got it, Raff, I—" She was going to tell him the whole truth when Hans lifted his finger warningly and whispered, "Remember what the *meester* told us. The father must not be worried."

"Speak to him, child," she answered, trembling.

Hans hurried to the bedside.

"I am glad you are feeling better," he said, leaning over his father. "Another day will see you quite strong again."

"Aye, like enough. How long did the money last, Hans? I could not hear your mother. What did she say?"

"I said, Raff," stammered Dame Brinker in great distress, "that it was all gone."

"Well, well, wife, do not fret at that. One thousand guilders is not very much for ten years and with children to bring up . . . but it has helped to make you all comfortable. Have you had much sickness to bear?"

"No, no," sobbed Dame Brinker, lifting her apron to her eyes.

"Tut, tut, woman, why do you cry?" said Raff kindly. "We will soon fill another pouch when I am on my feet again. Lucky I told you all about it before I fell."

"Told me what, man?"

"Why, that I buried the money. In my dream just now it seemed I had never said aught about it."

Dame Brinker started forward. Hans caught her arm.

"Hist! Mother," he whispered, hastily leading her away, "we must be very careful!" Then, while she stood with clasped hands waiting in breathless anxiety, he once more approached the cot. Trembling with eagerness he said, "That was a troublesome dream. Do you remember *when* you buried the money, Father?"

"Yes, my boy. It was before daylight on the same day I was hurt. Jan Kamphuisen said something, the sundown before, that made me distrust his honesty. He was the only one living besides Mother who knew we had saved a thousand guilders, so I rose up that night and buried the money—blockhead that I was ever to suspect an old friend!"

"I'll be bound, Father," pursued Hans in a laughing voice, motioning to his mother and Gretel to remain quiet, "that you've forgotten where you buried it."

"Ha, ha! Not I, indeed. But good night, my son, I can sleep again."

Hans would have walked away, but his mother's gestures were not to be disobeyed, so he said gently, "Good night, Father. Where did you say you buried the money? I was only a little one then."

"Close by the willow sapling behind the cottage," said Raff Brinker drowsily.

"Ah, yes. North side of the tree, wasn't it, Father?"

"No, the south side. Ah, you know the spot well enough,

you rogue. Like enough you were there when your mother lifted it. Now, son, easy. Shift this pillow so. Good night."

"Good night, Father!" said Hans, ready to dance for joy.

The moon rose very late that night, shining in, full and clear, at the little window, but its beams did not disturb Raff Brinker. He slept soundly; so did Gretel. As for Hans and his mother, they had something else to do.

After making a few hurried preparations they stole forth with bright, expectant faces, bearing a broken spade and a rusty implement that had done many a day's service when Raff was a hale worker on the dikes.

It was so light out of doors, they could see the willow tree distinctly. The frozen ground was hard as stone, but Hans and his mother were resolute. Their only dread was that they might disturb the sleepers in the cottage.

"This *ysbreeker* is just the thing, Mother," said Hans, striking many a vigorous blow, "but the ground has set so firm, it'll be a fair match for it."

"Never fear, Hans," she answered, watching him eagerly. "Here, let me try awhile."

They soon succeeded in making an impression. One opening and the rest was not so difficult.

Still they worked on, taking turns and whispering cheerily to one another. Now and then Dame Brinker stepped noiselessly over the threshold and listened, to be certain that her husband slept.

"What grand news it will be for him," she said, laughing, "when he is strong enough to bear it. How I should like to put the pouch and the stocking, just as we find them, all full of money, near him this blessed night, for the dear man to see when he wakens."

"We must get them first, Mother," panted Hans, still tugging away at his work.

"There's no doubt of that. They can't slip away from us now," she answered, shivering with cold and excitement as she crouched beside the opening. "Like enough we'll find them stowed in the old earthen pot I lost long ago."

By this time Hans, too, began to tremble but not with cold. He had penetrated a foot deep for quite a space on the south side of the tree. At any moment they might come upon the treasure. Meantime the stars winked and blinked at each other as if to say, "Queer country, this Holland! How much we do see, to be sure!"

"Strange that the dear father should have put it down so woeful deep," said Dame Brinker in rather a provoked tone. "Ah, the ground was soft enough then, I warrant. How wise of him to mistrust Jan Kamphuisen, and Jan in full credit at the time. Little I thought that handsome fellow with his gay ways would ever go to jail! Now, Hans, let me take a turn. It's lighter work, d'ye see, the deeper we go? I'd be loath to kill the tree, Hans. Will we harm it, think you?"

"I cannot say," he answered gravely.

Hour after hour mother and son worked on. The hole grew larger and deeper. Clouds began to gather in the sky, throwing elfish shadows as they passed. Not until moon and stars faded away and streaks of daylight began to appear did Meitje Brinker and Hans look hopelessly into each other's faces.

They had searched thoroughly, desperately, all around the tree; south, north, east, west. *The hidden money was not there!*

Chapter 39

Glimpses

*A*nnie Bouman had a healthy distaste for Janzoon Kolp. Janzoon Kolp, in his own rough way, adored Annie. Annie declared she could not "to save her life" say one civil word to that odious boy. Janzoon believed her to be the sweetest, sauciest creature in the world. Annie laughed among her playmates at the comical flapping of Janzoon's tattered and dingy jacket; he sighed in solitude over the floating grace of her jaunty blue petticoat. She thanked her stars that her brothers were not like the Kolps, and he growled at his sister because she was not like the Boumans. They seemed to exchange natures whenever they met. His presence made her harsh and unfeeling, and the very sight of *her* made him gentle as a lamb. Of course, they were thrown together very often. It is thus that in some mysterious way we are convinced of error and cured of prejudice. In this case, however, the scheme failed. Annie detested Janzoon more and more at each encounter; and Janzoon liked her better and better every day.

He killed a stork, the wicked old wretch! she would say to herself.

She knows I am strong and fearless, thought Janzoon.

How red and freckled and ugly he is! was Annie's secret comment when she looked at him.

How she stares and stares! thought Janzoon. Well, I am a fine, weather-beaten fellow, anyway.

"Janzoon Kolp, you impudent boy, go right away from me!" Annie often said. "I don't want any of your company."

Ha! ha! laughed Janzoon to himself. Girls never say what they mean. I'll skate with her every chance I can get.

And so it came to pass that the pretty maid would not look up that morning when, skating homeward from Amsterdam, she became convinced that a great burly boy was coming down the canal toward her.

Humph! If I look at him, thought Annie, I'll—

"Good morrow, Annie Bouman," said a pleasant voice.

How a smile brightens a girl's face!

"Good morrow, Master Hans, I am right glad to meet you."

How a smile brightens a boy's face!

"Good morrow, again, Annie. There has been a great change at our house since you left."

"How so?" she exclaimed, opening her eyes very wide.

Hans, who had been in a great hurry and rather moody, grew talkative and quite at leisure in Annie's sunshine.

Turning about, and skating slowly with her toward Broek, he told the good news of his father. Annie was so true a friend that he told her even of their present distress, of how money was needed and how everything depended upon his obtaining work, and he could find nothing to do in the neighborhood.

All this was not said as a complaint but just because she was looking at him and really wished to know. He could not speak of last night's bitter disappointment, for that secret was not wholly his own.

"Good-bye, Annie!" he said at last. "The morning is going fast, and I must hasten to Amsterdam and sell these skates.

Mother must have money at once. Before nightfall I shall certainly find a job somewhere."

"Sell your new skates, Hans?" cried Annie. "You, the best skater around Broek! Why, the race is coming off in five days!"

"I know it," he answered resolutely. "Good-bye! I shall skate home again on the old wooden ones."

Such a bright glance! So different from Janzoon's ugly grin— and Hans was off like an arrow.

"Hans, come back!" she called.

Her voice changed the arrow into a top. Spinning around, he darted, in one long, leaning sweep, toward her.

"Then you really are going to sell your new skates if you can find a customer?"

"Of course I am," he replied, looking up with a surprised smile.

"Well, Hans, if you *are* going to sell your skates," said Annie, somewhat confused, "I mean if you—well, I know somebody who would like to buy them, that's all."

"Not Janzoon Kolp?" asked Hans, flushing.

"Oh, no," she said, pouting, "he is not one of my friends."

"But you *know* him," persisted Hans.

Annie laughed. "Yes, I know him, and it's all the worse for him that I do. Now, please, Hans, don't ever talk anymore to me about Janzoon. I hate him!"

"Hate him! *You* hate anyone, Annie?"

She shook her head saucily. "Yes, and I'll hate you, too, if you persist in calling him one of my friends. You boys may like him because he caught the greased goose at the *kermis* last summer and climbed the pole with his great, ugly body tied up in a sack, but I don't care for such things. I've disliked him ever since I saw him try to push his little sister out of the merry-go-round at Amsterdam, and it's no secret up *our* way who killed the stork on your mother's roof. But we mustn't talk about such a bad, wicked fellow. Really, Hans, I know somebody who would be glad to buy your skates. You won't get half a price for them in Amsterdam. *Please* give them to me. I'll take you the money this very afternoon."

If Annie was charming even when she said *hate*, there was no withstanding her when she said *please*; at least Hans found it to be so.

"Annie," he said, taking off the skates and rubbing them carefully with a snarl of twine before handing them to her, "I am sorry to be so particular, but if your friend should not want them, will you bring them back to me today? I must buy peat and meal for the mother early tomorrow morning."

"My friend *will* want them." Annie laughed, nodding gaily, and skated off at the top of her speed.

As Hans drew forth the wooden "runners" from his capacious pockets and fastened them on as best he could, he did not hear Annie murmur, "I wish I had not been so rude. Poor, brave Hans. What a noble boy he is!" And as Annie skated homeward, filled with pleasant thoughts, she did not hear Hans say, "I grumbled like a bear. But bless her! Some girls are like angels!"

Perhaps it was all for the best. One cannot be expected to know everything that is going on in the world.

Chapter 40

Looking for Work

*L*uxuries unfit us for returning to hardships endured before. The wooden runners squeaked more than ever. It was as much as Hans could do to get on with the clumsy old things; still, he did not regret that he had parted with his beautiful skates but resolutely pushed back the boyish trouble that he had not been able to keep them just a little longer, at least until after the race.

Mother surely will not be angry with me, he thought, for selling them without her leave. She has had care enough already. It will be full time to speak of it when I take home the money.

Hans went up and down the streets of Amsterdam that day, looking for work. He succeeded in earning a few stivers by assisting a man who was driving a train of loaded mules into the city, but he could not secure steady employment anywhere. He would have been glad to obtain a situation as a porter or an errand boy, but though he passed on his way many a loitering, shuffling urchin, laden with bundles, there was no place for him. Some shopkeepers had just supplied themselves; others needed a trimmer, more lightly built fellow (they meant better dressed but did not choose to say so); others told him to call again in a month or two, when the canals would probably be broken up; and many shook their heads at him without saying a word.

At the factories he met with no better luck. It seemed to him that in those great buildings, turning out respectively such tremendous quantities of woolen, cotton, and linen stuffs, such world-renowned dyes and paints, such precious diamonds cut from the rough, such supplies of meal, of bricks, of glass and china—that in at least one of these, a strong-armed boy, able and eager to work, could find something to do. But no—nearly the same answer met him everywhere. No need of more hands just now. If he had called before Saint Nicholas's Day, they might have given him a job as they were hurried then; but at present they had more boys than they needed. Hans wished they could see, just for a moment, his mother and Gretel. He did not know how the anxiety of both looked out from his eyes, and how, more than once, the gruffest denials were uttered with an uncomfortable consciousness that the lad ought not to be turned away. Certain fathers, when they went home that night, spoke more kindly than usual to their own youngsters, from memory of a frank, young face saddened at their words, and before morning one man actually resolved that he would instruct his head man Blankert to set the boy from Broek at something if he should come in again.

But Hans knew nothing of all this. Toward sundown he started on his return to Broek, uncertain whether the strange choking sensation in his throat arose from discouragement or resolution. There was certainly one more chance. Mynheer van Holp might have returned by this time. Master Peter, it was reported, had gone to Haarlem the night before to attend to something connected with the great skating race. Still, Hans would go and try.

Fortunately Peter had returned early that morning. He was at

home when Hans reached there and was just about starting for
the Brinker cottage.

"Ah, Hans!" he cried as the weary boy approached the door.
"You are the very one I wished to see. Come in and warm
yourself."

After tugging at his well-worn hat, which always *would* stick
to his head when he was embarrassed, Hans knelt down, not by
way of making a new style of Oriental salute, nor to worship
the goddess of cleanliness who presided there, but because his
heavy shoes would have filled the soul of a Broek housewife
with horror. When their owner stepped softly into the house,
they were left outside to act as sentinels until his return.

Hans left the Van Holp mansion with a lightened heart.
Peter had brought word from Haarlem that young Brinker was
to commence working upon the summer-house doors immediately. There was a comfortable workshop on the place and it
was to be at his service until the carving was done.

Peter did not tell Hans that he had skated all the way to
Haarlem for the purpose of arranging this plan with Mynheer
van Holp. It was enough for him to see the glad, eager look rise
on young Brinker's face.

"I *think* I can do it," said Hans, "though I have never learned
the trade."

"I am *sure* you can," responded Peter heartily. "You will find
every tool you require in the workshop. It is nearly hidden
yonder by that wall of twigs. In summer, when the hedge is
green, one cannot see the shop from here at all. How is your
father today?"

"Better, *mynheer*. He improves every hour."

"It is the most astonishing thing I ever heard of. That gruff
old doctor is a great fellow after all."

"Ah, *mynheer*," said Hans warmly, "he is more than great.

He is good. But for the *meester*'s kind heart and great skill my poor father would yet be in the dark. I think, *mynheer*," he added with kindly eyes, "surgery is the very noblest science in the world!"

Peter shrugged his shoulders. "Very noble it may be, but not quite to my taste. This Dr. Boekman certainly has skill. As for his heart—defend me from such hearts as his!"

"Why do you say so, *mynheer*?" asked Hans.

Just then a lady slowly entered from an adjoining apartment. It was Mevrouw van Holp arrayed in the grandest of caps and the longest of satin aprons ruffled with lace. She nodded placidly as Hans stepped back from the fire, bowing as well as he knew how.

Peter at once drew a high-backed oaken chair toward the fire, and the lady seated herself. There was a block of cork on each side of the chimney place. One of these he placed under his mother's feet.

Hans turned to go.

"Wait a moment, if you please, young man," said the lady. "I accidentally overheard you and my son speaking, I think, of my friend Dr. Boekman. You are right, young man. Dr. Boekman has a very kind heart. You perceive, Peter, we may be quite mistaken in judging of a person solely by their manners, though a courteous deportment is by no means to be despised."

"I intended no disrespect, Mother," said Peter, "but surely one has no right to go growling and snarling through the world as they say he does."

"They say. Ah, Peter, 'they' means everybody or nobody. Surgeon Boekman has had a great sorrow. Many years ago he lost his only child under very painful circumstances. A fine lad, except that he was a thought too hasty and high-spirited. Before then Gerard Boekman was one of the most agreeable gentleman I ever knew."

So saying, Mevrouw van Holp, looking kindly upon the two boys, rose, and left the room with the same dignity with which she had entered.

Peter, only half convinced, muttered something about "the sin of allowing sorrow to turn all one's honey into gall" as he conducted his visitor to the narrow side door. Before they parted he advised Hans to keep himself in good skating order, "for," he added, "now that your father is all right, you will be in fine spirits for the race. That will be the prettiest skating show ever seen in this part of the world. Everybody is talking of it: you are to try for the prize, remember."

"I shall not be in the race, *mynheer*," said Hans, looking down.

"Not be in the race! Why not, indeed?" And immediately Peter's thoughts swept on a full tide of suspicion toward Carl Schummel.

"Because I cannot, *mynheer*," answered Hans as he bent to slip his feet into his big shoes.

Something in the boy's manner warned Peter that it would be no kindness to press the matter further. He bade Hans good-bye and stood thoughtfully watching him as he walked away.

In a minute Peter called out, "Hans Brinker!"

"Yes, *mynheer*."

"I'll take back all I said about Dr. Boekman."

"Yes, *mynheer*."

Both were laughing. But Peter's smile changed to a look of puzzled surprise when he saw Hans kneel down by the canal and put on the wooden skates.

"Very queer," muttered Peter, shaking his head as he turned to go into the house. "Why in the world doesn't the boy wear his new ones?"

Chapter 41

The Fairy Godmother

*T*he sun had gone down quite out of sight when our hero—with a happy heart but with something like a sneer on his countenance as he jerked off the wooden "runners" —trudged hopefully toward the tiny hutlike building, known of old as the idiot's cottage.

Duller eyes than his would have discerned two slight figures moving near the doorway.

That gray well-patched jacket and the dull blue skirt covered with an apron of still duller blue, that faded, close-fitting cap, and those quick little feet in their great boatlike shoes, they were Gretel's, of course. He would have known them anywhere.

That bright coquettish red jacket, with its pretty skirt, bordered with black, that graceful cap bobbing over the gold earrings, that dainty apron, and those snug leather shoes that seemed to have grown with the feet—why, if the Pope of Rome had sent them to him by express, Hans could have sworn they were Annie's.

The two girls were slowly pacing up and down in front of the cottage. Their arms were entwined, of course, and their heads were nodding and shaking as emphatically as if all the affairs of the kingdom were under discussion.

With a joyous shout Hans hastened toward them.

"Huzza, girls, I've found work!"

This brought his mother to the cottage door.

She, too, had pleasant tidings. The father was still improving. He had been sitting up nearly all day and was now sleeping as Dame Brinker declared, "Just as quiet as a lamb."

"It is my turn now, Hans," said Annie, drawing him aside after he had told his mother the good word from Mynheer van Holp. "Your skates are sold, and here's the money."

"Seven guilders!" cried Hans, counting the pieces in astonishment. "Why, that is three times as much as I paid for them."

"I cannot help that," said Annie. "If the buyer knew no better, it is not our fault."

Hans looked up quickly.

"Oh, Annie!"

"Oh, Hans!" she mimicked, pursing her lips and trying to look desperately wicked and unprincipled.

"Now, Annie, I know you would never mean that! You must return some of this money."

"But I'll not do any such thing," insisted Annie. "They're sold, and that's an end of it." Then, seeing that he looked really pained, she added in a lower tone, "Will you believe me, Hans, when I say that there has been no mistake—that the person who bought your skates *insisted* upon paying seven guilders for them?"

"I will," he answered, and the light from his clear blue eyes seemed to settle and sparkle under Annie's lashes.

Dame Brinker was delighted at the sight of so much silver, but when she learned that Hans had parted with his treasures to obtain it, she sighed and then exclaimed, "Bless thee, child! That will be a sore loss for thee!"

"Here, Mother," said the boy, plunging his hands far into his pockets, "here is more—we shall be rich if we keep on!"

"Aye, indeed," she answered, eagerly reaching forth her hand. Then, lowering her voice, added, "We *would* be rich but for that Jan Kamphuisen. He was at the willow tree years ago, Hans. Depend on it!"

"Indeed, it seems likely," sighed Hans. "Well, Mother, we must give up the money bravely. It is certainly gone. The father has told us all he knows. Let us think no more about it."

"That's easy saying, Hans. I shall try, but it's hard and my poor man wanting so many comforts. Bless me! How girls fly about. They were here but this instant. Where did they run to?"

"They slipped behind the cottage," said Hans, "like enough to hide from us. Hist! I'll catch them for you! They both can move quicker and softer than yonder rabbit, but I'll give them a good start first."

"Why, there *is* a rabbit, sure enough. Hold, Hans, the poor thing must have been in sore need to venture from its burrow in this bitter weather. I'll get a few crumbs for it within."

So saying, the good woman bustled into the cottage. She soon came out again, but Hans had forgotten to wait, and the rabbit, after taking a cool survey of the premises, had scampered off to unknown quarters. Turning the corner of the cottage, Dame Brinker came upon the children. Hans and Gretel were standing before Annie, who was seated carelessly upon a stump.

"That is as good as a picture!" cried Dame Brinker, halting in admiration of the group. "Many a painting have I seen at the grand house at Heidelberg not a whit prettier. My two are rough chubs, Annie, but *you* look like a fairy."

"Do I?" laughed Annie, sparkling with animation. "Well, then, Gretel and Hans, imagine I'm your godmother just paying you a visit. Now I'll grant you each a wish. What will you have, Master Hans?"

A shade of earnestness passed over Annie's face as she looked up at him; perhaps it was because she wished from the depths of her heart that for once she could have a fairy's power.

Something whispered to Hans that, for a moment, she was more than mortal. "I wish," said he solemnly, "that I could find something I was searching for last night."

Gretel laughed merrily. Dame Brinker moaned. "Shame on you, Hans!" And she went wearily into the cottage.

The fairy godmother sprang up and stamped her foot three times.

"Thou shalt have thy wish," said she. "Let them say what they will." Then, with playful solemnity, she put her hand in her apron pocket and drew forth a large glass bead. "Bury this," said she, giving it to Hans, "where I have stamped, and ere moonrise thy wish shall be granted."

Gretel laughed more merrily than ever.

The godmother pretended great displeasure.

"Naughty child," said she, scowling terribly. "In punishment for laughing at a fairy, thy wish shall not be granted."

"Ha!" cried Gretel in high glee, "better wait till you're asked, godmother. I haven't made any wish!"

Annie acted her part well. Never smiling through all their merry laughter, she stalked away, the embodiment of offended dignity.

"Good night, fairy!" they cried again and again.

"Good night, mortals!" she called out at last as she sprang over a frozen ditch and ran quickly homeward.

"Oh, isn't she just like flowers—so sweet and lovely!" cried Gretel, looking after her in great admiration. "And to think how many days she stays in that dark room with her grandmother! Why, brother Hans! What is the matter? What are you going to do?"

"Wait and see!" answered Hans as he plunged into the cottage and came out again, all in an instant, bearing the spade and *ysbreeker* in his hands. "I'm going to bury my magic bead!"

Raff Brinker still slept soundly. His wife took a small block of peat from her nearly exhausted store and put it upon the embers. Then, opening the door, she called gently, "Come in, children."

"Mother! Mother! See here!" shouted Hans.

"Holy St. Bavon!" exclaimed the dame, springing over the doorstep. "What ails the boy!"

"Come quick, Mother," he cried in great excitement, working with all his might and driving in the *ysbreeker* at each word. "Don't you see? *This* is the spot—right here on the south side of the stump. Why didn't we think of it last night? *The stump* is the old willow tree—the one you cut down last spring because it shaded the potatoes. That little tree wasn't here when father . . . Huzza!"

Dame Brinker could not speak. She dropped on her knees beside Hans just in time to see him drag forth *the old stone pot*!

He thrust in his hand and took out a piece of brick, then another, then another, then the stocking and the pouch, black and moldy but filled with the long-lost treasure!

Such a time! Such laughing! Such crying! Such counting after they went into the cottage! It was a wonder that Raff did not awaken. His dreams were pleasant, however, for he smiled in his sleep.

Dame Brinker and her children had a fine supper, I can assure you. No need of saving the delicacies now.

"We'll get Father some nice fresh things tomorrow," Dame Brinker said as she brought forth cold meat, wine, bread, and jelly and placed them on the clean pine table. "Sit by, children, sit by."

*　　*　　*

That night Annie fell asleep wondering whether it was a knife Hans had lost and thinking how funny it would be if he should find it, after all.

Hans had scarcely closed his eyes before he found himself trudging through a thicket; pots of gold were lying all around, and watches and skates, and glittering beads were swinging from every branch.

Strange to say, each tree, as he approached it, changed into a stump, and on the stump sat the prettiest fairy imaginable, clad in a scarlet jacket and blue petticoat.

Chapter 42

The Mysterious Watch

Something else than the missing guilders was brought to light on the day of the fairy godmother's visit. This was the story of the watch that for ten long years had been so jealously guarded by Raff's faithful *vrouw*. Through many an hour of sore temptation she had dreaded almost to look upon it, lest she might be tempted to disobey her husband's request. It had been hard to see her children hungry and to know that the watch, if sold, would enable the roses to bloom in their cheeks again. "But nay," she would exclaim, "Meitje Brinker is not one to forget her man's last bidding, come what may."

"Take care of this, mine *vrouw*," he had said as he handed it to her—that was all. No explanation followed, for the words were scarcely spoken when one of his fellow workmen rushed into the cottage, crying, "Come, man! The waters are rising! You're wanted on the dikes."

Raff had started at once, and that was the last Dame Brinker saw of him in his right mind.

On the day when Hans was in Amsterdam looking for work, and Gretel, after performing her household labors, was wandering about in search of chips, twigs, anything that could be burned, Dame Brinker, with suppressed excitement, had laid the watch in her husband's hand.

"It wasn't in reason," as she afterward said to Hans, "to wait any longer when a word from the father would settle all. No woman living but would want to know how he came by that watch." Raff Brinker turned the bright polished thing over and over in his hand, then he examined the bit of smoothly ironed black ribbon fastened to it. He seemed hardly to recognize it. At last he said, "Ah, I remember this! Why, you've been rubbing it, *vrouw*, till it shines like a new guilder."

"Aye," said Dame Brinker, nodding her head complacently.

Raff looked at it again. "Poor boy!" he murmured, then fell into a brown study.

This was too much for the dame. "Poor boy!" she echoed somewhat tartly. "What do you think I'm standing here for, Raff Brinker, and my spinning awaiting, if not to hear more than that?"

"I told ye all, long since," said Raff positively as he looked up in surprise.

"Indeed, and you never did!" retorted the *vrouw.*

"Well, if not, since it's no affair of ours, we'll say no more about it," said Raff, shaking his head sadly. "Like enough while I've been dead on the earth, all this time, the poor boy's died and been in heaven. He looked near enough to it, poor lad!"

"Raff Brinker! If you're going to treat me this way, and I nursing you and bearing with you since I was twenty-two years old, it's a shame. Aye, and a disgrace," cried the *vrouw,* growing quite red and scant of breath.

Raff's voice was feeble yet. "Treat you *what* way, Meitje?"

"What way," said Dame Brinker, mimicking his voice and manner. "What way? Why, just as every woman in the world is treated after she's stood by a man through the worst, like a—"

"Meitje!"

Raff was leaning forward with outstretched arms. His eyes were full of tears.

In an instant Dame Brinker was at his feet, clasping his hands in hers.

"Oh! What have I done! Made my good man cry, and he not back with me four days! Look up, Raff! Nay, Raff, my own boy, I'm sorry I hurt thee. It's hard not to be told about the watch after waiting ten years to know, but I'll ask thee no more, Raff. Here, we'll put the thing away that's made the first trouble between us, after God just giving thee back to me."

"I was a fool to cry, Meitje," he said, kissing her, "and it's no more than right ye should know the truth. But it seemed like it might be telling the secrets of the dead to talk about the matter."

"Is the man—the lad—thou wert talking of dead, think thee?" asked the *vrouw*, hiding the watch in her hand but seating herself expectantly on the end of his long foot bench.

"It's hard telling," he answered.

"Was he so sick, Raff?"

"No, not sick, I may say; but troubled, *vrouw*, very troubled."

"Had he done any wrong, think ye?" she asked, lowering her voice.

Raff nodded.

"Murder?" whispered the wife, not daring to look up.

"He said it was like to that, indeed."

"Oh! Raff, you frighten me. Tell me more, you speak so strange and you tremble. I must know all."

"If I tremble, mine *vrouw*, it must be from the fever. There is no guilt on my soul, thank God!"

"Take a sip of wine, Raff. There, now you are better. It was like to a crime, you were saying."

"Aye, Meitje, like to murder. *That* he told me himself. But I'll never believe it. A likely lad, fresh and honest-looking as our own youngster but with something not so bold and straight about him."

"Aye, I know," said the dame gently, fearing to interrupt the story.

"He came upon me quite suddenly," continued Raff. "I had never seen his face before, the palest, frightenedest face that ever was. He caught me by the arm. 'You look like an honest man,' says he."

"Aye, he was right in that," interrupted the dame emphatically. Raff looked somewhat bewildered.

"Where was I, mine *vrouw*?"

"The lad took hold of your arm, Raff," she said, gazing at him anxiously.

"Aye, so. The words come awkward to me, and everything is half like a dream, ye see."

"S-stut! What wonder, poor man." She sighed, stroking his hand. "If ye had not head enough for a dozen, the wit would never have come to ye again. Well, the lad caught ye by the arm and said ye looked honest (well he might!). What then? Was it noontime?"

"Nay, before daylight—long before early chimes."

"It was the same day you were hurt," said the dame. "I know it seemed you went to work in the middle of the night. You left off where he caught your arm, Raff."

"Yes," resumed her husband, "and I can see his face this minute—so white and wild-looking. 'Take me down the river a way,' says he. I was working then, you'll remember, far down on the line, across from Amsterdam. I told him I was no boatman. 'It's an affair of life and death,' says he. 'Take me on a few miles—yonder skiff is not locked, but it may be a poor man's boat and I'd be loath to rob him!' (The words might differ some, *vrouw*, for it's all like a dream.) Well, I took him down—it might be six or eight miles—and then he said he could run the rest of the way on shore. I was in haste to get the boat back. Before he jumped out, he says, sobbing-like, 'I can trust you. I've done a thing—God knows I never intended it, but the man is dead. I must fly from Holland.' "

"What was it? Did he say, Raff? Had he been shooting at a comrade, like they do down at the University of Göttingen?"

"I can't recall that. Mayhap he told me, but it's all like a dream. I said it wasn't for me, a good Hollander, to cheat the laws of my country by helping him off that way, but he kept saying, 'God knows I am innocent!' And he looked at me in the starlight as fair now, and clear-eyed as our little Hans might—and I just pulled away faster."

"It must have been Jan Kamphuisen's boat," remarked Dame Brinker dryly. "None other would have left his oars out that careless."

"Aye, it was Jan's boat, sure enough. The man will be coming in to see me Sunday, likely, if he's heard, and young Hoogsvliet too. Where was I?"

"Where were you? Why, not very far, forsooth—the lad hadn't yet given ye the watch—alack, I misgive whether he came by it honestly!"

"Why, *vrouw*," exclaimed Raff in an injured tone, "he was dressed soft and fine as the prince himself. The watch was his own, clear enough."

"How came he to give it up?" asked the dame, looking uneasily at the fire, for it needed another block of peat.

"I told ye just now," he answered with a puzzled air.

"Tell me again," said Dame Brinker, wisely warding off another digression.

"Well, just before jumping from the boat, he says, handing me the watch, 'I'm flying from my country as I never thought I could. I'll trust you because you look honest. Will you take this to my father—not today but in a week—and tell him his unhappy boy sent it, and tell him if ever the time comes that he wants me to come back to him, I'll brave everything and come. Tell him to send a letter to—to—there, the rest is all gone from me. I *can't* remember where the letter was to go. Poor lad! Poor lad," resumed Raff, sorrowfully taking the watch from his *vrouw*'s lap. "And it's never been sent to his father to this day."

"I'll take it, Raff, never fear—the moment Gretel gets back. She will be in soon. What was the father's name, did you say? Where were you to find him?"

"Alack!" answered Raff, speaking very slowly, "it's all slipped me. I can see the lad's face and his great eyes just as plain—and I remember his opening the watch and snatching something from it and kissing it—but no more. All the rest whirls past me; there's a kind of sound like rushing waters that comes over me when I try to think."

"Aye. That's plain to see, Raff, but I've had the same feeling after a fever. You're tired now. I must get you straight on the bed again. Where *is* the child, I wonder?"

She opened the door and called, "Gretel! Gretel!"

"Stand aside, *vrouw*," said Raff feebly as he leaned forward and endeavored to look out upon the bare landscape. "I've half a mind to stand beyond the door just once."

"Nay, nay." She laughed. "I'll tell the *meester* how ye tease and fidget and bother to be let out in the air; and, if he says it, I'll bundle ye warm tomorrow and give ye a turn on your feet. But I'm freezing you with this door open. I declare if there isn't Gretel with her apron full, skating on the canal like wild. Why, man," she continued almost in a scream, as she slammed the door, "thou'rt walking to the bed without my touching thee! Thou'lt fall!"

The dame's *thee* proved her mingled fear and delight, even more than the rush which she made toward her husband. Soon he was comfortably settled under the new cover, declaring, as his *vrouw* tucked him in snug and warm, that it was the last daylight that should see him abed.

"Aye! I can hope it myself," laughed Dame Brinker, "now you have been frisking about at that rate." As Raff closed his eyes the dame hastened to revive her fire, or rather to dull it, for Dutch peat is like a Dutchman, slow to kindle but very good at a blaze when once started. Then, putting her neglected spinning wheel away, she drew forth her knitting from some invisible pocket and seated herself by the bedside.

"If you could remember that man's name, Raff," she began cautiously, "I might take the watch to him while you're sleeping. Gretel can't but be in soon."

Raff tried to think but in vain.

"Could it be Boomphoffen?" suggested the dame. "I've heard how they've had two sons turn out bad—Gerard and Lambert?"

"It might be," said Raff. "Look if there's letters on the watch; that'll guide us some."

"Bless thee, man," cried the happy dame, eagerly lifting the watch. "Why, thou'rt sharper than ever! Sure enough. Here's letters! L.J.B. That's Lambert Boomphoffen, you may depend. What the J is for I can't say, but they used to be grand kind o' people, high-feathered as fancy fowl. Just the kind to give their children all double names, which isn't Scripture, anyway."

"I don't know about that, *vrouw*. Seems to me there's long mixed names in the Holy Book, hard enough to make out. But you've got the right guess at a jump. It was your way always," said Raff, closing his eyes. "Take the watch to Boompkins and try."

"Not Boompkins. I know no such name. It's Boomphoffen."

"Aye, take it there."

"Take it there, man! Why, the whole brood of 'em's been gone to America these four years. But go to sleep, Raff, you look pale and out of strength. It'll all come to you, what's best to do, in the morning.

"So, Mistress Gretel! Here you are at last!"

Before Raff awoke that evening, the fairy godmother, as we know, had been at the cottage, the guilders were safely locked in the big chest, and Dame Brinker and the children were faring sumptuously on meat and white bread.

So the mother, in the joy of her heart, told them the story of the watch as far as she deemed it prudent to divulge it. It was no more than fair, she thought, that the poor things should know after keeping the secret so safe, ever since they had been old enough to know anything.

Chapter 43

A Discovery

*T*he next sun brought a busy day to the Brinkers. In the first place the news of the thousand guilders had, of course, to be told to the father. Such tidings as that surely could not harm him. Then while Gretel was diligently obeying her mother's injunction to "clean the place fresh as a new brewing," Hans and the dame sallied forth to revel in the purchasing of peat and provisions.

Hans was careless and contented; the dame was filled with delightful anxieties caused by the unreasonable demands of ten thousand guilders' worth of new wants that had sprung up like mushrooms in a single night. The happy woman talked so largely to Hans on their way to Amsterdam and brought back such little bundles after all that he scratched his bewildered head as he leaned against the chimney piece, wondering whether "Bigger the pouch, tighter the string" was in Jakob Cats, and therefore true, or whether he had dreamed it when he lay in a fever.

"What thinking on, Big-eyes?" chirruped his mother, half reading his thoughts as she bustled about, preparing the dinner. "What thinking on? Why, Raff, would ye believe it, the child thought to carry half Amsterdam back on his head. Bless us! He would have bought as much coffee as would have filled this fire pot. 'No, no, my lad,' says I. 'No time for leaks when the ship is rich laden.' And then how he stared—aye—just as he stares this minute. Hoot, lad, fly around a mite! Ye'll grow to the chimney place with your staring and wondering. Now, Raff, here's your chair at the head of the table, where it should be, for there's a man to the house now—I'd say it to the king's face. Aye, that's the way—lean on Hans. There's a strong staff for you! Growing like a weed, too, and it seems only yesterday since he was toddling. Sit by, my man, sit by."

"Can you call to mind, *vrouw*," said Raff, settling himself cautiously in the big chair, "the wonderful music box that cheered your working in the big house at Heidelberg?"

"Aye, that I can," answered the dame. "Three turns of a brass key and the witchy thing would send the music fairly running up and down one's back. I remember it well. But, Raff"— growing solemn in an instant—"you would never throw our guilders away for a thing like that?"

"No, no, not I, *vrouw*, for the good Lord has already given me a music box without pay."

All three cast quick, frightened glances at one another and at Raff. Were his wits on the wing again?

"Aye, and a music box that fifty pouchfuls would not buy from me," insisted Raff. "And it's set going by the turn of a mop handle, and it slips and glides around the room, every-where in a flash, carrying the music about till you'd swear the birds were back again."

"Holy St. Bavon!" screeched the dame. "What's in the man?"

"Comfort and joy, *vrouw*, that's what's in him! Ask Gretel, ask my little music box Gretel if your man has lacked comfort and joy this day."

"Not he, Mother," laughed Gretel. "He's been *my* music box too. We sang together half the time you were gone."

"Aye, so," said the dame, greatly relieved. "Now, Hans, you'll never get through with a piece like that, but never mind, chick, thou'st had a long fasting. Here, Gretel, take another slice of the sausage. It'll put blood in your cheeks."

"Oh! Oh, Mother," laughed Gretel, eagerly holding forth her platter. "Blood doesn't grow in girls' cheeks—you mean roses. Isn't it roses, Hans?"

While Hans was hastily swallowing a mammoth mouthful in order to give a suitable reply to this poetic appeal, Dame Brinker settled the matter with a quick, "Well, roses or blood, it's all one to me, so the red finds its way on your sunny face. It's enough for mother to get pale and weary-looking without—"

"Hoot, *vrouw*," spoke up Raff hastily, "thou'rt fresher and rosier this minute than both our chicks put together."

This remark, though not bearing very strong testimony to the clearness of Raff's newly awakened intellect, nevertheless afforded the dame intense satisfaction. The meal accordingly went on in the most delightful manner.

After dinner the affair of the watch was talked over and the mysterious initials duly discussed.

Hans had just pushed back his stool, intending to start at once for Mynheer van Holp's, and his mother had risen to put the watch away in its old hiding place when they heard the sound of wheels upon the frozen ground.

Someone knocked at the door, opening it at the same time.

"Come in," stammered Dame Brinker, hastily trying to hide the watch in her bosom. "Oh, is it you, *mynheer!* Good day! The father is nearly well, as you see. It's a poor place to greet you in, *mynheer,* and the dinner not cleared away."

Dr. Boekman scarcely noticed the dame's apology. He was evidently in haste.

"Ahem!" he exclaimed. "Not needed here, I perceive. The patient is mending fast."

"Well he may, *mynheer*," cried the dame, "for only last night we found a thousand guilders that's been lost to us these ten years."

Dr. Boekman opened his eyes.

"Yes, *mynheer*," said Raff. "I bid the *vrouw* tell you, though it's to be held a secret among us, for I see you can keep your lips closed as well as any man."

The doctor scowled. He never liked personal remarks.

"Now, *mynheer*," continued Raff, "you can take your rightful pay. God knows you have earned it, if bringing such a poor tool back to the world, and his family, can be called a service. Tell the *vrouw* what's to pay, *mynheer*. She will hand out the sum right willingly."

"Tut, tut!" said the doctor kindly. "Say nothing about money. I can find plenty of such pay anytime, but gratitude comes seldom. That boy's thank-you," he added, nodding sidewise toward Hans, "was pay enough for me."

"Like enough ye have a boy of your own," said Dame Brinker, quite delighted to see the great man becoming so sociable.

Dr. Boekman's good nature vanished at once. He gave a growl (at least, it seemed so to Gretel) but made no actual reply.

"Do not think the *vrouw* meddlesome, *mynheer*," said Raff. "She has been sore touched of late about a lad whose folks have gone away—none know where—and I had a message for them from the young gentleman."

"The name was Boomphoffen," said the dame eagerly. "Do you know aught of the family, *mynheer*?"

The doctor's reply was brief and gruff.

"Yes. A troublesome set. They went long since to America."

"It might be, Raff," persisted Dame Brinker timidly, "that the *meester* knows somebody in that country, though I'm told they are mostly savages over there. If he could get the watch to the Boomphoffens with the poor lad's message, it would be a most blessed thing."

"Tut, *vrouw*, why pester the good *meester*, and dying men and women wanting him everywhere? How do ye know ye have the true name?"

"I'm sure of it," she replied. "They had a son Lambert, and there's an L for Lambert and a B for Boomphoffen on the back, though, to be sure, there's an odd J, too, but the *meester* can look for himself."

So saying, she drew forth the watch.

"L.J.B!" cried Dr. Boekman, springing toward her.

Why attempt to describe the scene that followed! I need only say that the lad's message was delivered to his father at last— delivered while the great surgeon was sobbing like a little child.

"Laurens! My Laurens!" he cried, gazing with yearning eyes at the watch as he held it tenderly in his palm. "Ah, if I had but known sooner! Laurens a homeless wanderer—great heaven! He may be suffering, dying at this moment! Think, man, where is he? Where did my boy say the letter must be sent?"

Raff shook his head sadly.

"Think!" implored the doctor. Surely the memory so lately awakened through his aid could not refuse to serve him in a moment like this.

"It is all gone, *mynheer*," sighed Raff.

Hans, forgetting distinctions of rank and station, forgetting everything but that his good friend was in trouble, threw his arms around the doctor's neck.

"I can find your son, *mynheer*. If alive, he is *somewhere*. The earth is not so very large. I will devote every day of my life to the search. Mother can spare me now. You are rich, *mynheer*. Send me where you will."

Gretel began to cry. It was right for Hans to go, but how could they ever live without him?

Dr. Boekman made no reply, neither did he push Hans away. His eyes were fixed anxiously upon Raff Brinker. Suddenly he lifted the watch and, with trembling eagerness, attempted to open it. Its stiffened spring yielded at last; the case flew open, disclosing a watch paper in the back bearing a group of blue forget-me-nots. Raff, seeing a shade of intense disappointment pass over the doctor's face, hastened to say, "There was something else in it, *mynheer,* but the young gentleman tore it out before he handed it to me. I saw him kiss it as he put it away."

"It was his mother's picture," moaned the doctor. "She died when he was ten years old. Thank God! The boy had not forgotten. Both dead? It is impossible!" he cried, starting up. "My boy is alive. You shall hear his story. Laurens acted as my assistant. By mistake he portioned out the wrong medicine for one of my patients—a deadly poison—but it was never administered, for I discovered the error in time. The man died that day. I was detained with other bad cases until the next evening. When I reached home, my boy was gone. Poor Laurens!" sobbed the doctor, breaking down completely. "Never to hear from me through all these years. His message disregarded. Oh, what must he have suffered!"

Dame Brinker ventured to speak. Anything was better than to see the *meester* cry.

"It is a mercy to know the young gentleman was innocent. Ah, how he fretted! Telling you, Raff, that his crime was like unto murder. It was sending the wrong physic he meant. Crime indeed! Why, our own Gretel might have done that! Like enough the poor young gentleman heard that the man was dead—that's why he ran, *mynheer.* He said, you know, Raff, that he never could come back to Holland again, unless"—she hesitated—"ah, your honor, ten years is a dreary time to be waiting to hear from—"

"Hist, *vrouw!*" said Raff sharply.

"Waiting to hear"—the doctor groaned—"and I, like a fool, sitting stubbornly at home, thinking he had abandoned me. I never dreamed, Brinker, that the boy had discovered the mistake. I believed it was youthful folly, ingratitude, love of adventure, that sent him away. My poor, poor Laurens!"

"But you know all now, *mynheer*," whispered Hans. "You know he was innocent of wrong, that he loved you and his dead mother. We will find him. You shall see him again, dear *meester*."

"God bless you!" said Dr. Boekman, seizing the boy's hand. "It may be as you say. I shall try—I shall try—and Brinker, if ever the faintest gleam of recollection concerning him should come to you, you will send me word at once?"

"Indeed we will!" cried all but Hans, whose silent promise would have satisfied the doctor even had the others not spoken.

"Your boy's eyes," he said, turning to Dame Brinker, "are strangely like my son's. The first time I met him it seemed that Laurens himself was looking at me."

"Aye, *mynheer*," replied the mother proudly. "I have marked that you were much drawn to the child."

For a few moments the *meester* seemed lost in thought, then, arousing himself, he spoke in a new voice. "Forgive me, Raff Brinker, for this tumult. Do not feel distressed on my account. I leave your house today a happier man than I have been for many a long year. Shall I take the watch?"

"Certainly, you must, *mynheer*. It was your son's wish."

"Even so," responded the doctor, regarding his treasure with a queer frown, for his face could not throw off its bad habits in an hour, "even so. And now I must be gone. No medicine is needed by my patient, only peace and cheerfulness, and both are here in plenty. Heaven bless you, my good friends! I shall ever be grateful to you."

"May Heaven bless you, too, *mynheer*, and may you soon find the dear young gentleman," said Dame Brinker earnestly, after hurriedly wiping her eyes upon the corner of her apron.

Raff uttered a hearty "Amen!" and Gretel threw such a wistful, eager glance at the doctor that he patted her head as he turned to leave the cottage.

Hans went out also.

"When I can serve you, *mynheer*, I am ready."

"Very well, boy," replied Dr. Boekman with peculiar mildness. "Tell them, within, to say nothing of what has just passed. Meantime, Hans, when you are with your father, watch his mood. You have tact. At any moment he may suddenly be able to tell us more."

"Trust me for that, *mynheer*."

"Good day, my boy!" cried the doctor as he sprang into his stately coach.

Aha! thought Hans as it rolled away, the *meester* has more life in him than I thought.

Chapter 44

The Race

*T*he twentieth of December came at last, bringing with it the perfection of winter weather. All over the level landscape lay the warm sunlight. It tried its power on lake, canal, and river, but the ice flashed defiance and showed no sign of melting. The very weathercocks stood still to enjoy the sight. This gave the windmills a holiday. Nearly all the past week they had been whirling briskly; now, being rather out of breath, they rocked lazily in the clear, still air. Catch a windmill working when the weathercocks have nothing to do!

There was an end to grinding, crushing, and sawing for that day. It was a good thing for the millers near Broek. Long before noon they concluded to take in their sails and go to the race. Everybody would be there—already the north side of the frozen Y was bordered with eager spectators. The news of the great skating match had traveled far and wide. Men, women, and children in holiday attire were flocking toward the spot. Some wore furs and wintry cloaks or shawls, but many, consulting their feelings rather than the almanac, were dressed as for an October day.

The site selected for the race was a faultless plain of ice near Amsterdam, on that great arm of the Zuider Zee, which Dutchmen, of course, must call the Eye. The townspeople turned out in large numbers. Strangers in the city deemed it a fine chance to see what was to be seen. Many a peasant from the north had wisely chosen the twentieth as the day for the next city trading. It seemed that everybody, young and old, who had wheels, skates, or feet at command had hastened to the scene.

There were the gentry in their coaches, dressed like Parisians, fresh from the boulevards; Amsterdam children in charity uniforms; girls from the Roman Catholic Orphan House, in sable gowns and white headbands; boys from the Burgher Asylum, with their black tights and short-skirted, harlequin coats. * There were old-fashioned gentlemen in cocked hats and velvet knee breeches; old-fashioned ladies, too, in stiff quilted skirts and bodices of dazzling brocade. These were accompanied by servants bearing foot stoves and cloaks. There were the peasant folk arrayed in every possible Dutch costume—shy young rustics in brazen buckles; simple village maidens concealing their flaxen hair under fillets of gold; women whose long, narrow aprons were stiff with embroidery; women with short corkscrew curls hanging over their foreheads; women with shaved heads and close-fitting caps; and women in striped skirts and windmill bonnets. Men in leather, in homespun, in velvet and broadcloth; burghers in model European attire, and burghers in short jackets, wide trousers, and steeple-crowned hats.

There were beautiful Friesland girls in wooden shoes and coarse petticoats, with solid gold crescents encircling their heads, finished at each temple with a golden rosette and hung with

---

*This is not said in derision. Both the girls and boys of this institution wear garments quartered in red and black, alternately. By making the dress thus conspicuous, the children are, in a measure, deterred from wrongdoing while going about the city. The Burgher Orphan Asylum affords a comfortable home to several hundred boys and girls. Holland is famous for its charitable institutions.

lace a century old. Some wore necklaces, pendants, and earrings of the purest gold. Many were content with gilt or even with brass, but it is not an uncommon thing for a Friesland woman to have all the family treasure in her headgear. More than one rustic lass displayed the value of two thousand guilders upon her head that day.

Scattered throughout the crowd were peasants from the Island of Marken, with sabots, black stockings, and the widest of breeches; also women from Marken with short blue petticoats and black jackets, gaily figured in front. They wore red sleeves, white aprons, and a cap like a bishop's miter over their golden hair.

The children often were as quaint and odd-looking as their elders. In short, one third of the crowd seemed to have stepped bodily from a collection of Dutch paintings.

Everywhere could be seen tall women and stumpy men, lively faced girls, and youths whose expression never changed from sunrise to sunset.

There seemed to be at least one specimen from every known town in Holland. There were Utrecht water bearers, Gouda cheesemakers, Delft pottery men, Schiedam distillers, Amsterdam diamond cutters, Rotterdam merchants, dried-up herring packers, and two sleepy-eyed shepherds from Texel. Every man of them had his pipe and tobacco pouch. Some carried what might be called the smoker's complete outfit—a pipe, tobacco, a pricker with which to clean the tube, a silver net for protecting the bowl, and a box of the strongest of brimstone matches.

A true Dutchman, you must remember, is rarely without his pipe on any possible occasion. He may for a moment neglect to breathe, but when the pipe is forgotten, he must be dying indeed. There were no such sad cases here. Wreaths of smoke were rising from every possible quarter. The more fantastic the smoke wreath, the more placid and solemn the smoker.

Look at those boys and girls on stilts! That is a good idea. They can see over the heads of the tallest. It is strange to see those little bodies high in the air, carried about on mysterious legs. They have such a resolute look on their round faces, what wonder that nervous old gentlemen with tender feet wince and tremble while the long-legged little monsters stride past them.

You will read in certain books that the Dutch are a quiet people—so they are generally. But listen! Did ever you hear such a din? All made up of human voices—no, the horses are helping somewhat, and the fiddles are squeaking pitifully (how it must pain fiddles to be tuned!), but the mass of the sound comes from the great vox humana that belongs to a crowd.

That queer little dwarf going about with a heavy basket, winding in and out among the people, helps not a little. You can hear his shrill cry above all other sounds, "*Pypen en tabac! Pypen en tabac!*"

Another, his big brother, though evidently some years younger, is selling doughnuts and bonbons. He is calling on all pretty children far and near to come quickly or the cakes will be gone.

You know quite a number among the spectators. High up in yonder pavilion, erected upon the border of the ice, are some persons whom you have seen very lately. In the center is Madame van Gleck. It is her birthday, you remember; she has the post of honor. There is Mynheer van Gleck, whose meerschaum has not really grown fast to his lips—it only appears so. There are Grandfather and Grandmother, whom you met at the Saint Nicholas fete. All the children are with them. It is so mild, they have brought even the baby. The poor little creature is swaddled very much after the manner of an Egyptian mummy, but it can crow with delight and, when the band is playing, open and shut its animated mittens in perfect time to the music.

Grandfather, with his pipe and spectacles and fur cap, makes quite a picture as he holds baby upon his knee. Perched high upon their canopied platforms, the party can see all that is going on. No wonder the ladies look complacently at the glassy ice; with a stove for a footstool one might sit cozily beside the North Pole.

There is a gentleman with them who somewhat resembles Saint Nicholas as he appeared to the young Van Glecks on the fifth of December. But the saint had a flowing white beard, and this face is as smooth as a pippin. His saintship was larger around the body, too, and (between ourselves) he had a pair of thimbles in his mouth, which this gentleman certainly has not. It cannot be Saint Nicholas after all.

Nearby, in the next pavilion, sit the Van Holps with their son and daughter (the Van Gends) from The Hague. Peter's sister is not one to forget her promises. She has brought bouquets of exquisite hothouse flowers for the winners.

These pavilions, and there are others besides, have all been erected since daylight. That semicircular one, containing Mynheer Korbes's family, is very pretty and proves that the Hollanders are quite skilled at tentmaking, but I like the Van Glecks' best—the center one—striped red and white and hung with evergreens.

The one with the blue flags contains the musicians. Those pagodalike affairs, decked with seashells and streamers of every possible hue, are the judges' stands, and those columns and flagstaffs upon the ice mark the limit of the race course. The two white columns twined with green, connected at the top by that long, floating strip of drapery, form the starting point. Those flagstaffs, half a mile off, stand at each end of the boundary line, cut sufficiently deep to be distinct to the skaters, though not enough so to trip them when they turn to come back to the starting point.

The air is so clear, it seems scarcely possible that the columns and flagstaffs are so far apart. Of course, the judges' stands are but little nearer together.

Half a mile on the ice, when the atmosphere is like this, is but a short distance after all, especially when fenced with a living chain of spectators.

The music has commenced. How melody seems to enjoy itself in the open air! The fiddles have forgotten their agony, and everything is harmonious. Until you look at the blue tent it seems that the music springs from the sunshine, it is so boundless, so joyous. Only when you see the staid-faced musicians do you realize the truth.

Where are the racers? All assembled together near the white columns. It is a beautiful sight. Forty boys and girls in picturesque attire darting with electric swiftness in and out among each other, or sailing in pairs and triplets, beckoning, chatting, whispering in the fullness of youthful glee.

A few careful ones are soberly tightening their straps; others halting on one leg, with flushed, eager faces suddenly cross the suspected skate over their knee, give it an examining shake, and dart off again. One and all are possessed with the spirit of motion. They cannot stand still. Their skates are a part of them, and every runner seems bewitched.

Holland is the place for skaters, after all. Where else can nearly every boy and girl perform feats on the ice that would attract a crowd if seen in Central Park? Look at Ben! I did not see him before. He is really astonishing the natives; no easy thing to do in the Netherlands. Save your strength, Ben, you will need it soon. Now other boys are trying! Ben is surpassed already. Such jumping, such poising, such spinning, such India-rubber exploits generally! That boy with the red cap is the lion now; his back is a watch spring, his body is cork—no, it is iron, or it would snap at that! He is a bird, a top, a rabbit, a corkscrew, a sprite, a flesh-ball, all in an instant. When you think he's erect, he is down, and when you think he is down, he is up. He drops his glove on the ice and turns a somersault as he picks it up. Without stopping he snatches the cap from Jacob Poot's astonished head and claps it back again "hindside before." Lookers-on hurrah and laugh. Foolish boy! It is arctic weather under your feet but more than temperate overhead. Big drops already are rolling down your forehead. Superb skater as you are, you may lose the race.

A French traveler, standing with a notebook in his hand, sees our English friend, Ben, buy a doughnut of the dwarf's brother and eat it. Thereupon he writes in his notebook that the Dutch take enormous mouthfuls and universally are fond of potatoes boiled in molasses.

There are some familiar faces near the white columns. Lambert, Ludwig, Peter, and Carl are all there, cool and in good skating order. Hans is not far off. Evidently he is going to join in the race, for his skates are on—the very pair that he sold for seven guilders! He had soon suspected that his fairy godmother was the mysterious "friend" who bought them. This settled, he had boldly charged her with the deed, and she, knowing well that all her little savings had been spent in the purchase, had not had the face to deny it. Through the fairy godmother, too, he had been rendered amply able to buy them back again. Therefore Hans is to be in the race. Carl is more indignant than ever about it, but as three other peasant boys have entered, Hans is not alone.

Twenty boys and twenty girls. The latter, by this time, are standing in front, braced for the start, for they are to have the first "run." Hilda, Rychie, and Katrinka are among them—two or three bend hastily to give a last pull at their skate straps. It is pretty to see them stamp, to be sure that all is firm. Hilda is speaking pleasantly to a graceful little creature in a red jacket and a new brown petticoat. Why, it is Gretel! What a difference those pretty shoes make, and the skirt and the new cap. Annie Bouman is there too. Even Janzoon Kolp's sister has been admitted, but Janzoon himself has been voted out by the directors, because he killed the stork, and only last summer was caught in the act of robbing a bird's nest, a legal offense in Holland.

This Janzoon Kolp, you see, was— There, I cannot tell the story just now. The race is about to commence.

Twenty girls are formed in a line. The music has ceased.

A man, whom we shall call the crier, stands between the columns and the first judges' stand. He reads the rules in a loud voice: "The girls and boys are to race in turn, until one girl and one boy have beaten twice. They are to start in a line from the united columns, skate to the flagstaff line, turn, and then come back to the starting point, thus making a mile at each run."

A flag is waved from the judges' stand. Madame van Gleck rises in her pavilion. She leans forward with a white handkerchief in her hand. When she drops it, a bugler is to give the signal for them to start.

The handkerchief is fluttering to the ground. Hark!

They are off!

No. Back again. Their line was not true in passing the judges' stand.

The signal is repeated.

Off again. No mistake this time. Whew! How fast they go!

The multitude is quiet for an instant, absorbed in eager, breathless watching.

Cheers spring up along the line of spectators. Huzza! Five girls are ahead. Who comes flying back from the boundary mark? We cannot tell. Something red, that is all. There is a blue spot flitting near it, and a dash of yellow nearer still.

Spectators at this end of the line strain their eyes and wish they had taken their post nearer the flagstaff.

The wave of cheers is coming back again. Now we can see! Katrinka is ahead!

She passes the Van Holp pavilion. The next is Madame van Gleck's. That leaning figure gazing from it is a magnet. Hilda shoots past Katrinka, waving her hand to her mother as she passes. Two others are close now, whizzing on like arrows. What is that flash of red and gray? Hurray, it is Gretel! She, too, waves her hand, but toward no gay pavilion. The crowd is cheering, but she hears only her father's voice. "Well done, little Gretel!" Soon Katrinka, with a quick, merry laugh, shoots past Hilda. The girl in yellow is gaining now. She passes them all, all except Gretel. The judges lean forward without seeming to lift their eyes from their watches. Cheer after cheer fills the air; the very columns seem to be rocking. Gretel has passed them. She has won.

"Gretel Brinker, one mile!" shouts the crier.

The judges nod. They write something upon a tablet each holds in his hand.

While the girls are resting—some crowding eagerly around our frightened little Gretel, some standing aside in high disdain—the boys form in a line.

Mynheer van Gleck drops the handkerchief this time. The buglers give a vigorous blast! The boys have started.

Halfway already! Did ever you see the like?

Three hundred legs flashing by in an instant. But there are only twenty boys. No matter, there were hundreds of legs, I am sure! Where are they now? There is such a noise, one gets bewildered. What are the people laughing at? Oh, at that fat boy in the rear. See him go! See him! He'll be down in an instant; no, he won't. I wonder if he knows he is all alone; the other boys are nearly at the boundary line. Yes, he knows it.

He stops! He wipes his hot face. He takes off his cap and looks about him. Better to give up with a good grace. He has made a hundred friends by that hearty, astonished laugh. Good Jacob Poot!

The fine fellow is already among the spectators, gazing as eagerly as the rest.

A cloud of feathery ice flies from the heels of the skaters as they "bring to" and turn at the flagstaffs.

Something black is coming now, one of the boys—it is all we know. He has touched the vox humana stop of the crowd; it fairly roars. Now they come nearer—we can see the red cap. There's Ben—there's Peter—there's Hans!

Hans is ahead! Young Madame van Gend almost crushes the flowers in her hand. She had been quite sure that Peter would be first. Carl Schummel is next, then Ben, and the youth with the red cap. The others are pressing close. A tall figure darts from among them. He passes the red cap, he passes Ben, then Carl. Now it is an even race between him and Hans. Madame van Gend catches her breath.

It is Peter! He is ahead! Hans shoots past him. Hilda's eyes fill with tears. Peter *must* beat. Annie's eyes flash proudly. Gretel gazes with clasped hands—four strokes more will take her brother to the columns.

He is there! Yes, but so was young Schummel just a second before. At the last instant Carl, gathering his powers, had whizzed between them and passed the goal.

"Carl Schummel, one mile!" shouts the crier.

Soon Madame van Gleck rises again. The falling handkerchief starts the bugle, and the bugle, using its voice as a bowstring, shoots off twenty girls like so many arrows.

It is a beautiful sight, but one has not long to look; before we can fairly distinguish them, they are far in the distance. This time they are close upon one another. It is hard to say as they come speeding back from the flagstaff who will reach the columns first. There are new faces among the foremost—eager, glowing faces, unnoticed before. Katrinka is there, and Hilda, but Gretel and Rychie are in the rear. Gretel is wavering, but when Rychie passes her, she starts forward afresh. Now they are nearly beside Katrinka. Hilda is still in advance. She is almost "home." She has not faltered since that bugle note sent her flying; like an arrow still she is speeding toward the goal. Cheer after cheer rises in the air. Peter is silent, but his eyes shine like stars. "Huzza! Huzza!"

The crier's voice is heard again.

"Hilda van Gleck, one mile!"

A loud murmur of approval runs through the crowd, catching the music in its course, till all seems one sound, with a glad, rhythmic throbbing in its depths. When the flag waves, all is still.

Once more the bugle blows a terrific blast. It sends off the boys like chaff before the wind—dark chaff, I admit, and in big pieces.

It is whisked around at the flagstaff, driven faster yet by the cheers and shouts along the line. We begin to see what is coming. There are three boys in advance this time, and all abreast. Hans, Peter, and Lambert. Carl soon breaks the ranks, rushing through with a whiff! Fly, Hans; fly, Peter; don't let Carl beat again. Carl the bitter, Carl the insolent. Van Mounen is flagging, but you are strong as ever. Hans and Peter, Peter and Hans; which is foremost? We love them both. We scarcely care which is the fleeter.

Hilda, Annie, and Gretel, seated upon the long crimson bench, can remain quiet no longer. They spring to their feet—so different and yet one in eagerness. Hilda instantly reseats herself. None shall know how interested she is, none shall know how anxious, how filled with one hope. Shut your eyes then, Hilda—hide your face rippling with joy. Peter has beaten.

"Peter van Holp, one mile!" calls the crier.

The same buzz of excitement as before, while the judges take notes; the same throbbing of music through the din, but something is different. A little crowd presses close about some object near the column. Carl has fallen. He is not hurt, though somewhat stunned. If he were less sullen, he would find more sympathy in these warm young hearts. As it is they forget him as soon as he is fairly on his feet again.

The girls are to skate their third mile.

How resolute the little maidens look as they stand in a line! Some are solemn with a sense of responsibility, some wear a smile half bashful, half provoked, but one air of determination pervades them all.

This third mile may decide the race. Still, if neither Gretel nor Hilda wins, there is yet a chance among the rest for the silver skates.

Each girl feels that this time she will accomplish the distance in one half the time. How they stamp to try their runners! How nervously they examine each strap! How erect they stand at last, every eye upon Madame van Gleck!

The bugle thrills through them again. With quivering eagerness they spring forward, bending, but in perfect balance. Each flashing stroke seems longer than the last.

Now they are skimming off in the distance.

Again the eager straining of eyes, again the shouts and cheering, again the thrill of excitement as, after a few moments, four or five, in advance of the rest, come speeding back, nearer, nearer to the white columns.

Who is first? Not Rychie, Katrinka, Annie, nor Hilda, nor the girl in yellow, but Gretel—Gretel, the fleetest sprite of a girl that ever skated. She was but playing in the earlier race, *now* she is in earnest, or rather, something within her has determined to win. That lithe little form makes no effort, but it cannot stop—not until the goal is passed!

In vain the crier lifts his voice. He cannot be heard. He has no news to tell—it is already ringing through the crowd. *Gretel has won the silver skates!*

Like a bird she has flown over the ice, like a bird she looks about her in a timid, startled way. She longs to dart to the sheltered nook where her father and mother stand. But Hans is beside her—the girls are crowding round. Hilda's kind, joyous voice breathes in her ear. From that hour none will despise her. Goose girl or not, Gretel stands acknowledged queen of the skaters!

With natural pride Hans turns to see if Peter van Holp is witnessing his sister's triumph. Peter is not looking toward them at all. He is kneeling, bending his troubled face low, and working hastily at his skate strap. Hans is beside him at once.

"Are you in trouble, *mynheer?*"

"Ah, Hans, that you? Yes, my fun is over. I tried to tighten my strap—to make a new hole—and this botheration of a knife has cut it nearly in two."

"*Mynheer,*" said Hans, at the same time pulling off a skate, "you must use my strap!"

"Not I, indeed, Hans Brinker," cried Peter, looking up, "though I thank you warmly. Go to your post, my friend, the bugle will sound in a minute."

"*Mynheer,*" pleaded Hans in a husky voice, "you have called me your friend. Take this strap—quick! There is not an instant to lose. I shall not skate this time. Indeed, I am out of practice. *Mynheer,* you *must* take it." And Hans, blind and deaf to any remonstrance, slipped his strap into Peter's skate and implored him to put it on.

"Come, Peter!" cried Lambert from the line, "we are waiting for you."

"For madame's sake," pleaded Hans, "be quick. She is motioning to you to join the racers. There, the skate is almost on. Quick, *mynheer*, fasten it. I could not possibly win. The race lies between Master Schummel and yourself."

"You are a noble fellow, Hans!" cried Peter, yielding at last. He sprang to his post just as the white handkerchief fell to the ground. The bugle sends forth its blast—loud, clear, and ringing. Off go the boys!

"Mine Gott," cries a tough old fellow from Delft. "They beat everything, these Amsterdam youngsters. See them!"

See them indeed! They are winged Mercuries, every one of them. What mad errand are they on? Ah, I know. They are hunting Peter van Holp. He is some fleet-footed runaway from Olympus. Mercury and his troop of winged cousins are in full chase. They will catch him! Now Carl is the runaway, the pursuit grows furious—Ben is foremost!

The chase turns in a cloud of mist. It is coming this way. Who is hunted now? Mercury himself. It is Peter, Peter van Holp; fly, Peter—Hans is watching you. He is sending all his fleetness, all his strength into your feet. Your mother and sister are pale with eagerness. Hilda is trembling and dares not look up. Fly, Peter! The crowd has not gone deranged, it is only cheering. The pursuers are close upon you! Touch the white column! It beckons—it is reeling before you—it—

"Huzza! Huzza! Peter has won the silver skates!"

"Peter van Holp!" shouted a hundred voices, for he was the favorite boy of the place. "Huzza! Huzza!"

Now the music was resolved to be heard. It struck up a lively air, then a tremendous march. The spectators, thinking something new was about to happen, deigned to listen and to look.

The racers formed in single file. Peter, being tallest, stood

first. Gretel, the smallest of all, took her place at the end.
Hans, who had borrowed a strap from the cake boy, was near
the head.

Three gaily twined arches were placed at intervals upon the
river facing the Van Gleck pavilion.

Skating slowly and in perfect time to the music, the boys and
girls moved forward, led on by Peter.

It was beautiful to see the bright procession glide along like a
living creature. It curved and doubled and drew its graceful
length in and out among the arches—whichever way Peter,
the head, went, the body was sure to follow. Sometimes it
steered direct for the center arch, then, as if seized with a new
impulse, turned away and curled itself about the first one, then
unwound slowly and, bending low, with quick, snakelike curv-
ings, crossed the river, passing at length through the farthest
arch.

When the music was slow, the procession seemed to crawl
like a thing afraid. It grew livelier, and the creature darted
forward with a spring, gliding rapidly among the arches, in and
out, curling, twisting, turning, never losing form until, at the
shrill call of the bugle rising above the music, it suddenly
resolved itself into boys and girls standing in a double semicircle
before Madame van Gleck's pavilion.

Peter and Gretel stand in the center in advance of the
others. Madame van Gleck rises majestically. Gretel trembles
but feels that she must look at the beautiful lady. She cannot
hear what is said, there is such a buzzing all around her. She is
thinking that she ought to try to make a curtsy, such as her
mother makes to the *meester*, when suddenly something so
dazzling is placed in her hand that she gives a cry of joy.

Then she ventures to look about her. Peter, too, has something in his hands. "Oh! Oh! How splendid!" she cries, and
"Oh! How splendid!" is echoed as far as people can see.

Meantime the silver skates flash in the sunshine, throwing dashes of light upon those happy faces.

Mevrouw van Gend sends a little messenger with her bouquets. One for Hilda, one for Carl, and others for Peter and Gretel.

At sight of the flowers the queen of the skaters becomes uncontrollable. With a bright stare of gratitude she gathers skates and bouquets in her apron, hugs them to her bosom, and darts off to search for her father and mother in the scattering crowd.

Chapter 45

Joy in the Cottage

*P*erhaps you were surprised to learn that Raff and his *vrouw* were at the skating race. You would have been more so had you been with them on the evening of that merry twentieth of December. To see the Brinker cottage standing sulkily alone on the frozen marsh, with its bulgy, rheumatic-looking walls and its slouched hat of a roof pulled far over its eyes, one would never suspect that a lively scene was passing within. Without, nothing was left of the day but a low line of blaze at the horizon. A few venturesome clouds had already taken fire, and others, with their edges burning, were lost in the gathering smoke.

A stray gleam of sunshine slipping down from the willow stump crept stealthily under the cottage. It seemed to feel that the inmates would give it welcome if it could only get near them. The room under which it hid was as clean as clean could be. The very cracks in the rafters were polished. Delicious odors filled the air. A huge peat fire upon the hearth sent flashes of harmless lightning at the somber walls. It played in turn upon the great leather Bible, upon Gretel's closet-bed, the household things on their pegs, and the beautiful silver skates and the flowers upon the table. Dame Brinker's honest face shone and twinkled in the changing light. Gretel and Hans, with arms entwined, were leaning against the fireplace, laughing merrily, and Raff Brinker was dancing!

I do not mean that he was pirouetting or cutting a pigeon-wing, either of which would have been entirely too undignified for the father of a family. I simply affirm that while they were chatting pleasantly together, Raff suddenly sprang from his seat, snapped his fingers, and performed two or three flourishes very much like the climax of a highland fling. Next he caught his *vrouw* in his arms and fairly lifted her from the ground in his delight.

"Huzza!" he cried. "I have it! I have it! It's Thomas Higgs. That's the name! It came upon me like a flash. Write it down, lad, write it down!"

Someone knocked at the door.

"It's the *meester*," cried the delighted dame. "Goede Gunst! How things come to pass!"

Mother and children came in merry collision as they rushed to open the door.

It was not the doctor, after all, but three boys, Peter van Holp, Lambert, and Ben.

"Good evening, young gentlemen," said Dame Brinker, so happy and proud that she would scarcely have been surprised at a visit from the king himself.

"Good evening, *jufvrouw*," said the trio, making magnificent bows.

Dear me, thought Dame Brinker as she bobbed up and down like a churn dasher, it's lucky I learned to curtsy at Heidelberg!

Raff was content to return the boys' salutations with a respectful nod.

"Pray be seated, young masters," said the dame as Gretel bashfully thrust a stool toward them. "There's a lack of chairs, as you see, but this one by the fire is at your service, and if you don't mind the hardness, that oak chest is as good a seat as the best. That's right, Hans, pull it out."

By the time the boys were seated to the dame's satisfaction, Peter, acting as spokesman, had explained that they were going to attend a lecture at Amsterdam and had stopped on the way to return Hans's strap.

"Oh, *mynheer*," cried Hans earnestly, "it is too much trouble. I am very sorry."

"No trouble at all, Hans. I could have waited for you to come to work tomorrow, had I not wished to call. And, Hans, talking of your work, my father is much pleased with it. A carver by trade could not have done it better. He would like to have the south arbor ornamented, also, but I told him you were going to school again."

"Aye!" put in Raff Brinker emphatically. "Hans must go to school at once—and Gretel as well—that is true."

"I am glad to hear you say so," responded Peter, turning toward the father, "and very glad to know that you are again a well man."

"Yes, young master, a well man, and able to work as steady as ever, thank God!"

Here Hans hastily wrote something on the edge of a time-worn almanac that hung by the chimney place. "Aye, that's right, lad, set it down. Figgs! Wiggs! Alack! Alack!" added Raff in great dismay, "it's gone again!"

"All right, Father," said Hans, "the name's down now in black and white. Here, look at it, father. Mayhap the rest will come to you. If we had the place as well, it would be complete." Then, turning to Peter, he said in a low tone, "I have an important errand in town, *mynheer*, and if—"

"Wist!" exclaimed the dame, lifting her hands. "Not to Amsterdam tonight, and you've owned your legs were aching under you. Nay, nay—it'll be soon enough to go at early daylight."

"Daylight, indeed!" echoed Raff. "That would never do. Nay, Meitje, he must go this hour."

The *vrouw* looked for an instant as if Raff's recovery was becoming rather a doubtful benefit; her word was no longer sole law in the house. Fortunately the proverb "Humble wife is husband's boss" had taken deep root in her mind. Even as the dame pondered, it bloomed.

"Very well, Raff," she said smilingly, "it is thy boy as well as mine. Ah! I've a troublesome house, young masters."

Just then Peter drew a long strap from his pocket.

Handing it to Hans, he said in an undertone, "I need not thank you for lending me this, Hans Brinker. Such boys as you do not ask for thanks, but I must say you did me a great kindness, and I am proud to acknowledge it. I did not know," he added laughingly, "until fairly in the race how anxious I was to win."

Hans was glad to join in Peter's laugh; it covered his embarrassment and gave his face a chance to cool off a little. Honest, generous boys like Hans have such a stupid way of blushing when you least expect it.

"It was nothing, *mynheer*," said the dame, hastening to her son's relief. "The lad's whole soul was in having you win the race, I know it was!"

This helped matters beautifully.

"Ah, *mynheer*," Hans hurried to say, "from the first start I felt stiff and strange on my feet. I was well out of it so long as I had no chance of winning."

Peter looked rather distressed.

"We may hold different opinions there. That part of the business troubles me. It is too late to mend it now, but it would be really a kindness to me if—"

The rest of Peter's speech was uttered so confidentially that I cannot record it. Enough to say, Hans soon started back in dismay, and Peter, looking very much ashamed, stammered out something to the effect that he would keep them, since he won the race, but it was "all wrong."

Here Van Mounen coughed, as if to remind Peter that lecture hour was approaching fast. At the same moment Ben laid something upon the table.

"Ah," exclaimed Peter, "I forgot my other errand. Your sister ran off so quickly today that Madame van Gleck had no opportunity to give her the case for her skates."

"S-s-t!" said Dame Brinker, shaking her head reproachfully at Gretel, "she was a very rude girl, I'm sure." Secretly she was thinking that very few women had such a fine little daughter.

"No, indeed"—Peter laughed—"she did exactly the right thing—ran home with her richly won treasures. Who would not? Don't let us detain you, Hans," he continued, turning around as he spoke, but Hans, who was eagerly watching the father, seemed to have forgotten their presence.

Meantime, Raff, lost in thought, was repeating under his breath, "Thomas Higgs, Thomas Higgs, aye, that's the name. Alack! If I could but tell the place as well."

The skate case was elegantly made of crimson morocco, ornamented with silver. If a fairy had breathed upon its tiny key, or Jack Frost himself designed its delicate tracery, they could not have been more daintily beautiful. "For the Fleetest" was written upon the cover in sparkling letters. It was lined with velvet, and in one corner was stamped the name and address of the maker.

Gretel thanked Peter in her own simple way, then, being quite delighted and confused and not knowing what else to do, lifted the case, carefully examining it in every part. "It's made by Mynheer Birmingham," she said after a while, still blushing and holding it before her eyes.

"Birmingham!" replied Lambert van Mounen, "that's the name of a place in England. Let me see it.

"Ha! ha!" He laughed, holding the open case toward the firelight. "No wonder you thought so, but it's a slight mistake. The case was made at Birmingham, but the maker's name is in smaller letters. Humph! they're so small, I can't read them."

"Let me try," said Peter, leaning over his shoulder. "Why, man, it's perfectly distinct. T-H—it's T—"

"Well," exclaimed Lambert triumphantly, "if you can read it so easily, let's hear it, T-H, what?"

"T. H-T.H. Oh! Why, Thomas Higgs, to be sure," replied Peter, pleased to be able to decipher it at last. Then, feeling they had been behaving rather unceremoniously, he turned toward Hans.

Peter turned pale! What was the matter with the people? Raff and Hans had started up and were staring at him in glad amazement. Gretel looked wild. Dame Brinker, with an unlighted candle in her hand, was rushing about the room, crying, "Hans! Hans! Where's your hat? Oh, the *meester*! Oh, the *meester*!"

"Birmingham! Higgs!" exclaimed Hans. "Did you say Higgs? We've found him! I must be off."

"You see, young masters." The dame was panting, at the same time snatching Hans's hat from the bed. "You see—we know him. He's our—no, he isn't. I mean—oh, Hans, you must go to Amsterdam this minute!"

"Good night, *mynheers*," Hans said, panting and radiant with sudden joy. "Good night. You will excuse me, I must go. Birmingham—Higgs—Higgs—Birmingham." And, seizing his hat from his mother and his skates from Gretel, he rushed from the cottage.

What could the boys think but that the entire Brinker family had suddenly gone crazy!

They bade an embarrassed "Good evening" and turned to go. But Raff stopped them.

"This Thomas Higgs, young masters, is a—a person."

"Ah!" exclaimed Peter, quite sure that Raff was the most crazy of all.

"Yes, a person. A—ahem—a friend. We thought him dead. I hope it is the same man. In England, did you say?"

"Yes, Birmingham," answered Peter. "It must be Birmingham in England."

"I know the man," said Ben, addressing Lambert. "His factory is not four miles from our place. A queer fellow—still as an oyster—doesn't seem at all like an Englishman. I've often seen him—a solemn-looking chap with magnificent eyes. He made a beautiful writing case once for me to give Jenny on her birthday. Makes pocketbooks, telescope cases, and all kinds of leatherwork."

As this was said in English, Van Mounen of course translated it for the benefit of all concerned, noticing meanwhile that neither Raff nor his *vrouw* looked very miserable, though Raff was trembling and the dame's eyes were swimming with tears.

You may believe the doctor heard every word of the story, when later in the evening he came driving back with Hans. "The three young gentlemen have been gone some time," Dame Brinker said, "but like enough, by hurrying, it will be easy to find them coming out from the lecture, wherever that was."

"True," said Raff, nodding his head, "the *vrouw* always hits upon the right thing. It would be well to see the young English gentleman, *mynheer*, before he forgets all about Thomas Higgs. It's a slippery name, d'ye see? One can't hold it safe a minute. It come upon me sudden and strong as a pile driver, and my boy writ it down. Aye, *mynheer*, I'd haste to talk with the English lad. He's seen your son many a time—only to think on't!"

Dame Brinker took up the thread of the discourse.

"You'll pick out the lad quick enough, *mynheer*, because he's in company with Master Peter van Holp, and his hair curls all up over his forehead like foreign folk's, and, if you hear him speak, he talks kind of big and fast, only it's English, but that wouldn't be any hindrance to your honor."

The doctor had already lifted his hat to go. With a beaming face he muttered something about its being just like the young scamp to give himself a rascally English name, called Hans "my son," thereby making that young gentleman happy as a lord, and left the cottage with very little ceremony, considering what a great *meester* he was.

The grumbling coachman comforted himself by speaking his mind as he drove back to Amsterdam. Since the doctor was safely stowed away in the coach and could not hear a word, it was a fine time to say terrible things of folks who hadn't no manner of feeling for nobody, and who were always wanting the horses a dozen times of a night.

Chapter 46

Mysterious Disappearance of Thomas Higgs

*H*iggs's factory was a mine of delight for the gossips of Birmingham. It was a small building but quite large enough to hold a mystery. Who the proprietor was, or where he came from, none could tell. He looked like a gentleman, that was certain, though everybody knew he had risen from an apprenticeship, and he could handle his pen like a writing master.

Years ago he had suddenly appeared in the place a lad of eighteen, learned his trade faithfully, and risen in the confidence of his employer, and was taken in as a partner soon after the time was up. Finally, when old Willett died, he had assumed the business on his own hands. This was all that was known of his affairs.

It was a common remark among some of the good people that he never had a word to say to a Christian soul, while others declared that though he spoke beautifully when he chose to, there was something wrong in his accent. A tidy man, too, they called him, all but for having that scandalous green pond alongside of his factory, which wasn't deep enough for an eel and was "just a fever nest, as sure as you live."

His nationality was a great puzzle. The English name spoke plain enough for *one* side of his house, but of what manner of nation was his mother? If she'd been an American, he'd certainly have had high cheekbones and reddish skin; if a German, he would have known the language, and Squire Smith declared he didn't; if French (and his having that frog pond made it seem likely), it would come out in his speech. No, there was nothing he could be but Dutch. And, strangest of all, though the man always pricked up his ears when you talked of Holland, he didn't seem to know the first thing about the country when you put him to the point.

Anyhow, as no letters ever came to him from his mother's family in Holland, and as nobody living had ever seen old Higgs, the family couldn't be anything much. Probably Thomas Higgs himself was no better than he should be, for all he pretended to carry himself so straight; and for their parts, the gossips declared, they were not going to trouble their heads about him. Consequently Thomas Higgs and his affairs were never-failing subjects of discussion.

Picture, then, the consternation among all the good people when it was announced by "somebody who was there and ought to know," that the postboy had that very morning handed Higgs a foreign-looking letter, and the man had "turned as white as the wall, rushed to his factory, talked a bit with one of the head workmen, and without bidding a creature good-bye, was off, bag and baggage, before you could wink, ma'am." Mistress Scrubbs, his landlady, was in deep affliction. The dear soul became quite out of breath while speaking of him. "To leave lodgin's in that suddent way, without never so much as a day's warnin', which was what every woman who didn't wish to be trodden underfoot, which thank hevving wasn't *her* way, had a perfect right to expect; yes, and a week's warnin' now you mention it, and without even so much as sayin' 'Many thanks to you, Mistress Scrubbs, for all past kindnesses,' which was most numerous, though she said it who shouldn't say it; least-wise she wasn't never no kind of a person to be lookin' for thanks every minnit. It was really scanderlous, though to be sure, Mister 'iggs paid up everythin' to the last farthin' and it fairly brought tears to my eyes to see his dear empty boots lyin' there in the corner of his room, which alone showed trouble of mind for he always stood 'em up straight as solgers, though bein' half-soled twice they hadn't of course been worth takin' away."

Whereupon her dearest friend, Miss Scrumpkins, ran home to tell all about it. And, as everybody knew the Scrumpkinses, a shining gossamer of news was soon woven from one end of the street to the other.

An investigating committee met that evening, at Mrs. Snigham's—sitting in secret session over her best china. Though invited only to a quiet "tea," the amount of judicial business they transacted on the occasion was prodigious. The biscuits were actually cold before the committee had a chance to eat anything. There was so much to talk over, and it was so important that it should be firmly established that each member had always been "certain sure that something extraordinary would be happening to that man yet," that it was nearly eight o'clock before Mrs. Snigham gave anybody a second cup.

Chapter 47

Broad Sunshine

One snowy day in January Laurens Boekman went with his father to pay his respects to the Brinker family.

Raff was resting after the labors of the day; Gretel, having filled and lighted his pipe, was brushing every speck of ash from the hearth; the dame was spinning; and Hans, perched upon a stool by the window, was diligently studying his lessons. It was a peaceful, happy household whose main excitement during the past week had been the looking forward to this possible visit from Thomas Higgs.

As soon as the grand presentation was over Dame Brinker insisted upon giving her guests some hot tea; it was enough to freeze anyone, she said, to be out in such crazy, blustering weather. While they were talking with her husband she whispered to Gretel that the young gentleman's eyes and her boy's were certainly as much alike as four beans, to say nothing of a way they both had of looking as if they were stupid and yet knew as much as a body's grandfather.

Gretel was disappointed. She had looked forward to a tragic scene, such as Annie Bouman had often described to her, from storybooks; and here was the gentleman who came so near being a murderer, who for ten years had been wandering over the face of the earth, who had believed himself deserted and scorned by his father—the very young gentleman who had fled from his country in such magnificent trouble, sitting by the fire just as pleasant and natural as could be!

To be sure, his voice had trembled when he talked with her parents, and he had met his father's look with a bright kind of smile that would have suited a dragon killer bringing the waters of perpetual youth to his king, but after all, he wasn't at all like the conquered hero in Annie's book. He did not say, lifting his hand toward heaven, "I hereby swear to be forever faithful to my home, my God, and my country!" which would have been only right and proper under the circumstances.

All things considered, Gretel was disappointed. Raff, however, was perfectly satisfied. The message was delivered. Dr. Boekman had his son safe and sound, and the poor lad had done nothing sinful after all, except in thinking his father would have abandoned him for an accident. To be sure, the graceful stripling had become rather a heavy man. Raff had unconsciously hoped to clasp that same boyish hand again, but all things were changed to Raff, for that matter. So he pushed back every feeling but joy as he saw father and son sitting side by side at his hearthstone. Meantime, Hans was wholly occupied in the thought of Thomas Higgs's happiness in being able to be the *meester*'s assistant again, and Dame Brinker was sighing softly to herself, wishing that the lad's mother were alive to see him—such a fine young gentleman as he was—and wondering how Dr. Boekman could bear to see the silver watch getting so dull. He had worn it ever since Raff handed it over, that was evident. What had he done with the gold one he used to wear?

The light was shining full upon Dr. Boekman's face. How contented he looked; how much younger and brighter than formerly. The hard lines were quite melting away. He was laughing as he said to the father, "Am I not a happy man, Raff Brinker? My son will sell out his factory this month and open a warehouse in Amsterdam. I shall have all my spectacle cases for nothing."

Hans started from his reverie. "A warehouse, *mynheer*! And will Thomas Higgs—I mean, is your son not to be your assistant again?"

A shade passed over the *meester's* face, but he brightened with an effort as he replied, "Oh, no, Laurens has had quite enough of that. He wishes to be a merchant."

Hans appeared so surprised and disappointed that his friend asked good-naturedly, "Why so silent, boy? Is it any disgrace to be a merchant?"

"N-not a disgrace, *mynheer*," stammered Hans, "but—"

"But what?"

"Why, the other calling is so much better," answered Hans, "so much nobler. I think, *mynheer*," he added with enthusiasm, "that to be a surgeon, to cure the sick and crippled, to save human life, to be able to do what you have done for my father, is the grandest thing on earth."

The doctor was regarding him sternly. Hans felt rebuked. His cheeks were flushed; hot tears were gathering under his lashes.

"It is an ugly business, boy, this surgery," said the doctor, still frowning at Hans. "It requires great patience, self-denial, and perseverance."

"I am sure it does," cried Hans. "It calls for wisdom, too, and a reverence for God's work. Ah, *mynheer*, it may have its trials and drawbacks, but you do not mean what you say. It is great and noble, not ugly! Pardon me, *mynheer*. It is not for me to speak so boldly."

Dr. Boekman was evidently displeased. He turned his back on the boy and conferred aside with Laurens. Meanwhile the dame scowled a terrible warning at Hans. These great people, she knew well enough, never like to hear poor folk speak so pertly.

The *meester* turned around.

"How old are you, Hans Brinker?"

"Fifteen, *mynheer*" was the startled reply.

"Would you like to become a physician?"

"Yes, *mynheer*," answered Hans, quivering with excitement.

"Would you be willing, with your parents' consent, to devote yourself to study, to go to the university, and, in time, be a student in my office?"

"Yes, *mynheer*."

"You would not grow restless, think you, and change your mind just as I had set my heart upon preparing you to be my successor?"

Hans's eyes flashed.

"No, *mynheer*, I would not change."

"You may believe him there," cried the dame, who could remain quiet no longer. "Hans is like a rock when once he decides, and as for study, *mynheer*, the child has almost grown fast to his books of late. He can jumble off Latin already, like any priest!"

The doctor smiled. "Well, Hans, I see nothing to prevent us from carrying out this plan, if your father agrees."

"Ahem," said Raff, too proud of his boy to be very meek. "The fact is, *mynheer*, I prefer an active, out-of-door life myself. But if the lad's inclined to study for a *meester*, and he'd have the benefit of your good word to push him on in the world, it's all one to me. The money's all that's wanting, but it mightn't be long, with two strong pair of arms to earn it, before we—"

"Tut, tut!" interrupted the doctor. "If I take your right-hand man away, I must pay the cost, and glad enough will I be to do it. It will be like having *two* sons, eh, Laurens? One a merchant and the other a surgeon. I shall be the happiest man in Holland! Come to me in the morning, Hans, and we will arrange matters at once."

Hans bowed assent. He dared not trust himself to speak.

"And, Brinker," continued the doctor, "my son Laurens will need a trusty, ready man like you when he opens his warehouse in Amsterdam, someone to oversee matters, and see that the lazy clowns around the place do their duty. Someone to— Why don't you tell him yourself, you rascal!"

This last was addressed to the son and did not sound half as fierce as it looks in print. The rascal and Raff soon understood each other perfectly.

"I'm loath to leave the dikes," said the latter, after they had talked together awhile, "but it is such a good offer, *mynheer*, I'd be robbing my family if I let it go past me."

Take a long look at Hans as he sits there staring gratefully at the *meester*, for you shall not see him again for many years.

And Gretel—ah, what a vista of puzzling work suddenly opens before her! Yes, for dear Hans's sake she will study now. If he really is to be a *meester*, his sister must not shame his greatness.

How faithfully those glancing eyes shall yet seek for the jewels that lie hidden in rocky schoolbooks! And how they shall yet brighten and droop at the coming of one whom she knows of now only as the boy who wore a red cap on that wonderful day when she found the silver skates in her apron!

But the doctor and Laurens are going. Dame Brinker is making her best curtsy. Raff stands beside her, looking every inch a man as he grasps the *meester*'s hand. Through the open cottage door we can look out upon the level Dutch landscape, all alive with the falling snow.

Conclusion

*O*ur story is nearly told. Time passes in Holland just as surely and steadily as here. In that respect no country is odd.

To the Brinker family it has brought great changes. Hans has spent the years faithfully and profitably, conquering obstacles as they arose and pursuing one object with all the energy of his nature. If often the way has been rugged, his resolution has never failed. Sometimes he echoes, with his good friend, the words said long ago in that little cottage near Broek: "Surgery is an ugly business," but always in his heart of hearts lingers the echo of those truer words: "It is great and noble! It awakes a reverence for God's work!"

Were you in Amsterdam today, you might see the famous Dr. Brinker riding in his grand coach to visit his patients, or, it might be that you would see him skating with his own boys and girls upon the frozen canal. For Annie Bouman, the beautiful, frank-hearted peasant girl, you would inquire in vain; but Annie Brinker, the *vrouw* of the great physician, is very like her—only, as Hans says, she is even lovelier, wiser, more like a fairy godmother than ever.

Peter van Holp, also, is a married man. I could have told you before that he and Hilda would join hands and glide through life together, just as years ago they skimmed side by side over the frozen, sunlit river.

At one time I came near hinting that Katrinka and Carl would join hands. It is fortunate now that the report was not started, for Katrinka changed her mind and is single to this day. The lady is not quite so merry as formerly, and, I grieve to say, some of the tinkling bells are out of tune. But she is the life of her social circle, still. I wish she would be in earnest, just for a little while, but no; it is not her nature. Her cares and sorrows do nothing more than disturb the tinkling; they never waken any deeper music.

Rychie's soul has been stirred to its depths during these long years. Her history would tell how seed carelessly sown is sometimes reaped in anguish and how a golden harvest may follow a painful planting. If I mistake not, you may be able to read the written record before long; that is, if you are familiar with the Dutch language. In the witty but earnest author whose words are welcomed at this day in thousands of Holland homes, few could recognize the haughty, flippant Rychie who scoffed at little Gretel.

Lambert van Mounen and Ludwig van Holp are good Christian men and, what is more easily to be seen at a glance, thriving citizens. Both are dwellers in Amsterdam, but one clings to the old city of that name and the other is a pilgrim to the new. Van Mounen's present home is not far from Central Park, and he says that if the New Yorkers do their duty the park will, in time, equal his beautiful Bosch, near The Hague. He often thinks of the Katrinka of his boyhood, but he is glad now that Katrinka, the woman, sent him away, though it seemed at the time his darkest hour. Ben's sister Jenny has made him very happy, happier than he could have been with anyone else in the wide world.

Carl Schummel has had a hard life. His father met with reverses in business, and as Carl had not many warm friends, and, above all, was not sustained by noble principles, he has been tossed about by fortune's battledore until his gayest feathers are nearly all knocked off. He is a bookkeeper in the thriving Amsterdam house of Boekman and Schimmelpenninck. Voostenwalbert, the junior partner, treats him kindly; and he, in turn, is very respectful to the "monkey with a long name for a tail."

Of all our group of Holland friends, Jacob Poot is the only one who has passed away. Good-natured, truehearted, and unselfish to the last, he is mourned now as heartily as he was loved and laughed at while on earth. He grew to be very thin before he died; thinner than Benjamin Dobbs, who is now portliest among the portly.

Raff Brinker and his *vrouw* have been living comfortably in Amsterdam for many years—a faithful happy pair, as simple and straightforward in their good fortune as they were patient and trustful in darker days. They have a *zommerhuis* near the old cottage and thither they often repair with their children and grandchildren on the pleasant summer afternoons when the pond lilies rear their queenly heads above the water.

The story of Hans Brinker would be but half told, if we did not leave him with Gretel standing near. Dear, quick, patient little Gretel! What is she now? Ask old Dr. Boekman, he will declare she is the finest singer, the loveliest woman, in Amsterdam. Ask Hans and Annie, they will assure you she is the dearest sister ever known. Ask her husband, he will tell you she is the brightest, sweetest little wife in Holland. Ask Dame Brinker and Raff, their eyes will glisten with joyous tears. Ask the poor and the air will fill with blessings.

But, lest you forget a tiny form trembling and sobbing on the mound before the Brinker cottage, ask the Van Glecks; they will never weary telling of the darling little girl who won the silver skates.

Afterword

E. L. Konigsburg

*D*id you read the whole book? Or did you skip? Paragraphs? Whole chapters, maybe.

I assume that anyone choosing to read a book written over a hundred years ago, one that qualifies as a classic, is nostalgic, has an assignment from school, or is a good reader. If you are in the first category, you won't want to skip; if you are in the second, you won't dare; and if you are in the third, you probably have. It's perfectly all right if you did. Good readers do skip passages. Part of being a good reader is knowing what to skip and what to read.

For example, if you didn't read Chapters Nine through Twelve, Sixteen through Twenty, and Twenty-four through Twenty-nine, you did not lose track of Hans Brinker or the silver skates. Those chapters are full of information and purpose, the first of Mrs. Mary Mapes Dodge's two stated purposes: "to combine the instructive features of a book of travels with the interest of a domestic tale" and to "free [her readers] from certain current prejudices concerning that noble and enterprising people [of Holland]." I say, "Good for you, Mrs. Dodge, good for you." But I ask, "What about your prejudices, Mrs. Dodge?"

Consider Chapter Ten, "What the Boys Saw and Did in Amsterdam." "[Ben] peeped into the Jews' Quarter of the city, where the rich diamond cutters and squalid old-clothesmen dwell, and wisely resolved to keep away from it." Mrs. Dodge thought he was wise to keep away from the Jews' Quarter because she is a victim of a prejudice that, fortunately, most of the people of Holland did not have. Jews had long ago settled in Amsterdam because of a policy of religious toleration there. In Chapter Two, Mrs. Dodge herself mentions this openmindedness. There are many modern readers—I among them—who don't think it was at all wise of Ben to keep away from that part of town, for by doing so, he missed seeing the ancestors of a particularly wonderful young Jew named Anne Frank.

With a phrase, a word, or a footnote Mrs. Dodge reveals other prejudices as well. For example, a footnote in Chapter Twenty-seven tells us that "In Holland women of the lower grades of society do not take the title of Mrs. (or *mevrouw*) when they marry, as with us. They assume their husband's name but are still called miss (*jufvrouw*, pronounced *yuffrow*)." Jufvrouw Brinker is loyal, thrifty, honest, industrious, and proud; those qualities would put her at the top of the social order in any book of mine, but she has no money, and in Mrs. Dodge's time, that blasts her smack into the lower grades of society.

So, dear reader, if you skipped those history-and-travelogue chapters, you will have missed a lot of Mrs. Dodge's snobbishness and outdated prejudices, but you will also have missed the story of the little boy who saved his town by putting his finger in the dike (it was Haarlem, not Amsterdam) and two accounts of how Antwerp got its name, one of which is brutal. You will also have missed a picture of Christmas as it was celebrated in Holland before there was advertising, plus a word picture of a forest of elms before there was Dutch elm disease, as well as an explanation of what smoking a pipe meant to a man before it meant increasing his chances of cancer.

What you will not have missed by skipping those chapters is the story of Hans Brinker.

The story is why this book endures, for among the traditions that Mrs. Dodge inherited was one that said that to keep a reader turning pages, an author should tell a story. And what a story she has to tell! She has story enough to make two average young adult novels.

Think of all the elements she corrals into a plot and think how cleverly she does it. First she marks off a playing field; there will be a race. Almost without our being aware of it we are roped in, for in the very first chapter we meet Hans and Gretel. They are brave, and we admire them. Why did the father throw Gretel's new shoes into the fire? We are intrigued. Mrs. Dodge has driven in the pilings that have staked out her territory.

We begin to want things for our young hero and his sister. Please, let them get some decent skates so they can participate in the race. Gretel gets skates, and a while later, Hans does too. But the getting of them is not easy, and once they have them, Mrs. Dodge has us hooked. We have paid our admission, and we are ready for the race. We know that it will not be smooth skating, for the playing field has been sown with the seeds of two mysteries: that of some lost money and that of a silver watch. But Mrs. Dodge has collected our tickets, and we take our seats, when, right before our eyes, she plows up the entire field with a terrifying tale of madness.

Finally the ground is smoothed over enough for the contestants to appear, and the race is run. Hans has been allowed to overcome all the obstacles Mrs. Dodge has put in his path, but he is tripped up, not by circumstances but by his own noble character. Only after the race is lost and won are we allowed to roam over the playing field to pick up the last of the pieces and walk to the finishing line with the two mysteries solved.

And what a sense of accomplishment we have when we get there! True to her times and traditions, Mrs. Dodge is there to greet us and give us a report of the future of our heroes and our heroine, news of the happily-ever-afters.

I wish Mrs. Dodge were here now. I would like very much to shake her hand, to congratulate her for telling such a rousing good story and to tell her that her book is still read and enjoyed. I would like to invite her to pull up a chair and come sit by me, and then I would like to help her catch up with what has happened in the world.